Also recommended...

You may also enjoy these other ForbiddenFiction works:

Taking Flight - an erotic anthology with wings!
Flight has captured the human imagination for centuries, inspiring poets and lovers alike to greater heights. Is the exhilaration of soaring better even than sex? Is the ecstasy of a lover's touch worth more than all the feathers in heaven? Is one moment of passion on the wind worth the risk of a lifetime? Here are seven erotic flights of fantasy, from gritty dystopian futures and surreal urban discoveries to mythic romances and fleeting moments of enchantment.
http://forbiddenfiction.com/library/collection/SPC-1.100004

Held in Dreams by Ava Burquette
Elaine is an ordinary human with ordinary dreams, maybe a little too shy for her own good. At least that's what she tells herself, until she is kidnapped by a strange and charismatic man named Ghalib who has come looking specifically for her. Ghalib definitely isn't ordinary. He isn't even human. He's a Dream Architect, one of the beings who create dreams for humanity. His world is the realm of passion, imagination and nightmares, where humans may be kept as pets or slaves. Ghalib is obsessed with Elaine, whose vivid, erotic dreams he finds irresistible. If Elaine is to contend with Ghalib on her own terms, she'll have to do more than let go of her shy, inhibited waking manner. She will have to realize her own dreams. (F/M, F/F, M/M)
http://forbiddenfiction.com/library/story/AB1-1.000093

Sam cannot bring himself

to pass up what will certainly be his last chance to work with Jessica, even if she appears now in this much-changed form.

Sam peers into her dark, empty eyes. He agrees with Deborah that there is more to them than there ought to be. Jessica Savage might be in there somewhere. His hand tightens around hers.

The rational part of Sam's mind knows this means he ought to step away and signal Tommy and Dave to riddle her with bullets. But the likelihood she is somehow still Jessica — even if this version of Jessica would tear him limb from limb with her molars if given the chance — appeals deeply to the part of Sam that has longed for Jessica Savage since he came to Hollywood, the part that made an obscure aspiring actress into a private obsession and deeply held fantasy.

Liquid Longing

an Erotic Anthology of
the Sacred and Profane

by Annabeth Leong

ForbiddenFiction
www.forbiddenfiction.com

an imprint of

Fantastic Fiction Publishing
www.fantasticfictionpublishing.com

LIQUID LONGING
A Forbidden Fiction book

Fantastic Fiction Publishing
Hayward, California

CREDITS
Editors: Lon Sarver, Rylan Hunter, Elizabeth A. Tanner
Cover Design: Siolnatine, D.M. Atkins
Cover: Illustration and collage by Siolnatine, from public domain sources
Internal cover design: D.M. Atkins and Siolnatine
Internal cover art: Illustrations by Siolnatine. Collages by Siolnatine using public domain elements and illustrations by Arthur Rackham, Leonardo DaVinci, and Master Tsukioka Yoshitoshi. Photographs by Mimage at Dreamstime, Chu-x at Shutterstock and kovalvs at Pixmac.
Production Editor: Erika L Firanc
Proofreading: Jae Knight, Kailin Morgan, JhP323, Todd Michaels, Kira O'Hara

SKU: AL1-100010-02 FFP
ISBN: 978-1-62234-223-5

Published in the United States of America

DISCLAIMER

This book is a work of fiction which contains explicit erotic content; it is intended for mature readers. Do not read this if it's not legal for you.

All the characters, locations and events herein are fictional. While elements of existing locations or historical characters or events may be used fictitiously, any resemblance to actual people, places or events is coincidental.

This book depicts depicts fictional BDSM; it is not intended to be used as an instruction manual. It contains descriptions of erotic acts that may be immoral, illegal, or unsafe. The characters are not models for the Safe, Sane and Consensual forms embraced by most current practitioners of BDSM. The authors take license with the use of BDSM for dramatic effect. Do not take the events in this story as proof of the plausibility or safety of any particular practice.

For R. and I., dark and light, shameless, dangerous, and powerful.

Author's Foreword

Certain old stories have fascinated me throughout my life. For example, I cannot remember a time when I wasn't chilled and intrigued by Bluebeard's gory closet and the temptation of a small key. When I began writing erotica, I often found myself returning to those stories, getting inside them and remaking them in the process of trying to understand what about them had gotten so deep into me. One of the things I like most about these retellings is that the end result often feels more three-dimensional to me than the original, well-removed from the "morality tale" that can linger behind a fairy story. So *The Three Wives of Bluebeard* is an exploration of vengeance, anger, curiosity, and sexual awakening, but I hope it offers no easy answers.

The language of the erotic provides my imagination the vocabulary for expressing the most vulnerable and most profound feelings. That is the way I most naturally explore shame and longing, worship and humiliation, and desire of all types. Take the story of Icarus and Daedalus — it concerns innovation, achievement, and hubris, but to me its dark heart lies in wanting what can't be kept, moments of bliss that come at a terrible price, and a wish to transform the body into something else entirely. *Icarus Bleeds* treats those themes sexually, seen through the eyes of a world-weary Daedalus whose desire for Icarus is no less overreaching and impossible than Icarus's desire for wings.

My riffs on mythological themes have sometimes stayed close to the original — *The Snake and the Lyre* follows the plot of the myth of Orpheus and Eurydice fairly faithfully — but other times, I've gone much farther afield. *Fires of Edo* is based on my research into Tokyo's past, when the shogunate was fading, and superstitions among firefighters about protective spirits. The water dragon Ryo, however, is my own invention, a possibility that embodies the ultimate aspiration. *Screen Siren* is based on my observation that after a zombie apocalypse, people would inevitably get on with things. *The Miracles of Dorothea of Andrine* is a love letter to the historical church (which fascinates me) at the same time that it's terrible blasphemy – in that way, I, the writer, share the contradictions of the story's main character.

For all the historical and mythological themes I've borrowed, I've tried to make them my own. I see a circle, the universal becoming personal and then, if done right, universal again. I want to dive into the collective unconscious, come up with something interesting, and leave something valuable behind.

I should talk about the sex as well. The stories here do not represent the safe, sane, and consensual – not at all. Much of this sex is ugly or disturbing or fraught with shame or lacking kindness. I always write to turn myself on, but sometimes I am also turning my own stomach. Being able to explore this sort of material is very important to me as an erotica writer. My own experience of sex is decidedly not all hearts and flowers. I have given myself orgasms only to begin crying a moment later. I have been in situations that confused me and made me angry, only to find I was also more turned on than I'd ever been in my life. I have crossed lines I shouldn't have crossed, and I've learned from that.

In real life, I very much believe in consent and negotiation. I believe in overcoming shame and pursuing one's own honest desires. Getting to that place hasn't been an easy journey, though, and it's required looking into many dark corners. Those dark corners are sometimes interesting places that I think are worth talking about. So *Less Than a Day* concerns the violent carnality that can accompany grief and impending loss, *Screen Siren* allows revulsion to overcome longstanding desire, and *Touching Freedom* tells the story of a young woman trying to lose her innocence on her own terms while everyone around her is essentially trying to force themselves on her. This book contains several scenes of rape, and several more of dubious consent. To me, that profanity needs to be addressed. It is too simplistic to say, as some do, that it's okay to write about these things as long as it's not done for the purpose of titillation. I am always titillated when I read about these things, even if I'm having other feelings at the same time, and I have to admit that if I'm going to be honest about anything at all.

There are also moments of the sacred and the profound in these pages. In *Andromache's Prize*, the sexual connection Briseis shares with Andromache transforms her from slave to leader. In the *Fires of Edo*, the appearance of Ryo at long last is not only a fantasy fulfilled, it's an affirmation of strength and purpose. *In the Death of Winter* demands a sacrifice, but returns a lost divinity. Through every story, I intend for even the darkest moments to be bittersweet and ultimately revealing. I offer my deepest gratitude and best wishes to all who have been traveling companions on this adventure into unknown spaces, and to all just setting out. Most especially, I'd like to thank Lon Sarver, who was my editor for most of these. He is as unflinching as they come and has never let me get away with pulling back or copping out. These stories would be much less brave if not for him. My thanks to all the staff at ForbiddenFiction as well. I believe the world needs fiction that takes real risks, and I can't think of anyone more committed to providing that.

— Annabeth Leong

Contents

Hunting Artemis

Dedicated to remain virginal for Artemis, it is not until Nikia meets the hunter Theron that she realizes what she has given up with her vows to the goddess. In the heat of her newly-discovered passion, no touch but Theron's can remove Nikia's lust. Nikia and Theron form an uneasy kinship, united by the cruelty of unrequited desire. Together, they will make unlikely sacrifices for Artemis, and together, they will receive an impossible reward. (M/F, F/F, M/F/F)

Chapter 1
Forbidden Glimpses of the Goddess

The day I came to Delos, as a girl of ten, to dedicate myself to Artemis, my mentor took me out beside the stable before the ceremony. Most of her advice washed past me. I had eyes only for the barren earth around the temple, the gleam of forest beyond, and the girls in white who whispered and giggled and peered at the newcomer.

I do remember one thing she said: "We run so hard and shoot so sure, Nikia, not only for love of the goddess and the hunt, but also because we must take revenge for all we sacrifice."

A dry, brown woman, she had skin the gray-brown color of a nut husk. I glanced up and found unexpected heat in her eyes. She cackled and thumped me on the shoulder, making me buckle under the strength of her arm.

"When the fire between your legs awakens, you'll call my words wise," she said.

Ten years passed before I did—when Theron came. On the first day of autumn, I went with the temple's delegation to greet him. Theron sat foremost in a fleet of smaller boats dropped into the water from the decks of his black ship. The sun glinted off the hard curves of his muscles as he steered toward shore with great sweeps of the oars. I couldn't make out his features from where I stood, but my body thrilled at his perfect, manly geometry. Even in the noonday heat, his brown hair gleamed with a touch of moonlight. I wondered if the goddess' fingers had recently touched his brow and brushed back his thick curls.

He disembarked with his hound at his heels, and as the high priestess spoke a welcome, I went to him and knelt in the sand, holding the ritual cup before me. He smelled of leaves and rain, as if fresh from the hunt. I tried to fix my eyes on one of his sleek calves, but they wandered up and mapped the lines of his thighs. I wondered what lay between his legs. Theron took the cup from my hands without a glance at me, without the slightest brush of flesh to flesh. He drank to the goddess' honor, his tall, lean body upright and quivering faintly with devotion. His bright brown eyes and pointed nose gave his pretty, noble face a hungry look. I breathed him in, imagining my body falling against him and my hands winding around the places my eyes had been.

Theron stepped past me and spoke the next words in the ritual.

I asked Eurydice about him at dinner, but my friend had little to say. "He is some great follower of Artemis from Thessaly. He brought a dozen steeds with him as a gift to the temple." She shrugged, whipped her black hair off her thin shoulders and looked at me suspiciously.

I tried to keep my voice light. "How long will he stay?"

"How long do any of these travelers stay? They come by the sun and leave by the moon. Who knows?"

Theron entered, and I snapped my mouth shut, swallowing what I planned to say. A hush fell over the room, reminding me I wasn't the only woman in awe of him. I smiled at Eurydice, and spent the rest of the meal focusing on the arch leading up to the white ceiling, and the carvings on the pillars around the hall. I could do without her curiosity.

My charade aside, I noticed every movement of his hands, and every change in the tilt of his head. I wished I sat beside him. I lingered after dinner rather than retire to the room I shared with Eurydice. When the moon rose above the forest trees, he crept to the stable. I wandered in after him with my bow slung over my back.

Theron's black-eared hound raced in circles at his feet. His fine black horse edged sideways as he saddled it. I watched him reassure it with strong, sure fingers and wished he caressed me instead. Theron narrowed his eyes and looked at me.

"Do you go alone on a midnight hunt?" I said, fingering my bow.

He turned away and mounted without a word, but I stopped him with a hand on the horse's neck. I knew better than to touch Theron. "Let me ride beside you," I said. "My duties multiply, and I do not often hunt."

"The ritual hunts are not the same as the real thing." He nodded. "I won't wait long."

I grinned, chose my horse, and saddled her in a rush before he had time to change his mind. When I returned, Theron gave another short nod and headed for the forest. Though I tried to hunt, I cared nothing for the flash of deer between the trees. I raced after the rich, male scent of him, strong and big enough to fill the forest. I could have followed him with my eyes closed, and yet I did not want to. I felt grateful for every moment he rode ahead of me, leaving me free to stare at his elbow, the tip of his ear, or the start of his spine above his shirt. In my heart, I feared Artemis would judge me for paying more attention to a man than to the chase.

Finally, the familiar rhythms of the hunt took over, and I found myself sighting and stalking deer. Theron, however, blundered on despite the silvery animal bodies, never touched his weapons, and made no particular effort to ride quietly. After the third time he startled my quarry, I turned on him, surprised at the anger in my voice. "What is it you're seeking here?"

His guilty eyes met mine. His brash confidence had fallen away, and beneath the veneer, he seemed haunted and harried. With an urge to lay my hand over his, I pressed my horse forward, but he pulled his mount into shadows illuminated only by the barest dusting of moonlight.

I went on the attack. "You're not really on a hunt, and it's clear you're not in this to be alone with me."

Theron swallowed. "It's the goddess," he said, his deep voice full of shame. "I dreamed of her the night before we landed at Delos. I must ride every night seeking Artemis."

"You know as well as I that Artemis will suffer the touch of no man." I didn't really mind his heresy, but I wanted to shame him as punishment for ignoring me.

His head snapped up, then dropped a moment later. "Then there's only one thing left to do."

He cleared his throat, dug his heels into his steed, and bolted off into the forest, so suddenly my horse shied. I collected her and tore after him, keeping my body low to avoid being flung from the saddle by a low-hanging branch.

Caught up in the chase, I felt his speed, as the lingering howl of his heart's desire joined with mine in longing. The leaves whipping about my face became his hair, the wind tearing at my clothes became his hands, and the horse between my legs, his body. I closed my eyes. His distinct scent seemed to spread through the forest. I breathed him in, bucking against the saddle and riding ever wilder. Surpassing him in speed, only the moon watched me.

When the mare and I tired, I fell against her neck, crazy for the touch of a lover. Theron, not yet spent, charged past me, crested the hill beyond, and hurtled down the other side like lightning. His horse's hooves ripped over the ground like thunder. His hound, staying abreast of his wild ride, yipped an otherworldly challenge to the night.

We tell a story among the girls of the temple about a man named Actaeon, a Theban prince and hunter. One day, he followed his quarry into a vale on Mount Cithaeron. As soon as Actaeon entered the vale, his animals went strange. His horse balked at some unseen thing and threw him, and his hounds lost the scent of the quarry, circling Actaeon in confusion before wandering away into the undergrowth.

Actaeon scarcely knew why he had come to that place. The air intoxicated him, and he walked on as though dreaming.

After an hour, he heard water nearby, and followed the sound to a hidden pool. Before stepping out into the clearing around the water, he froze at the sight of a woman bathing there. Tall and powerful, she stood in the center of the pool, snatching handfuls of water and sluicing her bare skin. Her short hair curled tightly about her head, and dark eyes burned from her face. Actaeon became entranced by the glow of her skin and the patch of dark curls between her strong thighs. He could not tear his eyes from her large nipples, covering half the surface of the small breasts perched atop her muscled chest.

And though we imagine the goddess Artemis does not wish to be described thus, we do it all the same, lingering on every beauty Actaeon saw. In hushed tones we talk about how Artemis stepped out of the pool and sunned herself on the rocks at the edge, running her hands over her face and neck. Before Actaeon's astonished eyes, the goddess teased her nipples, pulling and pinching them until her sharp breathing filled the clearing. Her pink tongue licked the edges of her mouth as she gasped and trailed her right hand down her belly and between her legs. Slowly, she spread her cunt and slid one long finger into the opening. The goddess writhed upon the rock as she stuffed her sex with more fingers, reveling in her private ecstasy.

Her muscles rippled gloriously, bunching in her sides as her body strained toward satisfaction. She exhausted herself before achieving bliss, however, and uncurled her body and rested on the rock, one hand still cupping her sex. Breathing hard, she turned her head to the side and saw Actaeon in his hiding place. The prince's hand pumped his straining cock. In truth, it took all his control not to charge into the clearing and take her into his arms. Artemis snatched her hands away from her cunt and leapt to her feet, turning a furious gaze upon him.

Ignoring his stammered apology with a wave of her hand, she turned Actaeon into a stag, and as the creature wobbled away on its new feet, she set his own hounds upon him.

Seeing no sign of Theron again, I dismounted and walked my mare back to the stable. I prayed, begging the goddess to forgive him for what he wanted from her, and to forgive me for what I wanted from him. I tried to placate her with hymns, and even accused Aphrodite of plotting against us.

Nearing the stable, I spoke the truth of my heart into the night. "Lady of the hunt, I don't know if I am fit to be in your service. If there is something you would have from me, take it and release me."

At breakfast in the morning, Theron sat with eyes blackened and shadowed by the night's ride. I would come to know the look well, for every night he went riding after the goddess, and every night I followed him until my horse could no longer run. And though he rarely looked at me, our kinship grew.

Autumn faded and winter threatened every evening. The leaves fell and crunched sharply underfoot. The wind traded claws for teeth, biting ever deeper during the midnight rides I took in pursuit of Theron. The naked trees struck obscene poses against the sky, digging into the earth with fisted roots and spreading their branches apart like pairs of legs.

Theron hadn't eaten in days. The endless hunt had wasted him, wearing thin the beauty of his face. The hard man beneath attracted me even more than before.

A hand closed over my shoulder as I crept behind him one night. "Nikia," Eurydice said. "What are you doing?"

"I go riding at night."

"So I hear. They say it's him you ride." She jerked her chin toward the stable, where I knew Theron would be saddling his horse.

Would he notice my absence? Or had I been creating a bond that only mattered to me?

Eurydice misunderstood the blush in my face. "It's true, then," she said.

I flashed a smile. "Eurydice, any fool can see he cares only about the goddess."

"And what about you?"

"I see nothing but him."

Her hand clutched mine. "Walk with me."

We walked behind the stables, in the direction opposite Theron's nightly ride. The trees thinned until the shore appeared and the pale beach beyond it. Barely in sight, the mast of Theron's black ship poked up into the darkness. We stepped onto the beach. She darted ahead on bare feet, but my shoes gathered sand until I stopped to remove them.

"They say they built the temple here in Delos because this is the place where Leto birthed Artemis, and where Artemis in turn played midwife for her twin brother Apollo," Eurydice said in a tiresome, pious voice.

"I know the story," I said.

She silenced me with a sharp slash of her white hand through the night. "On her birthday nights, when the moon is dark, they say

Artemis comes to bathe here in honor of her mother." To my surprise, Eurydice cast her robes aside and stepped toward the chilly water. She gasped as the first of the waves reached her feet, but pressed onward until they slapped her knees, her thighs, then between her legs. Her body glowed, framed by the ocean, and her nipples stood dark and hard against her breasts when she beckoned to me. I shed my clothes and obeyed, allowing her to take me in her arms.

"We are like the goddess," Eurydice said. "Strong and brave. Forget that man." She bathed me as she spoke, scooping up water and smoothing it over my skin, holding me up against the force of the crashing tide. Her touch, though innocent, ignited a fire between my legs. I shivered as my flesh awakened beneath her chaste, teasing fingers. She ran her hands through my hair and over my face, her fingers fluttering against my eyelids, lips, and nostrils. She drew light circles over my back, but did not touch me any of the places where I most wanted to be touched. I clung to her and pressed my breasts against her breasts, sliding so her thigh slipped between my legs. Nearly sobbing from the tension, I pressed against her thigh and she allowed it. Soon I crashed against it, even as the waves crashed against me, until the breath shuddered out of me in a long spasm.

Eurydice kissed me on the forehead as the pulsing between my legs continued. "Forget him," she said again and patted me on the shoulder blade.

Confused, I moved to kiss her on the lips, but she stepped back as the water churned and filled the space between us. Without her body against mine, I trembled.

She waded back to shore and retrieved her clothing, wrapping it around her body as if nothing had happened. I longed to lie down at the edge of the waves and press my fist between my thighs, but I climbed up after her and collected my own clothes. From the look on her face, she thought she had saved me from my lust for Theron. She didn't know that the relief bursting forth like a long-held breath transformed back to desire the moment I breathed in again. He would have understood. Nothing could replace him for me, just as nothing could replace the goddess for him.

Chapter 2
Sacrifices Made for Artemis

Eurydice caught me going after Theron every night for a week. Each time, she took me to the ocean. Finally, my shaming need and her indifference became unbearable. The next night I didn't go out, but lay in my bed and pretended to sleep.

When the moon reached its height, I could stand no more. I went to the stable and took a fresh horse, hoping to catch the second part of Theron's nightly ride.

Flashes of silver peeked out between the trees, but tonight I would not stop to watch the deer. I rode on carelessly, sparing no glance to anything but the trail before my eyes. My guts tangled and twisted as I pictured Theron's face. In my dreams, he smiled when I approached and pulled me into his arms. Awake, I imagined him sneering, sending me back to my bed alone.

I passed beyond the area that I had traveled well with him, and the path before me grew rockier. I slowed for fear of harming the horse. A stone's throw ahead, between two slender trunks, silver flashed again, then stayed and glowed. It was no deer.

Catching my breath, I followed Artemis' beckoning finger, cursing myself for allowing thoughts of Theron to blind me. I knew not why she called to me, her unworthy servant, but I followed, wondering if she planned to punish me or banish me from her temple. I saw only the curving finger, the strong hand, and the well-muscled forearm used to handling a bow. She led me into the forest's darkest heart where the smell of animals crowded thick and close upon my senses. The moon failed to reach this place, and I had to trust the finger to lead me on a path my horse could manage.

The smell of sex, sharp and wild as the sea, spiraled up my nose, making my body throb. My horse shied and threw me into the bushes. I walked on, following the silver glow without reservation. A hound—the tilt of its black ears familiar to me—burst from the undergrowth, whining at my heels and running ahead to guide me. I followed, not understanding the dog's urgency.

A long time later, I heard water nearby, followed the sound, and crept up to a hidden pool. Before stepping out into the clearing there, I froze. The fog lifted from my brain, and I saw Theron, a deep wound in his gut leaking into the pool, staining the water with a thick red swirl. I rushed to his side while his hound whimpered and licked its master's forehead. I dared not look into Theron's face, for fear I'd collapse into useless sobs.

I gathered him in my arms, pressed my hand against his neck, and prayed life still flowed in him. A breath, weak but warm, fluttered the hair beside my face, and I cried aloud. I wrapped a rough bandage around his wound, tearing my attention from the feel of his soft skin. His distinct scent had been polluted by the acrid stench of blood and pain. I needed a horse. I could barely lift him, much less carry him back to the temple.

His horse, the fine steed from Thessaly, stepped into the clearing then, and I did not pause to question why. It came easily at my call. I coaxed it to kneel so I could roll the man into the saddle. After a struggle, I let the horse rise again and climbed up behind Theron.

I held him on the long ride back to the temple, my desire for him pushed to the back of my mind. I didn't cry. Instead, my eyes felt drier than seven deserts. If he died in my arms, I might be free at last, and so would he. I spent the next hours regretting the thought.

Daylight loomed on the horizon by the time we returned, and the sun's rays scattered gloriously over the land. I saw only how pale Theron looked in that exuberant light. Though he breathed and sometimes mumbled, his mind lay somewhere far away. At the last bare stretch from the tree line to the temple, the horse and I wanted to break into a run, but I held us back since it seemed Theron could not withstand it.

From a distance, the priestesses ran, bringing aid. I gave Theron over to their care and stumbled numbly to the room I shared with

Eurydice. They could ask their questions later. For now, I would let them tend to him.

The sun streamed through the windows of the room, striking me in the face with light as pitiless as the heel of a palm. I'd never been in my room this time of day before. Eurydice sat beside me. She took my hand and began to relay a strange story. "A bird came into the high priestess's window late at night. The creature made such a nuisance and racket of itself that, still half-asleep, the high priestess took her hunting knife and killed it. But the bird's death cry rang with the voice of prophecy, and the priestess got up at once, carried its body out into the courtyard, and sliced it open to see what message the gods had written within.

"At the sight of its entrails, the high priestess entered a trance. She saw Artemis bathing alone, with none of her maidens present to attend to her. Ares, god of war, stalked the goddess of the hunt, hoping to slake his lust. The priestess saw a warrior sacrificing himself for the goddess, and a maiden sacrificing herself for the warrior."

I stirred and shook off Eurydice's hand. "I've never heard this story."

"It's the story they're telling about you."

"What's this talk of sacrifice? Is Theron—"

"Alive, and they sing your praises for saving him."

Her expression resigned, Eurydice's fine features hardened. She knew those nights in the ocean hadn't abated my longing for Theron at all. I smiled, an offering of peace, and to my relief, she returned it. "Do they plan to ask me why I was out there?"

"You were led by the goddess," Eurydice said and winked at me. "It won't stop the young girls from talking, but nothing does."

"I have to see him."

"Artemis appeared to the priestesses in a vision," Eurydice said with a smirk. "You, and you alone, are to tend to him. And when he is well, you are to leave Delos forever."

"Banished?"

She nodded and watched my face for a reaction. It should have destroyed me to think of leaving the island that had been my home for half my life. Instead, I felt exhilarated. I'd loved hunting night after night, but the thought of the wide world before me, free of vows, made my heart soar more than any midnight ride could. I kissed Eurydice on the cheek to say goodbye, and her answering sigh made me wonder if I had read her wrong on our nights together. It didn't matter now. I went to him.

Pale and weak, Theron tossed in anxious sleep. Though rest healed me, it left him untouched. The healers assured me he would live, but most of winter would be over before he recovered.

They left me alone with him, no questions asked. I soon got over the shock and began to come to terms with the realities of his body, which needed to be fed, washed, lifted, and turned. I saw his every ugliness and scar. I saw his face by evening light, by morning light, by noon light, and in the darkness. Sleeping in the corner of his room, I never spoke except to murmur to him or pray to Artemis.

What spell had controlled me through autumn? At the time, I'd thought I loved Theron, but now my feverish longing faded as I attended to his care day after day. When the healthy Theron spoke, walked, and hunted, I dreamed about his body. Now, with his body in my charge, I dreamed of the man. I wanted to see expression in his face. I wanted to see his lips curve into a smile or a frown. I still marveled at his body, but what obsessed me now were the memories of his wild laughing as he charged through the woods. I would stare for hours at his features, trying to tease out the history of his life. Childhood play, I imagined, left as its mark the old scar on his elbow. A badly-made sandal shaped his crooked second toe, I decided. Love, to me, meant knowing every inch of him, and at the same time knowing him to be a mystery.

Desire no longer drove me. I waited for him patiently, trusting he would one day return.

Theron's eyes opened one day in late winter as I dressed the wound on his familiar body. He caught my wrist.

"Nikia," he said.

I answered with a smile.

"How long have you been here?"

"Most of a season."

"And the goddess?"

"She led me to you."

Theron shook his head. "Ares tore me in half. His body blazed so I couldn't see him. I couldn't do anything to protect Artemis."

"What you did must have been enough."

I tried to calm myself by turning my attention back to the routines I had built around his inert form. I couldn't. Meeting his eyes and hearing his voice restored my desire, and my anger at his obsession with Artemis. I blushed as I ran my hands over the wound, averting my eyes from the bare skin of his stomach and the trail of fur leading down below. He caught my hand again. "She wanted me there, watching her," Theron said. "I would never have dared to be there without her knowledge."

White-hot jealousy crowded out my vision, and rage as deep as the ancient anger of the Titans pounded through me. I went on with my work, trying and failing to lock him out of my heart.

Theron grew stronger every day, and I knew I would soon leave Delos. Tendrils of spring peered around doorways like timid little girls. The sun, which had sneered down on us like a cold and distant monarch through winter, turned to gentler pursuits, taking an interest in tracking soft shadows over sloping meadows and wind-blown beaches.

I took Theron outside. Obeying the order of the goddess, everyone hid from us. "What is her plan for us?" he said into the eerie silence. I shrugged, avoiding the thought of losing him.

"Will you stay on Delos?" I said. My face gave more meaning than my words.

"Yes," he said. "I'm sorry, Nikia."

I shrugged again. It would never satisfy me for him to submit to

13

my caress as Eurydice had done. I'd had months to resign myself to this.

The priestess came one evening. "The temple will prepare a boat for you in the morning," she said.

I did not speak of this to Theron. I cooked his evening meal, waving off his attempts to help. At the end of the meal he took my hand and pressed it to his cheek. I stared at him, heart pounding in my chest.

Emptiness woke me in the middle of the night. I couldn't smell him. Remembering autumn, I pressed the sleep from my eyes with my fist and got up to follow him to the stable. He waited there with two of his fine black horses saddled. He tossed me the reins of the mare. "You'll need to be able to keep up with me tonight," Theron said.

I nodded, feeling self-conscious. We mounted, and our horses rushed from the stable as if from the starting gates of the games at Olympus. We raced faster than the first horses rushing up to shore from sea foam under the whip of Poseidon. The magnificent horses of Achaean heroes, which pulled bright and deadly chariots behind them as they thundered toward Trojan enemies, could not have caught us. The moon witnessed our ride, our horses as sure on the night trails as at the height of noonday, and the forest sounds fading to a whisper as we gave ourselves over to the thrill of speed.

We came once again to Artemis's secret place in the heart of the forest. Intoxicated by the heady scent of the goddess's body, we dismounted just outside the clearing. Theron took my hand before we passed through the undergrowth and onto the wet brown earth beside the pool.

She appeared then, her body deadly and glorious. She wore nothing but bow and hunting knife. Her eyes flashed at our intertwined hands. I pulled away from Theron, but she stopped me with a gesture. "I won't be jealous," Artemis said, her voice large as battle but soft as a flower. Theron fell to his knees, pulling me with him.

"Rise and come here," she said to me. When I obeyed, she took me in her arms. The pleasure of her touch pounded through me, too strong for my body. "I will know the touch of no man," Artemis purred. "But my Theron deserves some reward. Give him this for me." She bent her head and kissed me full on the mouth, her sweet tongue pressing my lips open and slipping into me. I would have fallen, except the goddess held me up and pushed me into Theron's waiting arms.

Trembling, I wound both arms around his neck, letting him support my weight. He shook, too. Even in the full presence and terror of Artemis, I smelled Theron's body and longed for him. I gave him her kiss, and a little of mine, too.

His eyes on the goddess, he caught his breath, still holding me, and said, "If the goddess will accept it, I would have you repay her this in turn from me." Theron loosened my robe and let it drop from my shoulders and into the mud. He picked me up and wrapped my legs around his waist, then lifted my breasts to his lips, kissing and sucking on the nipples. I groaned and ground against him, my blood thudding in my ears. *At last.* I didn't mind being a vessel for her, as long as he touched me that way. When he set me on the ground again, I turned back to Artemis in a daze. Her eyes flashed, but she nodded her permission, and I took her nipples in my mouth one after the other, nibbling them gently as Theron had nibbled mine, trying to transmit to the goddess every nuance of the lips and teeth I had dreamed of for so many nights.

I ferried caresses between them for what felt like hours. I trailed kisses down his chest for her, ending by dragging teasing fingers up both his thighs. For him, I pressed my lips to the insides of her elbows, the flesh behind each knee, and the place where her neck met her shoulder. I vibrated with the touch of mortal and immortal alike, until my mind thrummed with pleasure and power. My fingers explored Artemis's sex, as Theron had explored mine. When I didn't think I could walk another step, Artemis made me lie down in the earth beside the pool and beckoned Theron closer.

"Look at me but do not touch," she said, this time to him. The goddess looked down at me then. "Do you give yourself to me and him?" she asked. I swallowed hard and nodded. Artemis settled her sex over my face, her scent going straight to my head. I gripped her thighs with both my hands and opened my mouth wide to her, letting my nose press into her opening as I suckled the hard nub between her legs. She gasped and laid her hands over mine, squeezing. Theron probed the wetness between my legs, then replaced his fingers with his long, hard cock. The sensation as the two consummated their love through me filled me more than to the brim. I forgot myself as man and goddess gasped above me.

I think the orgasm started in Artemis, but it passed from her into my mouth and down my body, until I shuddered and rolled my hips up to meet Theron's thrusts. Then it caught hold of him, too, and he clawed at my hips at his own release. Almost before Theron finished pouring out his seed, Artemis disappeared, leaving us alone in each other's arms, and yet not lonely.

We fell asleep at once, exhausted by the force of her immortal presence. I had no dreams, only the sensation of his warm arms around me, holding me up even in the land of sleep.

The light of the next morning's sun brushed against us like feathers. I opened my eyes to Theron. I feared he would be disgusted by me, since I no longer served as channel for the goddess. But he stroked my hair as he woke and smiled into my gaze, meeting my lips with a kiss meant only for me. "We are much the same, the two of us," he said.

If you enjoyed this story, you can sign up for a free membership at
ForbiddenFiction and discuss it with other readers
and the author at the *Hunting Artemis* story page
at http://forbiddenfiction.com/library/story/AL1-1.000228.

Touching Freedom

Natalie hates living in Wesley House, where tentacles boil up from the shower drains and girls sigh suspiciously above the hiss of running water. She's not one of the perverted Hentai girls; there's no place in her controlled life for that sort of pleasure or abandon. She petitions for a new room assignment.

When she is forced her to encounter the tentacles, however, Natalie discovers a scientific puzzle. Instead of the beast she expected, she finds a vulnerable creature in need. Trying to help it leads to Natalie's first taste of rebellion, her first experiences of being seen as a "hot girl," and her first awakening to sexual pleasure. (F/?)

Chapter 1

Hentai Girls

Natalie knew it had come back when all the girls on her floor started taking really long showers again. Buildings and Grounds said they'd permanently fixed any problems or infestations after Natalie's last complaint, but she just knew if she went into the shared bathroom, she'd see piles of tentacles boiling under the shower curtains and hear girls sighing suspiciously above the hiss of running water.

Rumors about the origin of the creature living in the pipes of Wesley House held that it was an ancient horror from beyond the stars, an out-of-control waterproof robot built by horny engineering students, the chemically altered product of runoff from the college cafeteria, or a collective delusion caused by unusual mold that grew on Wesley's old bricks. The most persistent story claimed it had grown from a rich girl's unauthorized pet octopus, bred specifically to be a masturbation toy. When campus security caught the girl with the pet — supposedly because of her loud moaning — the girl dumped it down the shower drain to avoid getting in trouble. It resurfaced years later in its current form.

Natalie hadn't believed the stories before she lived in Wesley. They all sounded too nutty to relate to anything real. But she'd seen the thing in the Wesley showers, and she didn't need an origin story to know she didn't want anything to do with it. The idea of a creature coming up through the plumbing sounded like the stuff of nightmares to her — and that was even without considering where it might try to put its tentacles.

She packed her toiletries into a neon green basket and started showering in Davis, the next dorm over. She visited the dean's office every day, begging for a change in her room assignment. She rushed quickly in and out of her building, avoiding encounters in the hallway with the Hentai girls, the ones who liked living in Wesley.

Natalie's routine worked without too much trouble until the night she returned to her dorm late on a Saturday, exhausted from a long trip to an out-of-town violin recital. Trudging up the stairs to her floor, hauling her purse and her instrument, she heard music and drunken laughter. She cringed. The party spilled into the hallways, blocking the way to her room.

Even under normal circumstances, Natalie wouldn't have wanted to participate. She didn't like the idea of surrendering to anything, not even for a moment, and parties applied too much pressure to give up control. On top of that, though, the Hentai girls made her even more uncomfortable. They represented an ideal of femininity that had always seemed out of reach, and while boys seemed to find that alluring, Natalie was keenly aware of its claws and sharp edges.

She tried to pass through quickly without engaging the others, but someone cut the music. The suddenly silent Hentai girls arranged themselves into a gauntlet, their eyes burning into Natalie.

"Um. Hi," Natalie said. Her voice trembled despite her desire to seem cool and brave. The door to her room was only a few feet away, but the glaring girls standing in the way of it made the distance seem much farther. She told herself this was just a party prank, and that there was no need to get too scared.

No one responded to her tentative greeting, though. Instead, one set of girls locked hands across the hallway, preventing her progress. Natalie dropped her head to hide her growing fearfulness and addressed the group. "Please. I just want to get to my room. I'm tired."

Someone laughed. The cruelty of the sound made Natalie flinch. More girls reached for each other before and behind Natalie, trapping her in a web of linked arms.

She tightened her grip on her purse. "Could you... could you please let me through?" She hated the pathetic tone of her voice, but she'd never figured out how to handle direct confrontation. She'd been taught to stay out of the way, and to reach out to an authority figure if she needed help.

A sweet-faced redhead smiled, showing surprisingly sharp teeth.

"You can stay for one beer, right? We want to talk to you, but you never seem to want to talk to us." She held out a bottle, but the angle was wrong, as if she planned to pour its contents over Natalie's head rather than hand it to her.

Natalie's heart pounded. "I'll call campus security."

"You're good at that, aren't you? Making complaints? You threaten to call the authorities right away, and I bet you don't even know my name."

"It's Cora," Natalie said automatically, her good-student instincts strong as ever.

The redhead cocked her head and took a swig of the beer. "Oh, you do know who I am! That's sweet. But why don't you ever say hi?"

"I'm not really looking for friends." Her shoulder ached where the strap of her violin case pulled on it. Her mind flipped through the playbook of useless adult advice she'd received for threatening situations. She couldn't just ignore these girls—they were forcing her to pay attention to them. It was way too late to look for a buddy to accompany her down this hallway. Trying to fight seemed truly ridiculous. She wanted nothing more than to get out of this situation, but all she could think to do was plead for release. "Look, I'll make sure to say hi in the future. I'm sorry. Now, can I go to bed?"

The sea of linked arms rippled, allowing Cora to approach Natalie. "You're the one who called Buildings and Grounds, aren't you?"

Natalie said nothing.

"Living in Wesley is a privilege. Every year, girls fight to get in here. We're all upperclassmen. Even the doubles in this dorm disappear before the sophomores get to look at them. What are you doing here if you don't like it?"

"I had a violin recital the day of room drawing. My friend thought it would be funny to put me in Wesley."

"Right. Because you're so far above us. With your violin recitals and whatever your major is."

"Marine biology."

"Whatever. You're busy making Tiger Mommy love you. I bet you've got a merit scholarship."

Natalie glared back. She didn't like that she fit the Asian stereotype, but there it was. "I'm trying to get transferred. I'm sure I'll be out of here before it causes any trouble."

Cora's eyes narrowed. "It's already caused trouble. Do you know how often we have to protest to save Wesley? Some of the administrators want to tear this dorm down. They say there's a persistent infestation going down to the very roots of the plumbing. When you complain, it gives them ammunition."

Natalie let her violin case and purse slip to the floor. A hint of stomach acid crept into the back of her throat, and she swallowed hard to try to clear it. She could never think long about the creature and what the Hentai girls did with it. Even in the dark of her own room, orgasm struck her as unseemly, too bestial and unrestrained. Having an orgasm in a shared bathroom, where dozens of other girls had done the same thing, responding to the touch of a creature of unknown origin, letting it inside her—her belly gave a threatening heave. The Wesley girls might as well claim they *liked* running across cockroaches in the cafeteria. "There *is* a persistent infestation! We all know what's in the bathroom. It's sick. They *should* tear this building down!"

"That's very judgmental of you, Natalie. None of *us* are having a problem with any infestations. When was the last time you had a shower in this dorm?"

"I'm not going in there."

"You saw it once and ran away, didn't you?" Cora pressed. "Didn't you? First day the dorm opened after the summer, I bet?"

"Yes! That's what all of you ought to have done!" Remembering the first time she'd seen the creature made Natalie's calves itch, though she knew nothing was touching her. She knew she ought to keep her expression neutral, but she couldn't hold back the revulsion she felt as she stared Cora down.

Cora's lip curled. Her face reddened. As shameless as Cora sounded, Natalie's reaction seemed to have embarrassed her. She stepped closer and gripped Natalie's chin. "You think you're so perfect, don't you? You're above it all? You don't need the things the rest of us need?" Her hand shook against Natalie's jaw. She clenched tightly for a second, then snapped her palm open. Natalie braced herself for a slap that didn't come.

21

Instead of striking her, Cora sneered in Natalie's face. "I think you need a shower now. You look like you got pretty sweaty today."

Natalie glanced toward the floor's shared bathroom. Her stomach lurched at the idea of going in there at all. She didn't even use the toilets there, much less the shower stalls. Now, she regretted every defiant thing she'd said. "Look, I'm sorry about the complaint." Natalie's shoulders lifted around her ears. She had the sick sense it was too late to get out of this, but she had to try to placate Cora. "I promise I'll stay out of your way until I get transferred out of Wesley."

"We can't work this out until you stop thinking you're better than us. You need to get over this phobia of yours. The shower's fine." Cora grabbed Natalie's arm, separating her from the straps attached to her belongings. Natalie struggled, but other girls grabbed her, too. She looked around for help, but no one met her eyes. She screamed, but instead of giving her strength, desperation made her limbs freeze. Natalie searched Cora's face for any sign of compassion or mercy, but her tormentor's expression showed nothing but cold fury.

"Don't make me go in there! Please!" Her throat tightened at the idea of tentacles wrapping around her feet and making their slimy way up her legs.

"We're locking the bathroom door until you take a nice, long shower," Cora said. "It's for your own good."

"You can't let her do this! You can't let her!" The wilder Natalie got, the more the girls around her moved like forces of nature, controlling her with the indifference of a deadly ocean current. Natalie freed one arm, tearing Cora's shirt in the process. She tried to claw at the other girl's face. "You're a bunch of fucking perverts! You can't do this to me!"

Cora stopped abruptly, grabbing Natalie by the wrist and peeling her grasping hand away from her face. "Why? Because you'll tell Buildings and Grounds? You think a bunch of perverts care about that?" She looked to the other girls for support. "Do you ladies think this bitch is as clean and perfect as she pretends to be?"

"No way," said a brunette with an orange flower in her hair. She flipped Natalie's skirt up, revealing a pair of sagging cotton panties. "Oh, honey. You know you don't have to wait for your mommy to buy those for you." Natalie's body felt cold and hot at the same time.

She kicked, but her foot went nowhere. There was no way to cover herself, nowhere to hide. Everyone was paying attention to her underwear and her bare legs, and the shame of that fact made her tighten everywhere, until air could barely move in and out of her chest.

Cora snapped the elastic waistband of Natalie's panties. "Well, well. Maybe she's innocent after all." Her face softened for a moment, and Natalie hoped she would waver.

The other girls weren't having that, though. "She just needs encouragement," the brunette said. "She's probably creaming those little-girl panties thinking about what it'll be like in the Wesley shower. You're helping her. She's dirty, and she needs a shower."

The girls in the hall hooted at this declaration, celebrating it. They chanted: "You're dirty, and you need a shower." Natalie found her voice too late. The refrain drowned her protests completely.

Cora shrugged at Natalie and plunged again into the mood she had instigated. She dragged Natalie to the bathroom door. Other girls tore at her top and skirt. Cora gestured to Natalie's underwear, and the girls stripped that off, too, along with her sandals. They thrust Natalie into the bathroom on the third floor of Wesley, famous all over the campus for the regular appearance of tentacles from the shower drains, and held the door closed.

Chapter 2

Alone with a Monster

Instinct demanded that Natalie fling herself at the door, pounding on it and howling to be let out. That accomplished nothing, and all the while the center of her spine pricked. She glanced over her shoulder every few seconds, convinced that the creature had risen from the plumbing to stand directly behind her. The darkened bathroom made it seem as if the creature could be wound around every dingy pipe, or was about to pop out of every drain.

The chant dropped, and the sudden silence made Natalie's attempts to escape seem all the more futile. The grimy tile floor felt cool and gritty against the bottoms of her bare feet. Natalie took a deep breath, struggling for control of her voice. "Please," she whispered, making one last bid for sympathy from the girls out in the hall. "I don't want it to... do anything to me. Please let me out."

While she awaited a reply, she flipped on the light. She wanted to see anything that came for her.

"You won't know until you try it," Cora called through the door. "If you don't get wet, you don't come out." An animalistic shriek of approval went up at the double-entendre. Cora's voice strengthened and rose in volume. "And you'd better get good and wet. I'm going to smell your hair and make sure it's clean."

"You should smell her pussy and make sure it's salty!" Natalie didn't even know who that was. There were too many of them to resist, and too much of a mob mentality to allow the mood to change. They cheered and cat-called Natalie, trying to one-up each other.

"Cora, this is crazy," Natalie begged. "Please. You don't really want to do this."

"Sweetie, quit being coy." Natalie recognized the brunette. Her raucous voice came through the door, thick with the effects of alcohol. "We're giving you permission to do what you really want. Go on."

"No. I really don't want to."

"We don't believe you," one girl replied in singsong tones.

There was more laughter, then Cora said, "These girls are getting bored out here. If you don't do something entertaining soon, I'm going to have to come in there and make it interesting."

Natalie gripped the door handle involuntarily, wondering now if she could hold it closed. There was no way she could win that battle against the girls in the hallway, though. She searched for possible escape routes. The bathroom's one window might not be large enough to squeeze through, and even if she could, she had no way to get down three stories. If her shouting hadn't alerted anyone so far, she didn't see how it could help her now.

The thought of the shower stalls made Natalie's stomach roil again. She wondered if the girls would have mercy if they found her emptying her guts into one of the toilets.

"Natalie, I don't hear any water..." The sugary tone covering Cora's threat only made it more frightening. Adrenaline replaced nausea for Natalie.

She borrowed a set of toiletries from one of the bathroom's cubbies, selected a shower stall, and pulled back its curtain.

Nothing leaped out immediately. The light fixture hummed. The scariest thing Natalie saw was mildew gathered at the corners of the shower and around the drain. She allowed herself to hope the creature really was just a story after all. Or, even if it was real, Natalie thought there might be a chance it wouldn't appear this time. She stashed the toiletries within reach and turned on the water, ready to take the fastest shower of her life.

Natalie washed the makeup off her face as quickly as she could, figuring Cora would definitely check that. Before she could rinse the soap from her temples, the creature appeared, one thin, pale tentacle licking up through the drain cover.

Natalie screamed and jumped out of the shower, running to the door and pounding on it. "Let me out of here now, God damn it! This isn't funny! Please!" Tears of panic flooded her eyes.

The girls on the other side of the door only laughed. "Get back in the shower, Natalie, or I'll come in and watch you," Cora threatened.

"I can't. Please." She danced from foot to foot, afraid to remain still. She kept imagining slimy sensations, as if that tentacle was already touching her. It didn't matter that the scientist in her knew better—her horror at this creature had nothing to do with science.

"I can. And I will."

The girls howled with delight. "You'll thank us later!" someone promised.

Natalie knew she had no chance of talking Cora down from her determination—not with all the others there, feeding off Natalie's misery and egging Cora on.

Sobbing and hiccupping, Natalie made her way back to the shower stall, in time to see the thin tentacle complete an exploration of the stall's floor, then wind deftly through the holes in the drain cover and lift it away, creating an opening large enough to allow three much thicker tentacles to rise through the drain as well. These, too, began to feel around the shower. Rings of muscle rippled under pale skin as they moved, and occasionally a knob bubbled onto the surface, then disappeared. Natalie shivered. Could they be searching for her?

Even adrenaline and fear of the girls couldn't push Natalie to step any closer. She stood frozen, staring at the tentacles.

"If I don't hear a shower echo around your voice in thirty seconds, I'm coming in there," came her torturer's voice through the door. "It won't hurt you." The girls outside began to count.

Natalie knew she was probably lucky they hadn't already run into the bathroom. If they physically forced her into the shower, they would probably keep her there. They wouldn't let her avoid the tentacled creature, and they would probably watch whatever it did to her. She had barely endured the shame of them all looking at her panties. Natalie's brain shied away from thinking through whatever else they might see if they came into the shower with her. Wincing, Natalie ran in among the tentacles and shouted, "I'm in here!"

She stood on her tiptoes, watching the fleshy appendages continue their exploration. She wondered what it would feel like to step on one, and the arch of her foot spasmed. Natalie fought to keep her last meal down.

"You keep that up," Cora called. "Shout to me periodically so I know you're being good."

"Or moan to her," said another girl. Loud laughter echoed through the empty bathroom.

"Okay!" Natalie answered. The thin tentacle found her, prodding her foot, and Natalie's word ended in another scream as it wrapped her ankle. Seemingly alerted by the thin tentacle's discovery, the three thick tentacles followed suit before Natalie had time to react, their strong grip holding her in the shower now whether she liked it or not.

"Oh my God, get it off me! Get it off me!" She tried to pry them away from her legs, but whenever one of her hands touched their undulating, muscular surfaces, she recoiled, shaking.

"Sounds like it found her," said a girl outside. They had quieted, apparently eager for evidence of Natalie's distress. Natalie didn't want to give that to them, but she couldn't help whimpering. She didn't recognize her own voice. Desperation made it thin and high.

The tentacles began to crawl up Natalie's legs, squeezing and massaging her calves as they did. They felt rubbery, but not slimy, and they seemed more purposeful than they had any business being. Those tentacles would head up between her thighs.

Natalie retched and shuddered. Despite being a senior, she'd never let anyone touch her there. She'd barely touched herself. In Natalie's carefully controlled world, ruled by violin and the expectations of her parents and teachers, she had no room for letting go.

The tentacles moved higher, and Natalie's horror crystallized, leaving her mind strangely blank. This was the worst thing she could imagine, and there no longer seemed to be any point in screaming. She watched the creature's progress, and the only thing she felt now was deep hatred for Cora and the other Hentai girls. She hated their ostentatious displays. She hated their pleasure, and their assumption that she would learn to enjoy what they enjoyed.

Steely resolve filled her chest, and she got over her disgust for the tentacles enough to try one more time, forcefully, to peel them off. Clenching her teeth, she wound her hand around the thickest one and tugged it firmly away from her body.

To her surprise, it gave. Natalie tried the others, and each released her in response to one firm tug.

"It's gone quiet in there!" Cora howled. "She must be having a good time right about now, even if the stuck up bitch won't tell us about it."

Natalie ignored the taunt and stared at the tentacles. They were supposed to be an instrument of violence, the weapon Cora and the other girls were using against her, but they seemed uncertain now. Moving tentatively, they unwound from her body one by one, but remained hovering near her. There was an honesty to the hatred she'd discovered, and in her bones she understood now that the tentacles weren't really the enemy. They weren't really what she feared. They had released her willingly, doing what the Hentai girls would not.

The creature would have let her run out of the shower, but Cora and her friends would not let her out of the bathroom. Natalie edged into a position with a clear line to the door in case she needed to retreat, then touched one tentacle with the tip of her finger. Even having released her, the creature might be aggressive, or it might conceal other surprises.

It pressed toward her the way a cat would, though, and Natalie stroked slowly down its length. When she'd thought of the creature as a disgusting invader from the depths of the building's plumbing, she'd reacted like a stereotypical girl watching a horror movie. Now it seemed less like a monster and more like an object of research. Of course it wasn't slimy. She should have known.

She'd worked with an octopus for a while when volunteering at an aquarium. That creature was capable of learning and remembering, and craved human touch as much as the familiar varieties of human pets. "What do you want?" she murmured, studying the collection of tentacles while continuing to stroke one.

She knew the longer she stayed in the shower, the more the Hentai girls would believe they'd accomplished their goal. Natalie focused on the tension in her neck and shoulders, trying to unknot the muscles. The girls had unintentionally told her the truth—the creature wouldn't hurt her. It hadn't forced itself on her though they'd apparently believed it would. Ironically, she was probably safer at this moment, with the creature, than she'd been at any other point since she'd arrived at Wesley.

Natalie needed to sell the girls outside on the depth of her shame when she left the shower, but in the meantime she could indulge her growing curiosity about the creature. It occurred to her that its initial behavior, heading aggressively for her vagina, might be trained rather than instinctual. If it had been a living masturbation toy at one point—if that particular rumor turned out to be true—how did the person using it tell it what she wanted it to do? Had it become anything else now? How intelligent was it?

Natalie knelt in the shower and touched it some more, finding that it responded to her in a predictable fashion. She even managed to teach it a game, squeezing a tentacle in patterns that it repeated back to her.

No longer afraid, she finished the shower Cora had commanded, keeping the tentacles occupied by prodding them with her toes. They behaved like pets, and seemed eager to please. Watching them curl around her feet, Natalie felt suddenly sorry for them, the way she sometimes did for the trick dolphins at SeaWorld. She wasn't enjoying her own time at Cora's mercy, and she wondered how the girls treated this creature. What did it eat? What did it need?

The door opened as soon as she turned the water off, and Cora poked her head in. "Is little Natalie a woman now?"

The knowledge that she'd escaped what they'd intended made her feel stronger than she had all night, but she wasn't about to let that inflate her confidence. She hadn't forgotten that they'd overpowered her with ease. Natalie was glad Cora wouldn't get the satisfaction of seeing her broken, hurt, or sobbing, but she didn't want to inspire more confrontation. She kept her body hidden behind the shower curtain, her spine curled. The creature retreated as soon as the water stopped, and Natalie made a mental note that it seemed to need moisture. "You were right," she told Cora. "It didn't hurt me. It was a perfect gentleman."

The girls howled. "I bet it was," Cora said. She held out a bottle of beer, the offer genuine this time, recognition that Natalie had survived a hazing. The Hentai girls seemed to think she was one of them now, and Natalie wasn't sure if that made her want to curse at them or collapse on the floor in relief.

She shook her head at the beer. "I just want to go to my room now.

29

And I want my clothes."

The room seemed to hold its breath as the girls awaited Cora's reaction to this refusal. The redhead smiled, though, giving Natalie a mocking nod. "Our shrinking violet here's had quite a night. I'll bet she needs to curl up in bed alone." She gestured lewdly with the bottle. "You know, think about the creature."

Natalie's face flamed, though she knew the teasing wasn't true. The girls laughed again, but they let her duck out of the bathroom. The brunette handed her the balled-up remains of her clothing, and Natalie ran down the hall to safety at last.

Natalie didn't want to know what Cora would come up with as additional retribution if she reported the event to campus security. She said nothing.

She did, however, start showering in Wesley, paying no mind to the teasing that came from the Hentai girls. Their new acceptance of her improved her living situation a great deal, even if she still hated them for what they'd tried to do to her. The creature poked its tentacles out every time she turned the water on. Natalie had learned that it liked when she stroked her hand firmly down the length of its exposed flesh — or had she trained it to like that? She started a notebook where she tracked her observations of its behavior.

A few times, she started conversations with other girls in Wesley, trying to figure out what they did with it. For all the innuendo about the creature, no one seemed willing to talk specifics. Donna, for example, a tall, slim, volleyball-playing blonde who lived down the hall, rolled her eyes when Natalie raised the subject. "You know what we do with it."

"I mean, what specifically?" Natalie pressed.

Donna shrugged. "It grabs you and fucks you. Like... you know."

Natalie had trouble believing no other girl had discovered how responsive the tentacles could be. She waited in a bathroom stall late one night, hoping to get a chance to watch how someone else interacted with the creature.

She didn't have to wait too long. Cora came in, stripping off her clothes as soon as she passed through the door and heading straight for the showers. Natalie waited until the water started, then stepped out of the stall as quietly as she could. The school always skimped on shower curtains, probably in an effort to save money, so Natalie had an easy view of the redhead, almost to the knee. A clutch of tentacles wound around her calves, and Cora gripped them with red-manicured hands, urging them up.

"Come on," she muttered. "Don't get sluggish on me now. You were never shy before." She hauled the tentacles higher up her body, squeezing them so hard that bloodless patches spread out from around her grip.

Holding her breath, Natalie lowered herself to the floor, working soundlessly to find an angle where she could get a better view of Cora's shower. She crawled on her belly until she was just outside the shower stall, hoping Cora would be too occupied with the tentacles to notice her there.

Natalie peered upward. The redhead stood, legs wide, tentacles wrapped around all four limbs. Many more had come up for Cora than ever had for Natalie. They crammed through the shower drain in what looked to be a painful squeeze. Cora yanked them maniacally, guiding them around her waist, her upper thighs, and her bare breasts. She squeezed them hard and they squeezed her back, but she didn't seem satisfied. Cora wrung one tentacle with both hands, and the creature responded by tightening all around her. Her nipples stood out as her breasts protruded and reddened.

Cora sighed and rocked within the hold. Natalie noted the rocking, wondering if that effectively signaled the creature to perform a different action. Whatever the impetus, a tentacle unwound from Cora's thigh and probed her slit. Natalie's face heated and she wanted to look away, but she reminded herself of her scientific curiosity and kept her gaze fixed on the redhead.

Tentacles peeled loose from her waist and arms and joined their fellows at Cora's entrance. The girl rocked harder and faster, the muscles of her thighs straining to spread as wide as possible. Four thick tentacles, studded with fleshy knobs, charged into her, and Cora threw back her head in ecstasy, her mouth open in a cry that was choked off by another tentacle pressing between her lips. Powerful rings of muscles contracted rhythmically to drive the appendages that worked within Cora.

Natalie watched wide-eyed as Cora and the creature played out every move in a complex symphony of violation. If her training theory was true, the nuance of the creature's behavior with Cora seemed an incredible feat.

Not wanting to press her luck, Natalie retreated as rapidly as she dared. Only later, when she returned to her room to make her notes, did she realize how aroused she'd been by Cora's display. Furtively, Natalie slipped one finger into her panties. She drew it out covered with juices. For a moment, she wanted to lie in her bed and linger on the image of the creature with Cora, to rub herself until she shuddered in ecstatic oblivion the way Cora had.

She resisted the urge. Pleasure was for Cora and the others, and it bothered Natalie to submit to it. Cora's abandon had been impressive, but if Natalie imagined herself in the same position, her throat tightened and her stomach clenched. Natalie wanted answers. The elation of discovery was the only type of high she could allow herself.

"Natalie, are you distracted?"

"What?"

"Your technique is suffering. Have you been keeping up with your practicing?"

Natalie lowered her violin and forced herself to look her teacher in the eye. The woman's sharp features had haunted her day and night in the four years she'd attended college. Selected by Natalie's mother, Audra Simmons had an all-too-familiar severity. Even this minor criticism made Natalie's shoulders tense.

"I've had a lot of work for my major lately," Natalie said, trying to sound neutral. She didn't want Audra to fixate on this. She smiled briefly, a practiced half-confident "everything is fine" expression that had worked on authority figures for most of her life. "I promise I'll practice more."

"I hear you've gotten a room in Wesley." Audra's voice dripped disapproval. "I hope this doesn't mean you're distracted by the college lifestyle. Have you gotten a boyfriend? Are you taking time off on the weekends?"

"No," Natalie sighed. Longing crept into her tone despite her efforts to keep it suppressed. "I'm not taking time off." *Not ever.*

Chapter 3
Starfish and Freaks

"Wow, you live in *Wesley*?" Stuart flicked his eyes up and down Natalie's body, breaking his habitual slouch to lean forward. He took the pencil he'd been chewing out of his mouth and set it beside his computer's keyboard. He wasn't bad looking. He hadn't let himself go the way a lot of grad students did, and, behind his glasses, he had nice blue eyes. Streaks of gray behind his ears testified that during his time in grad school, he'd made the full transition from boy to man. But Natalie wasn't in his office for a date, and she wanted to get any potential for misunderstanding out of the way immediately.

She crossed her arms defensively over her breasts. "I didn't tell you to impress you, Stuart. I'm definitely not trying to hit on you. I'm asking because you've been at this school the longest. And because I thought, as a marine biologist, you might care to find out about it."

"Can you get me in to see it?"

"Yes, if you agree to help me." He seemed way too excited by this statement. "I'm not going to give you a demonstration or anything."

"Sure, sure." Stuart raised an eyebrow. "But you've tried it, right?"

"Forget it. I'm sorry I asked. I'll figure this out on my own."

Stuart hurled himself to the door before she could leave. "Wait, wait, wait. Look, Natalie, I'm sorry. I'm being a tool. I promise, I'll be cool."

She leaned back and waited.

"Okay, you need something. I understand that. I've looked up some papers, you know, out of curiosity. Maybe it's not just breeding, maybe it's genetic engineering."

"Genetic engineering? Seriously? How rich was this girl supposed to have been?"

He shrugged. "I'm just saying money can buy you a lot. Anyway, it does seem possible to modify an octopus the way the rumors describe. Certain kinds of genetic modifications can be ongoing and adaptive, increasing an organism's plasticity both in terms of neurons and at a cellular level. That might explain the way the creature seems to have... grown. Assuming, of course, that the stories I've heard are true. I could get the papers for you if you need help with the research."

"I'm a scientist, too, you know," Natalie said coldly. "I've got as much access to the papers on Elsevier as you do."

Stuart seemed about to protest, but then he collected himself and nodded. "Fair enough. I've got to show I've learned something in my time as a grad student." He drummed his fingers on his thighs and spun around on one heel. Natalie couldn't help smiling in response. His excitement, however perverted its motivation might be, was exactly what she'd been hoping for. Stuart turned back to her. "How about this? I question whether the creature is based entirely on an octopus."

"What? Why?"

"Well, Buildings and Grounds has cut it back several times, right? They must actually do something to it, because it disappears for a while. I wonder if it regenerates like a starfish, and has some of the corresponding genetic material. It could regrow tentacles if they're cut off or something, maybe even reattach to them if it gets the opportunity. That would explain why the administration hasn't gotten rid of it."

Natalie snorted. "I used to wish they'd just pour a couple hundred gallons of Drano down the pipes and take the thing out once and for all."

"Used to, huh?" Stuart grinned. "The creature changed your mind?"

"Shut up. Anyway, the Wesley girls must worry that toxic chemicals would kill the creature. All the officers of the Environmental Club live in Wesley, and they're super-active about protesting chemical use on campus."

"Makes sense. Even a genetically engineered starfish wouldn't be immortal."

"Okay," Natalie said. "So tell me more about this starfish theory." She allowed Stuart to coax her in the direction of his desk. She took the chair beside his even though, in his tiny office, that meant nearly sticking her head in one of his many fish tanks.

"Don't think I'm a perv for telling you this." His fingers crept toward her knee. "I've heard that some girls take cuttings of it when they graduate and leave Wesley for good. That wouldn't work unless it had some sort of regeneration capability."

"That *has* to be an urban legend!" Natalie protested. "Surely someone would notice if these things were spreading."

"The whole thing seems like an urban legend, doesn't it?" Stuart said. "Do I get to see it now?"

Cora caught Natalie going into the third-floor bathroom with Stuart. She whistled and looked them both up and down. "Why, Natalie! You've turned into a little *freak*! And an older guy, too. If I didn't know you'd had it in you, I wouldn't think you had it in you." The redhead winked theatrically and continued down the hall.

Natalie rolled her eyes and ignored Stuart's gaze until they got inside the bathroom. When she did glance at him again, he wore an awed expression that she didn't like at all. "So you *have* tried it," he said.

"Remember how you said having a girl let you into Wesley is every guy's dream? Don't ruin it for yourself, okay?"

"Right. Sorry."

"Just try to focus on the creature, and not... the rest of this."

"Sure. Totally."

Natalie took off her shoes, rolled up her pant legs, and stepped to the shower. "It seems to need moisture. It only comes out when the water's on." She started the water, and sure enough the pale, thin tentacle poked up through the drain cover.

Stuart gasped and stepped back. "Does it... does it just grab you and start... doing things?"

Natalie greeted the tentacle with a toe prod, it reciprocated, and a few others emerged. Keeping out of the water herself, she stroked them in her usual way. "They seem to respond to training," she said.

"I see that." Stuart's voice sounded strangled. She glanced back at him, and couldn't help noticing the erection filling the front of his jeans.

She looked at it pointedly. "Is that all you can think about?"

"I'm sorry. They're kind of phallic, and you're stroking them, and I can't stop thinking about where they've been."

"I had no idea I was that exciting." Natalie kept her voice sarcastic, but, actually, his reaction was sort of flattering. Stuart was treating her like a real Wesley girl, a hot girl, not a robot dedicated to academic achievement.

"You are *very* exciting," he said, but lifted his hands defensively. "Sorry, don't throw me out, okay? You asked. I'm focusing the best I can."

Natalie smiled a little to herself and went on stroking the tentacles. "I want to know how this creature survives. What do you think it eats?"

Stuart swallowed, his Adam's apple moving up and down in his throat. "God, this whole thing is probably making you think I'm a total creep, but I have an idea." When she didn't answer, he went on. "If I were designing a living masturbation toy, I would make the creature want to do whatever it's supposed to do. So I wonder if it lives off female secretions."

"I don't think it lives off soap." Natalie forced a smile after the joke and pretended to consider Stuart's suggestion objectively, nodding slowly. Her interest in the creature had forced her to think more about sex, but that didn't make her comfortable discussing female secretions with some guy. She cleared her throat. "That makes sense," she said as evenly as she could. "Could be. What do you think is its ideal environment?"

Stuart blinked and worked his jaw.

"I don't mean that. I mean, where do you think would be the healthiest place for it to live?"

He shrugged. "The ocean, maybe? Both octopuses and starfish live in salt water. It's hard to assess this thing's health, considering we can only access part of it. It's obviously surviving where it is — it's hard to say what would be best for it."

Natalie let one tentacle wind around her forearm. The sense of pity she'd been feeling for the creature welled up in her again. "I think it's craving something. It seems desperate."

"Are you *trying* to kill me with innuendo?"

"I'm being serious." She stroked the back of the tentacle. She imagined she could feel the creature sigh in response to her. "Stuart, do you have a salt-water fish tank?"

"What?"

"I want to take a cutting and test it in that environment."

"Even if it likes that, what are you going to do? You can't get the whole creature out of here and move it to the ocean."

"I know. I thought if you're right — if the creature can regenerate — maybe the cutting can merge back with the larger creature if it gets the chance, and maybe it'll at least feel healthier, have some better nutrients or something."

"Is this a girl thing? Like, it gave you a really hard orgasm and now you want to help it?"

She rolled her eyes. "Stuart, can I use your fish tank?"

He stared at her, his eyes traveling an obvious path to the tentacle on her arm. The naked desire on his face shocked Natalie. "God, yes. You can use anything you want."

Natalie waited until the middle of the night, when she had a good chance of being alone with the creature without interruption. She went into the bathroom, but didn't turn the light on this time. She didn't think she wanted to see herself doing what she was about to do.

She knew every corner of the room by now, and felt comfortable enough in her rapport with the creature that she didn't feel fear as she stripped herself, stepped into the shower, and turned on the water.

It came to her, and she lowered herself to a sitting position on the floor and sat beside it. Blind tentacles nosed at her chest, and she allowed them to encircle her. Before she'd touched the creature, she'd imagined it would feel slimy and cold, but in truth it wrapped her in a firm, warm hug. She sighed and rocked into its embrace, keeping a hand ready to redirect it if she accidentally triggered another girl's training.

"You don't know anything but being used, do you?" she whispered. "Your whole life, you've just done what people expected you to do. It looked like you got free and got big, but really, you're just as trapped as ever." The creature, of course, did not respond, but Natalie realized her cheeks were wet with tears.

She gripped a tentacle where it wrapped her shoulders and stroked it. "I guess I'm talking about myself, not just you. I used to think if I did well, people would be satisfied with me, but they aren't, are they? They always want more, and you can never let your guard down. Not ever." The creature returned her affection, a few thin tentacles fondling her back.

Natalie took a deep breath and tried to collect herself. "I swear I'm here for you. We need to figure out what you eat." She rested one hand on her inner thigh, gathering her resolve. "I wish I had a more scientific way to test this, but we're just going to have to do our best."

She swiped her finger through her folds. Even though she'd been crying, she'd gotten wet at some point. In the dim light from the window, Natalie's finger glistened. She held her hand near the tentacles, trying not to telegraph any particular sense of direction.

Knobs bubbled up on the tentacles wound around her body, and she recognized the phenomenon from the first time she'd seen the creature. Natalie reflected that she didn't generally see knobs when she interacted with the tentacles. Perhaps they were involved with feeding, and it didn't generally consider her a food source?

She touched her moistened finger to one of the knobs as an experiment. The knob gave in response to her touch, the tissue much spongier than what Natalie normally felt on the creature. Her heart beat with excitement. The knob seemed like a viable intake organ.

Natalie delved between her legs again. More knobs appeared on the surfaces of the tentacles, their studded texture massaging her where the tentacles wrapped her. Natalie moaned inadvertently, then admonished herself. She hadn't come for a sexual experience—she simply wanted to gather information about the creature's feeding habits. Still, she could not deny that the knobs' eager response to her touch affected her.

She relaxed and let the tentacles support her as she again dipped her finger between her legs. This time, instead of swiping through the folds, she worked her index finger inside herself. Gasping, she fed the resulting fluid to the tentacles. The tentacles did not overwhelm her. The knobs never seemed ravenous or rapacious.

Natalie repeated her gestures over and over, and gradually, she felt pleasure radiating through her pelvis whenever she touched herself. She allowed her hips to respond to her probing finger. She allowed her fingers to find her clit and massage it, savoring the trembling pleasure that tingled down her legs when she did.

Under the guise of feeding the creature, Natalie ever so slowly worked herself into a powerful orgasm, the first she had allowed herself in months. When she shuddered and threw back her head in ecstasy, a thick tentacle slid between her lips, and she sucked it without a thought.

"I'm not sure if you'll be fully prepared for your next recital," Audra Simmons said. The practice room where Natalie had met her felt too hot and too close.

Natalie tried fixing her eyes on Audra's severe bun so she wouldn't have to meet the woman's unsympathetic glare. "I'll practice harder."

"You've been promising that for weeks. I think you're becoming a Wesley girl, wasting your promise on frivolous entertainments."

Natalie blushed. Audra Simmons, like most officials, probably thought the rumors about the tentacles in Wesley weren't true. This clearly didn't stop her from accepting the popular reputation of the Hentai girls. "I've had a request in for a change of room since the beginning of the school year. I go to check on it in the dean's office every—" Natalie stopped. How long *had* it been since she'd followed up on that? "I check on it all the time," she finished lamely.

Her face might as well have been on fire. Dozens of recent furtive scenes in the showers at Wesley — *feeding the creature* — flashed through Natalie's mind. Was Audra right about her?

"I'll put in a word for you with the Dean," Audra said, softening. "We need to get you into an environment that supports your practice."

Chapter 4
Experiments with Boys and Tentacles

Knobbed tentacles darted up immediately to meet Natalie, arching toward her hand. She kept her dominant right hand, and the knife it held, out of the way, stroking them with her left hand instead.

"I'm still going to take care of you," Natalie whispered. "Just not the usual way. I'm sorry if this hurts."

She knelt and dropped a kiss on the nearest tentacle before severing it swiftly with the knife. It jerked and oozed in her hand, and the surrounding tentacles retracted suddenly, disappearing down the drain.

"I hope you won't be avoiding me now," Natalie said, stroking the piece she held. In case it would help it heal, she reached between her legs and smeared some of her juices over its surface before transferring it to the small carrier tank she'd borrowed from Stuart.

Cora caught her emerging from the bathroom with the piece of tentacle and raised an eyebrow. How did the redhead always manage to catch her at the worst moments? "You don't graduate for another seven months, you know. Don't you think it's a little early for that?"

Natalie could only stammer in reply.

"You here to visit your friend?" Stuart asked. "Or me?"

"Are you ever going to stop that?" Natalie asked, settling herself next to his tank of tropical fish.

"What? Hitting on you? Not until I get results."

"What if you never get results?"

He grinned. "I've got faith as long as you keep coming to see me." Recently, her body had started to respond to the way Stuart's cheeks creased when he smiled. Was this because of her late-night sessions feeding the creature? Natalie blushed.

"Actually," she said, "I came to check on it."

"It looks healthy. And come check this out. I think it's growing a part we can't see on the full-sized creature." Natalie followed him into the locked storage closet where he kept the smaller creature's saltwater tank.

The tentacle she'd cut still formed the bulk of its body, but a bulbous mass had formed at one end. "I think it's brain tissue," Stuart said. "The tentacle itself probably contains part of the nervous system, and maybe that includes the potential to grow a new brain if it gets separated from the main body."

"And if they're rejoined? What happens to the new brain?"

Stuart shrugged. "Maybe it merges with the old brain."

Natalie leaned close to the tank and peered at it. "Look at that color. That's a brilliant orange, not the pale shade we see in Wesley. I think it *is* healthier."

"Maybe it's just doing well on a concentrated diet of Natalie."

"Stuart, I swear."

He pressed close to her, and Natalie's body went stiff. "I think about you feeding it all the time," he whispered. One hand rested on her hip, and when she did not move, it slipped under her shirt and traveled up toward her breast. Stuart drew Natalie into his embrace. She tried to understand what she was feeling. It was hard to determine her own reaction when his was so obvious and overwhelming. The stubble on his cheek scratched the tip of her ear. "It drives me crazy. It makes me so fucking jealous. Do you take it out of the tank and put it inside you? I have to know. I want to watch."

He pulled her right breast out of the cup of her bra and pinched her nipple, and Natalie jerked. Her pulse pounded between her legs. Her nights feeding the creature had taught her about the kind of temptation Stuart offered. She knew she was still naive, though. Stuart wouldn't be content with merely tasting her arousal. Natalie didn't know how she would feel about offering him more.

43

She glanced at the creature in the tank, remembering the ecstasy she'd seen on Cora's face. Could sex with a man make her feel that much pleasure?

Natalie felt tired of being the good girl. Why had she come to Stuart in the first place? Was it really that she couldn't put together a salt-water tank herself? Maybe she'd been curious. Regaining her powers of movement and speech, she leaned up and whispered back to him, "Stuart, today I'll let you help."

"Jesus, yes. Just tell me what I have to do."

Keeping her eyes on the creature, she guided his hand under her skirt and into her panties. Stuart moaned loudly when he touched her wetness. "I've wanted this for so long," he said, and forced three fingers into her. Natalie yelped and jumped away from him. She'd never put so many fingers inside herself.

"What's the matter, baby?" He pulled her into a kiss, his tongue sweeping through her mouth and somehow managing to choke her more than the much thicker tentacle did when it pressed between her lips.

Natalie twisted her head away and snatched his hand from beneath her skirt. She locked eyes with Stuart. They were both panting. "Don't forget to feed it," she said. She didn't know if she wanted to go through with this, but she didn't know if Stuart would let her back out now that it had started.

"I'll help you feed it later, Natalie. I just need to get inside you, right now. Please." He fumbled with the zipper of his pants. She glimpsed the head of his cock and got the old heave in the stomach that the creature used to inspire.

"No," Natalie said. "Not like this."

"Come on." Stuart grabbed her. "You Wesley girls like this hentai shit, right? You want me to push you up against the wall and just take you? Maybe in the ass?"

Her temples ached. She tried to tell herself this wasn't happening, but she knew better. The creature had shown her unexpected mercy when the Hentai girls had tried to force her on it, but humans never seemed to back down. "No!" Natalie wailed. "Forget it! I changed my mind!"

Stuart ignored her and kept coming. Glancing around the closet desperately, Natalie lit on the salt-water tank. Fueled by adrenaline, she yanked it off its shelf and heaved it into Stuart's chest. He coughed when the thick glass caught his solar plexus, falling backwards. The tank dropped to the floor and shattered. Natalie paused only long enough to grab the small creature from amid the broken glass and puddles of water. She tucked it under her shirt and fled.

Natalie ran straight for the third-floor bathroom, turning on the shower water before she even peeled off her clothes. The creature cradled against her chest twitched wildly. She thought it might be dying.

Sobbing, she laid it on the drain cover while she got naked, then lay beside it and held it. Its muscles still twitched in response to her, so it wasn't dead. She let the water wash over her body, missing the certainty of life when she still trusted that people would appreciate her if she did the right thing. She missed the comfort she'd felt in the creature's embrace. She missed her belief in the harmlessness of Stuart's flirtation.

Natalie stroked the creature on her chest. "I want something for myself, just once," she whispered. "Just for me." Cora's ecstatic face flashed through her mind again, and one hand slipped between her legs. Realizing her juices might do the creature good, she transferred her arousal to its skin. It arched in response, knobs forming over its bright orange surface.

Natalie stared at it, still stroking, and made a decision. "You understand what I need, I think," she said, and guided the tentacle between her legs. It didn't plunge into her. It rested at her entrance, rubbing at her with a large knob, while Natalie spread herself slowly wider.

It went rigid when she guided it in a few inches, but did not move while she grew used to accommodating it. She didn't expect too much blood from its entry—she knew from visits to the gynecologist that she'd broken her hymen years ago in the course of normal activity. Still, she'd expected discomfort and soreness, not the gathering hunger that filled her now.

Gasping, lifting her pelvis as high as it could go off the shower floor, she pushed the tentacle deeper in. It curled, arching against a tender spot inside, and Natalie groaned aloud. She wanted more of that, and she stroked it encouragingly. Her other hand found its way to her clit. She rubbed, finding that this caused her to clench her muscles around the creature. It undulated within her, providing slow ripples of pressure to various points along her inner walls.

Natalie worked her clit frantically, straining her muscles and pointing her toes. She needed more. A familiar sensation in her mouth made her eyes pop open. The drain cover had moved aside, and a clutch of knobbed tentacles emerged, heading between her legs. Natalie exhaled and spread as wide as she could go. Tentacles wound her breasts, her waist, her arms, and her ankles, but others probed between her legs. They slipped into her slowly, carefully, slickly, entangling with the cutting as they did, and oscillating within her the way it did.

Sensing motion, she craned her neck and saw the creature had lifted her off the floor. She gave herself over to it, and its motions inside her became more forceful.

A tentacle nudged the hand at her clit, and Natalie let it push her away. A thick knob rolled up and down her clit in a smooth, muscular motion. Natalie sucked hard on the tentacle in her mouth, and her entire body heaved in time to the movements of the tentacles within her as she came for it, over and over again.

The creature seemed to know when Natalie got tired. It lowered her gently to the floor, taking Natalie's cutting with it. She hoped it understood she had tried to create a better life for at least that small part of it.

"Where are you going?" Cora asked, staring at the luggage Natalie was dragging down the hall.

"My violin teacher asked the Dean to move me to a new dorm. She said Wesley was distracting me from my studies."

"I *hope* it was!"

Natalie couldn't help but smile. Cora had never really understood what was going on. She thought about the hatred she'd felt for the Hentai girls. She hadn't forgiven Cora and the others for what they'd done to her—but she wouldn't trade the experience away either.

"You should come back and visit," Cora said. She lowered her voice. "The creature's learned this new rippling thing." She shuddered. "It's pretty amazing."

Natalie grunted as she hefted another suitcase. She didn't want to leave. On the other hand, she didn't know who she would become if she stayed. She might understand Cora a bit better, but Natalie wasn't really like her. She wasn't the hot girl Stuart had hoped for. Natalie suspected she was about to disappoint just about everyone. Her time at Wesley had taught her that she couldn't be what her mother and Audra Simmons wanted either, and she didn't think moving her out of the dorm would take that knowledge away.

"The creature is a good performer," Natalie said. "It knows how to do what's expected and please its audience." She paused, too conscious of the parallels between herself and that boiling mass of tentacles. "Do you ever wonder what *it* wants?"

"Does that matter? I mean, it's just a *thing*, right?"

Natalie's eyes dropped to the carpet. "Yeah. I guess you're right." Natalie couldn't envision a way to offer the creature a meaningful escape, and she feared the same would be true for her. She couldn't picture what freedom would be like for either of them—the best she could come up with seemed partial and fleeting. Maybe all it would ever have was a taste of that salt-water tank, and she would have to content herself with the memory of that one night of abandon. She doubted she would ever trust a person enough to give herself over as completely as she had with the creature.

She gave Cora a little wave, dismissing the redhead's puzzled expression. Natalie tried to put a brave face on the things she'd learned about herself. "Don't worry. A part of me will always be a Wesley girl."

If you enjoyed this story, you can sign up for a free membership at
ForbiddenFiction and discuss it with other readers
and the author at the *Touching Freedom* story page
at http://forbiddenfiction.com/library/story/AL1-1.000226.

Less Than a Day

Tod is a harbinger of imminent death. He doesn't use his powers for good—instead, he offers women a last fuck before they die. Jaded, Tod is surprised when one woman gets to him like no other. The last sex of her life is the best sex of his. (M/F)

Less Than a Day

"You've got less than a day to live," he whispered in her ear. "Want to fuck?"

Unlike most pickup lines, the setup was true. At first glance, she could have been any single woman at the bar with blonde hair, strappy shoes, and overdone makeup and expectations; but she was the one whose imminent passing he felt in his bones. He, on the other hand, could not have been just any man. He was over six feet tall, thin as a rail, with a stone face and a cock just as hard. His hair and eyes were blacker than emptiness, and his heart was emptier than space.

The woman he'd approached blinked and pulled back from him. As if his physical appearance wasn't enough to tell her he was different, he'd dressed like an apparition as well. He wore a tailored black suit, a blood-red tie, a silver watch, and shoes polished bright enough to reflect the bit of moonlight that crawled through the bar window.

"Want to what?" the woman said.

"You heard me," he said out loud, settling into the bar stool beside her. "Want. To. Fuck. Question mark."

He didn't use his powers for good–not particularly. He told himself he used them at face value. The women he liked best had terminal diseases. They already felt death's cold shadow, and they were desperate and hungry for him, whatever he offered. They didn't care if his pronouncement was true *per se*. He did not like the women who thought they were immortal, the ones who laughed and told him to talk to some muscle-bound boyfriend, the ones who brushed him off with a flip of their hair and didn't even remember him in their final moments.

This woman was neither. She stared. "I did hear that part," she said. "I think I asked the wrong question."

"I can repeat the first sentence also, if you'd like." He leaned close and smiled. Now was the time to set her at ease. If he'd thrown her sufficiently off guard with his bald opening, she would like him for an upturning of the lips here, a soft touch to the cheek there. If she believed what he said, she would need him then.

"Okay," she said.

He moved his stool closer. He gestured to the bartender and ordered two club sodas. He waited until he had the drinks before turning back to her. "You've got less than a day to live," he said.

"You'd think you'd order me a stiffer drink," she said. "How do you know?"

He just smiled and looked down at the bubbles in his drink. The bar was dark and noisy. He knew just how his face looked in shadow, and how quiet could spread in a ring around him in even the loudest places.

"Okay," she said again.

He glanced up quickly. Her eyes were green like the dress she wore, but he thought they'd be blue when she was naked. She nodded slowly, and he let the grin spread over his face.

He held out a hand and helped her off the stool, led her out of the bar with firm and rapid steps.

"You don't look like the type who came in a car," she said, once they'd ducked out of the bar's back entrance and smelled the comparatively fresh air of the alley outside.

"I didn't."

The night was warm, but he noticed that her nipples were hard under her dress, and the faint hairs on her arms stood on end. The moon was nearly full.

"We can take mine," she said. Now she led, with the same fearlessness he'd displayed. Her car was an expensive red number, nicer than her forlorn little cocktail dress had led him to expect. She walked to the passenger side to let him in — an oddly chivalrous gesture.

"What do you do?" he asked as he settled his long body into the front seat.

She fiddled with her purse and put on lip balm. "Do you really care?"

He blinked. "I suppose not."

"Don't ask me any questions like that. If what you say is true, I don't want to waste any time talking about things that don't matter." She adjusted her mirrors and started the car. "Do you have a name?"

"Tod."

"Todd?" she said hopefully.

"Tod," he repeated.

"That's cute." Her voice was dark. "I do know a little German, you know."

He didn't feel the need to respond. He watched her drive. She frowned as she looked at the road, hunched forward a little to grip the steering wheel.

"We're going to my place, in case you care," she said.

"I figured."

"You do this a lot," she said. It wasn't a question. "What do you usually do?"

"What do you mean?"

She shot her eyes in his direction. "I don't want a quickie."

"Of course not. You should make sure to get what you want."

"Is that what you always say?"

"Most people don't ask. They just expect me to fuck them."

"I think," she said slowly, "that *I* want to fuck *you*."

She wasn't urgent about any of it. They parked outside her house and she took him in, pausing to take off her shoes and put her jacket away tidily. Her house was full but orderly, with a lot of feminine touches like couch covers with blue embroidered flowers. She made them both tea, which he accepted.

"Am I going to find out who or what you actually are?" she asked. She sat in a light wooden chair at her kitchen table, her legs crossed at the ankles.

"No."

"Do you know anything about how I'm going to die?"

"No."

"Then I think I'm done talking. My room's around the corner to the left. Go take off your clothes and get in my bed. I'll be in as soon as I clean up the tea."

He almost offered to do it for her. Instead, he shook his head and did as she asked. He stroked himself slowly as he waited, idly reading the titles on her bookshelf. He felt her books must have all been gifts — they formed no cohesive picture of her.

She came in and paused in the doorway. "You look hot like that," she said. "Do people say that a lot?"

His hand stilled on his cock. "I don't think they usually care."

"I do. I wouldn't want my last fuck to be just anyone." She nodded toward his cock. "Don't let me stop you."

She stepped closer to the bed when he resumed stroking and pulled her dress up over her head. Her motions were slow and deliberate, but not lewd. Despite himself, he held his breath waiting for a glimpse of her nipples. She hadn't been wearing a bra. They popped out of the tight dress, dark and pointy, and he moaned in the back of his throat.

"You want me." She sounded surprised.

"Of course I do," he said. "Come here."

She stepped toward him before she'd gotten the dress off all the way. Her face still hidden in it, she shrieked when he pulled her down beside him and started biting those nipples. He let her struggle with the dress as he sucked and bit. He had her nipples poking out obscenely from each of her tits, her hips rolling against him.

She'd relaxed in his arms with her face still covered and her hands still tangled in the dress. He took the opportunity to find out how hard he could bite her breast. He fastened his teeth on her left nipple and slowly increased the pressure, listening to her whimper become a moan and her moan become a scream. He stopped short of drawing blood, but she never asked him for mercy — she only rubbed her cunt against his leg.

She fought free of the dress when he released her. "Are you going to laugh at me if I ask you to wear a condom?"

He produced one from where he'd stashed it under the pillow. "*I'm* not about to die," he said.

"Right. That makes sense." She took a deep breath. For a moment, he thought she would cry. Then she visibly hardened. "Put it on. I want to ride your cock."

He did as she asked. She didn't kiss him or make any romantic gestures. When he was ready, she supported herself with her right hand as she maneuvered herself into place. He helped her spread her cunt lips for him. She was dripping wet, and he wondered when she'd gotten that way.

She sank down onto his cock with one smooth gesture, grinding against him at the end. "Ah, God," she said, her head thrown back. "Do you know how long it's been?"

"There's only one thing I know about you," he said. He put his hands on her hips to help her, but she didn't need his help. She was already pounding him, one hand on the wall beside the bed and the other on his chest.

He watched her ride him. He was turned on and ready for her, but the way she moved relaxed him. She was content to fuck herself with his cock. He didn't need to do anything in particular for quite some time.

He toyed with her, pinching her thighs or her nipples or her sides. She fucked him, rubbing her clit, squeezing her nipples, slipping her fingers into her mouth and then down to her clit once they were spit-covered and then back to her mouth once they were cunt-covered.

Sometimes, she slowed. For a while, she lowered herself so she rested on his chest and ground her clit against his pelvis while she squeezed his cock hard with her cunt. She sat up after that and leaned back so her breasts thrust out, bracing herself with one hand on his thigh behind her. Keeping her body still, she brought her free hand to her clit and masturbated ostentatiously. He didn't think it was for his benefit. Instead, she masturbated with his body. The idea turned him on. He felt his cock getting harder inside her.

He couldn't believe her wrist wasn't tired. She circled her fingers over her clit with ferocious intensity, sweating, gasping in frustration every time she didn't quite climax. Eventually, she came so hard he could clearly feel her spasming even through the condom.

While she was still coming, she resumed fucking him, really slamming down on him now. For the first time he groaned, his eyelids falling closed. He reached out for her. He wanted to fuck her back. He wanted to arch up into her and come. He wanted to push deep into her, and pull back only so he could push into her again.

"Don't you dare come yet, you motherfucker," she said then, her voice coming tight through clenched teeth. "Don't you fucking dare come."

He opened his eyes and stared at her. She was biting her lower lip, gripping his shoulders while she fucked him hard. Her hair hung around her face in sweaty threads, and sweat dripped down her back and off the points of her tits. Her eyes were hooded and dazed, staring vacantly into his face and seeing something far beyond.

He couldn't help himself. He grabbed her and pulled her down into a hard thrust. Once. Twice. Three times, and that was it. He groaned and came while she still tried to ride him. He heard her above him, saying, "Damn it, damn it, damn it."

Feeling her tight pussy still moving while he came drained him all the way.

She came to a crashing stop on top of him. "You couldn't wait?"

He shook his head, his cock still throbbing with the pleasure of it.

"I was so close to coming again."

"I can take care of that." He wouldn't have said it normally, but he wanted to make it up to her.

She cocked her head, relenting a little.

He eased her gently off his cock and got rid of the condom. Then he pushed her onto her back and lowered his lips to her pussy. It tasted a little unpleasant there, what with the latex and the sweat and the smell of his own body. But she grabbed his head right away and pulled him in.

"Don't think you're doing me a favor just by licking it," she hissed.

Startled again, he wrapped both arms around her ass and thighs and dove in. He nibbled at her labia, and when she moaned and pushed up against his face, he bit them. He nipped her clit, drooled all over her, fucked her with his tongue.

He shoved fingers up her cunt. He put one in her ass and sucked her clit hard.

"Christ, yes!" she shouted. "Don't stop!" He sucked as hard as he could, sure that he must be hurting her. She screamed but never loosened her hand on his head. He felt her starting to come, her whole body convulsing, jackknifing at a pace all her own.

"Fuck, fuck, fuck," she said. "Can you fuck me again?"

Eating her had gotten him hard. He fumbled for a condom as she clutched at him. When he finally had it on, he grabbed her legs and held them up so he could really spear her.

"Just do it hard," she said. "Make yourself come."

"Yes, ma'am." He plunged in and out of her, pulling all the way out every time and shoving fiercely back in. Since he'd already come once, he couldn't have gone too fast if he'd wanted to. Besides, she was almost purring under him. He looked down at her, off in her own world with his cock.

He gripped her harder and drilled her more forcefully. He let himself make his own private world, too, one where all he had to think about was her cunt.

She had her hand down between them, working her clit, and then she was coming again, growling from the back of her throat as she did. For a moment after she came, she felt really loose around him. He pumped harder, trying for the bit of stimulation he got around his head when he drove in really far.

She screamed a little when he pushed in that deep, and soon her pussy was clenching so tight around his cock that the sensation traveled up to his lungs and he felt like he couldn't breathe.

She was talking to him again, a stream of obscenities and anonymous filth. He hadn't thought she had this in her. The dirtiness of it made him speed up, trying not to touch the bed at all. She moved her hand out of the way and held herself up for him with a fist under each hip.

He gasped and came again.

He resisted sagging onto her body until she pulled him down. His arms were weak from exertion and he couldn't hold himself up against her force. Everywhere their skin touched he felt hot and sticky.

She kissed his forehead and lay still beneath him. "You lasted longer than I thought you would."

"Thanks." He felt annoyed with her. He shifted so he could roll away.

She stopped him with a hand on his shoulder. "So what happens now? How long do I have left?"

"The thing I do isn't very precise," he said.

Her breath was slow, considering what had just passed between them. He was still panting. "So now you leave. And I wait here alone."

He sighed. He did roll off now, and she didn't try to prevent him. He got rid of the second condom and looked at her. She would probably have been embarrassed by what he saw — smeared makeup, wild hair, sweat-soaked skin, bruises starting on her breasts from where he'd been biting her. But he liked it.

He lay on his back with his head pillowed on his folded arms. "I always leave before I see the death," he said. "The actual death... leaves a bad taste in my mouth."

She stared at him, incredulous. Then she burst out laughing. She tried to stop herself with a fist in her mouth, then gave up and rolled over, burying her face in the pillow as her shoulders shook with it. He waited. Again, he felt the need to make it up to her, though he couldn't have explained why.

A moment later he realized she was crying, not laughing. He lifted a hand to touch her shoulder but did not.

"I'm such an idiot," she choked out finally. "Right up to the end. Idiot."

"What? Why? You seem like so much less of an idiot than–" He trailed off, certain the comparison would not please her.

"Less of an idiot than the other dumb, desperate girls you fuck?" She sat up now, wiping the last of her mascara off with vigorous fists digging into the corners of her eyes. "High praise, coming from you." She sagged a little. "But I'm not less of an idiot. You see, I thought you were going to keep me company until the end. I thought I wouldn't have to die alone. But that's not what you were promising at all, was it? You were just offering me a last fuck. Which is exactly what you said. And I thought I was so clever and so sexy."

He clutched at her, suddenly fervent. "You were sexy. You were sexy as hell."

She shivered. "Let's not talk about heaven and hell right now."

"Fine." He sighed. He felt heavier than usual.

Her eyes mauled his face. "So what could I offer that would get me a little more company? I've got some valuables here. You could take them if I really die."

"I'm not a thief."

"Of course not." She picked at her sweat-soaked bed-sheets. "Listen, if you're going to leave, you'd better get out of here."

He watched her eyes—blue now, as he'd guessed–shimmering with barely captured tears. She was right. Now was the time to leave.

But instead of getting up and looking for his clothes, he took her in his arms with a tenderness that surprised even him. He tilted her face up and kissed the corners of her eyes, flicking his tongue out to taste the salt there. He kissed her lips and her jaw and the hollow of her throat.

"What are you doing?" she whispered.

"I don't know."

He returned to her lips. She hesitated, but soon kissed back.

"Do you want to fuck me again?" she asked finally.

"I could, maybe, but I don't have to."

"Can I ask you for a favor?"

"You can ask."

"Will you sleep with me?"

He hesitated. She rolled away so he couldn't see her eyes. "Just for a few hours," she said quickly. "I'm tired, but I don't want to be alone. Then you can wake me up if you want, and—"

He put his hand over her mouth. He didn't want to hear her promises or her negotiations. Still silent, he turned her so her back was cradled against his chest, her ass against his pelvis. He draped one arm over her chest and palmed a breast. He lay there stiffly for a moment, then let his face roll forward into her hair.

"Do you swear you'll be here when I wake up?"

"You're going to have to trust me," he said. He wasn't going to swear.

Her body felt small and tight with tension. She smelled of sweat more than anything else. It wasn't a bad smell.

He counted her breaths, noticed the count getting slower. She uncoiled in his arms. He worried she might die that way and he wouldn't realize at first that he held a corpse. He wished death were as simple as this uncoiling, the relaxing that marked the crossing from waking to sleep.

He slipped into sleep beside her, so easily that he didn't know it until the dreams came.

"You don't have a wallet, or keys, or even money," she said. "What are you?"

He sighed. "Do you wake every man up by telling him you went through his clothes while he slept?"

"You were awake. I saw your breathing change."

"True." He opened his eyes. She had washed her face and put on a thin tank top that just covered her nipples and the curve of her ass.

"Were you having nightmares?"

He made his face as hard as he could.

"It woke me up," she admitted. "You were struggling in your sleep. And whimpering."

"Whimpering." He made the word drip with disapproval. He sat up in bed. His head felt heavy and foggy. For a moment, he wondered if she'd put something in the tea.

"You don't have to tell me." Her face began to close off from him. Absurdly, he had to stop that.

He reached for her, pulled her against his still naked chest. He stroked her hair and breathed the smell of her like she was something he would care to remember. "I did have a dream," he whispered finally. "A nightmare of you, of death in the pool."

She shivered in his arms. "Is that what's going to happen to me?"

He ignored her and went on. "I did other things, was with other people. But that image of you kept coming in. I started running, but everywhere I went, it was all I saw, and every voice I heard belonged to you."

She didn't speak for a long time. He thought she'd fallen asleep again, until she rolled to face him. "Thanks for staying." She kissed him slowly, her lips soft and warm against his, and just a little sticky.

His arms tightened around her. He realized how hard he held her when her back cracked. He jumped and released her, but he felt her shake her head into the kiss. He wrapped her again, as tightly as loneliness.

"I could love you, maybe," she whispered. "If I weren't about to die. I think you need that."

"Don't," he said.

"Sshh," she said. "Right now, I want to pretend." She rolled onto her back, pulling his weight onto her. "What if I loved you so much that you could do anything you wanted with me? What if every touch felt good, no matter what?"

"What are you talking about?" He stiffened with alarm. She made him feel young, inexperienced, uncertain. Ridiculous.

"Bite me," she breathed. "Right at the base of my neck. As hard as you can."

In her dark bedroom, her blue eyes looked black as his. Slowly, he lowered his teeth to her neck and bit hard. She gasped in pain, fisted her hands. "Make me bleed," she said.

It was harder than he would have thought. He bit and sucked and pulled, trying and failing for a long time to tear the skin of her neck. People seemed so fragile, always ready to die, and yet a body resisted damage so steadfastly. She sobbed and struggled, but every time he almost let up, she begged for more. Finally, a trickle of iron flavor at his lips alerted him to a little wound in her neck. She sucked air between her teeth. "It stings. Bite my tits."

He bit her nipple harder than he ever had with anyone. He took it firmly between his teeth and pulled back until she cried out and honestly fought him. He grabbed her hands to hold her down and pulled some more. He tore at her nipple until she called him every filthy name and her body arched against his, her thighs wrapped tightly around him and her slick cunt frantically rubbing against his leg. The nipple bled more than her throat had. When he switched to the other, she screamed that she would kill him. He ignored her and mauled it, chewing and tugging and feeling a type of lust he never had before.

By the time he released her and looked down at her two wounded breasts, she'd become passive. When he spread her legs and bit her clit, she didn't move to stop him—just turned her head and sobbed into the pillow. He fastened his teeth around that most sensitive spot and tightened his jaw slowly, until he'd sunk deep into her flesh. Her sobs turned high-pitched. He shoved three fingers up her cunt and felt it squeezing down around them.

"I love you," she breathed. "I love you. I love you." And came.

He couldn't stand it. He opened his mouth and let go of her, pulled his fingers out, and flipped her over so he didn't have to look at her face. He spread the cheeks of her ass.

"Please," she said. He wet his fingers and pushed them slowly into her asshole, relishing each jerk her body gave as they penetrated her. A tear fell onto the blanket, but she shifted feebly, opening herself to him a little more. He added another finger and another, listening to the way her breathing changed as he further filled her.

He eased his hand out of her ass and found another condom. He spat on it, and on her asshole as well, and worked himself into her. He could feel the pulse moving through her skin. His body rose and fell each time her lungs expanded and released. He kissed the nape of her neck and bore down with his cock until he'd made it all the way in.

She sighed and lifted her ass up to him. He dug his fingers into her shoulders and levered himself into her, harder and harder. Suddenly, he wanted to hurt her, to enjoy every desperate sound she made. He gave her everything he had. He pounded her until his muscles screamed. He nailed her to the bed beneath him. She'd stopped speaking words, moaning inarticulately as she found her clit with her fingers again.

She had nowhere to go. He had her completely. As his cock spurted, he whispered into her hair, making sure she couldn't hear, "You too."

The feeling that rose in his chest frightened him. He pulled his cock out and stood. He had to get away. "Don't leave," she whispered. "Stay with me until the end."

He didn't say a word, just found his clothes and pulled them on. He already felt the mess on his cock soiling his clothes and soaking through his underwear. Right then, he didn't care.

She lay still on the bed, face buried in her arms. Before he walked out of the room, he grabbed a fistful of her hair and lifted her head. Her eyes seared him, full of fire and betrayal, reflecting memories of his own that he couldn't stand to think about. He almost asked her name, but thought better of it. She didn't try to stop him again.

He would normally have left a long time before, maybe even whistling to himself as he walked down a black and silent street, smelling of sour sweat and feeling alive. He let himself out, crossed the street, but could go no further. The night looked different to him. Part of him had stayed inside his dream, and he imagined he heard her voice. For the first time in a long time, he wanted a cigarette. And a drink.

Would her house catch fire? Would she die of some medical condition, leaving no sign of when it had happened? Would a masked man come to her door and find his way inside?

He stood in the shadows across from her door and watched. It was not yet dawn. He had to go, before he learned answers he didn't want to know to questions he didn't want to have. She had threatened to love him. He shivered.

Several blocks away, a shadow lengthened under the streetlights and drifted closer. Death would be here soon. He could go back to her, hold her hand as she stared into those grave-hollow eyes — but he would have to see them, too. He watched the shadow grow, measuring his own courage and finding it wanting.

The first fingers of light grasped the bottom of the sky. He spat on the sidewalk and turned away.

The Three Wives of Bluebeard

The cruel captain Bluebeard marries Mollena moments after her father's burial, only to brutalize her and abandon her in his isolated mansion. Her only consolations are dream visits from two beautiful, seductive women and her explorations through her husband's mysterious house. But Bluebeard forbade Mollena from the door locked with the small, gold key—and that's the one place her dream lovers want her to go. (M/F, F/F)

Chapter 1
Taken to Wife

Bluebeard came to take Mollena to wife moments after she buried her father, the failed merchant Andre du Toussaint. He stepped up beside her in the church graveyard and gripped her upper arm with one of his big hands, rough and scarred from working the sails of ships in his youth. Ignoring her tears, he pulled her away from the fresh mound of earth atop her father's coffin and led her to the priest.

"Father Arsenault," Bluebeard said in his flat and gravelly voice. "I'm sure you're busy today, but I wondered if you would accept some coin in exchange for a quick wedding ceremony. I'm afraid there's a bit of a rush. I sail tomorrow, but I promised my bride's father that I would provide for her after his death."

The priest glanced from Bluebeard to Mollena. The girl tried not to let her terror show. She had begged her father not to promise her to the burly ship's captain, whose previous two wives had disappeared under mysterious circumstances. She had sworn that she could spin or take in laundry or serve in some family's house as a governess. But the dying old man had insisted that she become a respectable married woman, and Mollena knew she was poor and plain, with hair like a soiled dishrag, a hooked nose, long and awkward limbs, and close-set eyes. None but Bluebeard would have her.

She met the priest's eyes bravely and nodded. Bluebeard displayed an embarrassing quantity of coin. The priest pressed his lips together and took the money.

Two of her father's pallbearers served as witnesses, all but her new husband still dressed in black for mourning. The captain's midnight blue hair and beard shone, he rose two hands above the next tallest man there, and his black eyes were cold with secrets. He wore a tailored suit that must have cost more than Mollena's father had made in a year. The ring he shoved onto the third finger of her left hand might have been made of iron the way its weight pulled upon her arm and heart.

Then Bluebeard took her home. Mollena craned her neck, stunned by high ceilings, the scent of fine wood and exotic spices, and a multitude of doors. Bluebeard jerked her closer to him, wrapping one meaty arm around the back of her neck. "You'll have time to see the house later," he said, undoing his belt buckle.

A thin, dry servant came to take the leather strap, fixing Mollena with a lascivious, appraising glare in the process.

"She isn't much," the servant said.

"No," Bluebeard agreed. Mollena waited for him to soften the statement, but he did not. He squinted at her. "Let's get this over with."

They left the servant behind, Bluebeard dragging Mollena up the stairs to his bed chamber at a pace just faster than she could comfortably walk. She stumbled and strained to keep up. Fine baubles displayed in the hallways blurred together. She saw only Bluebeard's broad shoulders, his purposeful stride. He shouldered his bed chamber door open and thrust her inside.

"Strip, girl," he commanded, freeing himself of his own clothing. Bewildered, she began to undo buttons. "You're not making much of a show of it, are you?" Bluebeard grabbed her hands away from her collar and pinned them beside her hips.

He leaned in close. His bitter breath clogged the air around her face. Bluebeard gripped her right hand and guided it to the mass of flesh between his legs. She had tried not to look at it. It felt far softer than she expected, the skin downy, two balls flopping loosely in their sack, and his tool dangling between, limp and slightly hot.

Mollena choked at the thought of herself, mere hours after her father's death, naked in a strange man's room, caressing him intimately. Blood rose to her cheeks.

Bluebeard shook her right hand impatiently. He wrapped it around his soft member. "Listen, girl," he said. "You're no joy to behold. You've no money to speak of. You're no pleasant companion.

You'll live easily here and want for nothing. This is your only duty. Learn to do it well."

Mollena blinked up at him. She attempted to move her hand over his flaccid shaft, but her nerves turned her gestures into weird jerks. Bluebeard glared and slapped her hand aside, replacing her uncertain grip with his own well-practiced fingers.

"I'm sorry," she tried. "I don't know anything about–"

"You can end your sentence there," Bluebeard said, gasping a little and humping against his hand. "You don't know anything." His shaft had grown a great deal in a short time. It now sprouted alarmingly thick and long from his lower belly, barely covered by his large hands. Mollena stared at it, biting her lip. "Lie down on the bed and spread."

She hesitated, glancing from the bed to his bulky body and back.

"Now!" Bluebeard roared, releasing himself in order to grasp her and throw her down. He forced her legs apart and hooked them over his shoulders. Mollena gasped at the discomfort of the unnatural position and struggled to move them down. Bluebeard growled and held one foot in place with one hand. With the other, he probed her sex, spreading her and lining up his club of a member.

"Hold still and take it, wife," Bluebeard said between gritted teeth. He forced himself inside her. Mollena could not help but sob, shocked by his manner as much as by the intrusion. Bluebeard grunted and adjusted his grip, fastening both her ankles to his shoulders and driving into her hard.

"Stop crying," he snarled. "That face is ugly enough without your pathetic expression. I've bedded whores old enough to be your grandmother who were prettier than you, not to mention wetter between the legs."

Mollena could bear neither the pain in her body nor the pain of his words. Bluebeard pounded into her, his flesh slapping against hers, his wild motions catching and pinching the dry skin between her legs. She grunted and cried out as he stabbed into her depth, beating and bruising her on the inside.

She turned her face toward her arm to hide from him, silent tears dripping from her cheeks onto the bed. Bluebeard increased his pace, finally grinding hard against her with a roar. His seed pumped into her, dribbling out around his member and pooling between the cheeks of her buttocks.

Bluebeard released Mollena, wiped himself with the corner of the bedclothes, and flopped onto the bed beside her, clasping her tight against his hot, hairy chest. She lay awake after it was over, imprisoned by his big arms, trembling with grief and fear, and shocked by all that had changed.

A great clock in the hall outside the bedroom struck every hour with dour precision. At midnight – the witching hour – she began to hear footsteps, sighs, and weeping in addition to the clock.

"Hello?" Mollena whispered, wondering if she should wake the man who had married her.

The door swung open, and in stepped two achingly beautiful women, one like night and the other like day. They clasped each other's hands tightly, and tears streamed down both their faces.

Pearls and opals dripped from the dark woman's throat and wrists. She wore white, and her long, black hair wound about her head and ears in complicated braids. Big green eyes opened wide at the sight of Mollena and she gestured to her companion, the smell of lilies wafting from her slender wrists as she moved.

The light woman wore a daisy chain in curly red hair, and her yellow dress clung tightly to her ample curves. She was round as the earth, with thick thighs and a soft belly. Her skin ruddy with freckles, laugh lines warmed the corners of her blue eyes despite her tears. She smelled like sun-warmed linen. She smiled sadly at Mollena.

"Who are you?" Mollena said.

Both women glanced at Bluebeard and shook their heads. Each pressed a finger to her lips. Mollena and the women stared at each other until the new wife drifted off to sleep.

Birds began tentative songs as morning broke, sunlight tapping its fingers against the sky, testing. Bluebeard snored in Mollena's ear.

She twitched a stiff leg, her body sore from Bluebeard's attentions. Seeing the door to the room closed, she decided she must have dreamt the two women.

Growing pressure in her bladder forced her to attempt escape from Bluebeard's grasp. Barely daring to breathe, Mollena pressed at the meaty forearms to make enough space for her to wriggle out.

She had nearly gotten free when he woke and gripped her tighter. His member pressed against her belly, threatening her with his desire.

"Just a minute," she whispered. "I'll be right back."

Blushing, she slipped out of bed to relieve herself. Fluids from the night before caked her inner thighs. The lips of her sex burned when they rubbed together, irritated by the ferocity of her new husband's attentions. Mollena made a tentative attempt to wash herself, half hoping that Bluebeard would fall back to sleep if she took her time before returning to him.

"How long will you keep me waiting?" Bluebeard muttered roughly from the bed. Mollena jumped and ran to him. He pulled her under the covers and opened her legs unceremoniously. Still tender from the night before, his ministrations hurt more this second time. Mollena bit her lip and tried to endure it.

He rolled out of bed as soon as he had finished with her. "I hope you feel like a woman now," he said, "because I don't have time to do any more." He turned his back and began to dress. "I'll be away for a few months. This is your home; enjoy it and keep it warm and ready for my return. My servant's not much for talking, but perhaps you can convince him to listen to your woman's prattle."

He paused heavily in the doorframe before leaving. He looked over his shoulder at her. She could not resist pulling the blanket higher to cover herself.

He smirked. "In the nightstand, you'll find the keys to every room in this house. You can use any of them and go wherever you like. With one exception: if you use the small gold key we'll both be sorry."

He placed his broad black hat over his blue-black hair and slammed the carved oak door shut behind him.

Chapter 2

The Ladies of the House

Abandoned for the present by her husband, Mollena tried to enter social life as a married woman. She sent invitations into town, but received polite excuses and complaints about the distance of the journey. Only after she'd been rebuffed by everyone from childhood friends to desperately lonely spinsters did Mollena realize the truth: no one would come to visit Bluebeard's house. The stories about his first two wives had done their damage.

Mollena screwed up her courage and went to the old servant, who was polishing fine, filigreed silverware in the kitchen. "I want you to take me to town."

"The master said to watch you here," the old man replied. His thin, frail body bent nearly double, but the malice in his voice made her fall back a pace.

"Just to visit a friend," she pleaded. "Would you trap me in my own home?"

The servant laughed. "Did the master tell you it was yours?" He narrowed his eyes. "He didn't mean it. You don't want to make him angry like the others did, do you?" He tapped the piece of silverware in his hand with a gnarled finger. The sharp blade of the knife glimmered when it moved.

Mollena swallowed. "What are you saying?"

"Questions," the servant sighed, running his cloth lovingly over the blade. "Questions make him angry. Be a good girl and run along."

Mollena wasted no time escaping him. She did her best to accept being alone in the house with the old man. She locked the door to the bed chamber at night and stayed out of his way as much as possible, doing her own cooking and cleaning and washing whenever she could. She entertained herself by singing old songs and playing what little she could on the piano in the main hall.

If Bluebeard had not behaved so cruelly, Mollena might have believed she had married well. The house was well-appointed. She found he had left her a closet full of fine dresses and, through the servant, access to accounts in town that allowed her to order any food she desired.

After her encounter with the servant, she feared the keys. But finally the day came when she had scrubbed even the imagined spots on the windowsills in the bedroom, kitchen, and hall. Her throat ached from singing. She sat on the bed and opened the nightstand.

Dozens of keys of all colors, shapes, sizes, and materials testified to the size of the house. Awed, she poked at them with her finger. The mass of metal and wood shifted to reveal a tiny golden key, tarnished and dirty.

A wail rose from the passage outside the room, followed by a woman's sob that cut off abruptly. Mollena gasped and slammed the drawer shut. She sat absolutely still, heart pounding. Mollena found the courage to extricate herself from the drawer and investigate the source of the sounds.

She searched a long time and found nothing. Shaken, Mollena ran downstairs and out onto the lawn, feeling the house and its secrets hulking behind her all the while.

The two women opened the bedroom door again. This time, instead of weeping, they giggled. The dark woman stepped boldly into the bedroom and flung herself down beside Mollena. The bed creaked under her weight.

Nervously, Mollena dragged herself up onto her elbows. "Who are you?" she demanded of the dark woman. The light woman still lingered in the doorway. "Am I dreaming?" Mollena asked.

"It depends," the dark woman said with a smirk. She laid her hand delicately on Mollena's wrist. "If you decide you're dreaming, will you let me do this?" She leaned in and pressed her lips to Mollena's.

The startled sound Mollena made transformed into something throatier. She had endured Bluebeard with no understanding of the heat he seemed to feel. This woman's touch freshened the very air in the room. Mollena trembled, breathing in the smell of a garden in spring just before a lightning storm.

The woman's lips caressed Mollena until she opened beneath them. A soft, warm tongue slipped into Mollena's mouth, stroking gently. The woman's smooth black hair trapped the sweet fragrance of her breath and the heat of her skin against Mollena's cheek. Mollena tried, tentatively, to return the kiss, bringing her own tongue to meet the woman's. She ran through the limited knowledge she had gained during her night with Bluebeard. Feeling uncertain, she reached up and gripped the black-haired woman's dress at the upper arms, trying to get up the courage to reach into it or unfasten something.

Before long, all thought slipped out of her mind. That maddening, patient tongue possessed her. Its movement inside Mollena's mouth telegraphed to every part of her body. Finally, the woman released Mollena, who lay flat on her back and panting.

"Am I dreaming?" Mollena asked again.

"A little bit yes and a little bit no," the woman said.

Mollena had forgotten about the light woman until she laughed. "Cecily is so enjoying being mysterious with you," the light woman said. She, too, settled on the bed beside Mollena. The soft warmth from the two women's bodies set off a fierce longing in Mollena. "I'm Francine. You are dreaming, but this is a true dream, and we are not figments of your imagination."

"You live in this house?" Mollena asked.

"We used to," Francine said.

"Now who's being coy?" Cecily said. She flopped away from the group, rolling her eyes. "We still live here, in every way that matters." Cecily's delicate black eyebrow arched. "We live here body and soul."

"Why don't I see you when I'm awake?"

Francine stopped Cecily from answering and shushed Mollena with a soft, sweet kiss on the lips. She stroked her, slipping her hands into Mollena's nightgown and caressing her breasts and sides. After a

71

moment, Mollena surrendered to the sensation, letting her head press deep into the pillow and arching her back. "You want something, don't you?" Francine said, giggling.

"Yes," Mollena managed.

Francine's fingers began to move along her belly, tickling and teasing as they went. But Cecily sighed loudly and trapped Francine's wrist before the light woman could satisfy the desire that had begun to bud in Mollena. "Don't distract her," Cecily said. "Let her ask her question." She turned to Mollena, easing Francine's hands away in the process. "What was it you wanted to know, dear heart?"

"Do you live in some other part of the house?" Mollena said, looking from one to the other. "Why haven't I seen you during the day?"

"You could look for us," Cecily offered. "With all those keys, you'll certainly find something."

Francine scowled at the dark-haired woman. "Don't tell her to do that. Why don't you ask Bluebeard about us?"

"That idea's no better," Cecily said. "If you don't want her to look for us, then I suppose you should just go on distracting her."

Mollena shook her head. She couldn't think clearly through the haze of the dream and the intoxicating presence of the two women. "I don't understand," she said. "Who are you?"

Francine smiled sadly at Mollena. "There's no distracting her," she told Cecily.

"Well, of course not," Cecily said. "And you don't really want her distracted. You want her to look for us, you just don't want to admit it." Cecily patted Mollena's cheek. "You won't have any trouble finding us if you want to, my sweet."

Mollena tried to protest and ask more questions, but both women settled close to her, undoing her nightgown completely. Cecily nibbled Mollena's left nipple, while Francine suckled at the right. Thought fled Mollena completely as the clarity of the dream dissolved into a sensual swirl.

Mollena woke with her hand between her legs and an aching in her head. The set of keys gleamed dully from the nightstand drawer beside the bed, which she didn't remember opening. Mollena moved slowly. She sniffed the pillows on the bed and couldn't decide whether she imagined the scents of sun and lilies that she detected there.

She sat upright and steeled herself. Holding her breath, she snatched up the keys.

The small gold key came into her fingers without her having to look for it. She worried at it with her thumb and forefinger as she stepped out into the passage. A door opposite the bedroom led out onto the widow's walk, a thin balcony that spanned the outside of the second floor and looked down on the cliffs and water below the isolated house.

The master bedroom was on the second floor of Bluebeard's mansion, and Mollena hadn't explored the rest of that level at all. The corridor extended the length of a large ship. In the dim light from the widow's walk, Mollena could make out dozens of doorknobs, to both left and right.

She crept to the nearest, a round red door, not able to explain why her heart pounded so. Goosebumps rose on her skin as she ran her fingers along the painted wood and pressed her cheek to listen for noises from the other side. She heard nothing.

After a long pause, Mollena turned her attention to the ring of keys, trying one then another until at last she found one made of brass, fitted with an engraved, heart-shaped handle. She screamed a little when the door's lock turned over under her hands. Slowly, she swung the door open, half expecting to find Cecily and Francine waiting on the other side.

The women weren't there, but Mollena's eyes adjusted to the darkness to reveal a room outfitted to rival the finest, most fashionable theaters. She couldn't stop herself from smiling. Her father's fortunes had been good when she was very small, but she'd been too young at the time to appreciate fine fabrics and she hadn't had a woman's shape or the desire to flatter it.

Mollena took a step inside.

"Looking for something?" She jumped at the dry voice behind her. She hadn't been face to face with the servant since the day in the kitchen.

Bluebeard had given her permission to explore the house. He had given her the keys she held. Still, she could not prevent a guilty expression from forming on her face.

"Give me the keys," the servant commanded.

Mollena handed them over before she could think to question his tone. The old man sorted through them, singling out the small gold key and holding it close to his eyes to inspect it. "What are you doing?" she managed finally.

"Watching you for the master."

"He said not to use that key."

"He did indeed."

"Then why–"

The servant tossed the keys on the floor before her feet. "Women," he said, "do not always obey."

Only after she watched him plod heavily away down the hall did she lean over to pick up the keys. Her delight in the room had vanished. She closed the door and locked it behind her.

Mollena folded back the covers of Bluebeard's big bed with a sigh. Life had always been lonely, but never so much as this. Even her father in his illness had been better company than this gloomy house and the single, menacing servant.

She closed her eyes and prayed for her soul, but in her heart, she wished for another visit from Cecily and Francine. Sleep came grudgingly, in fits and starts, and at uncomfortable angles.

Noises in the hall reached her ears.

"She doesn't care for us," Cecily's voice said. "She's not really searching."

Mollena tried to turn her head toward the sound, but could not.

"Let her be," Francine replied. "Let her have what peace she can."

"You want to let her die without ever learning the truth? You want us to continue to rot unwept, with no hope of rest?"

Mollena struggled to rise from the bed. Her limbs would not obey.

"Perhaps it will not be so," said Francine.

Cecily snorted. "You think he cares for her? He will return to the house soon. She does not have much time to act."

Finally, Mollena managed to lift herself and turn. She saw nothing. She stepped out into the hall. She waited, shivering in the cold corridor, but the only sound was of the house settling deeper into its perch on the cliff.

Mollena stood in the hallway outside the bed chamber, holding the ring of keys. She would go mad without companionship. She needed to appease Cecily and Francine. And yet, the servant's observation and innuendo chilled her.

"You won't have any trouble finding us if you want to, my sweet," Cecily had said. Mollena traced the lines of the small gold key in her hand. But her mind did not wish to know what her fingers did.

There would be no harm, she reasoned, in trying the doors. If they opened with any other than the forbidden key, Bluebeard could not blame her for looking inside. Cecily and Francine would see her honestly searching, and might return to her bed. As for the door unlocked by the small gold key – when she found it, she could decide.

With plodding resolution, Mollena worked her way down the hall, opening one door at a time. Under different circumstances, she would have felt delighted. Rich things from Bluebeard's travels stuffed each room from floor to ceiling – exotic wooden statues from the other side of the world, aromatic stores of spices, books bound in animal skin, erotic paintings.

Without the memory of his cold, dark eyes, Mollena could imagine the wonders stored in this house persuading her to fall in love with the man who had collected them. But she thought of the way he had used and abandoned her along with the rest of his treasures, and the things in the rooms took on an air of mourning. Bluebeard knew how to collect things, she thought, but he didn't know how to care for them. Dust covered all his splendid prizes, hiding their rich colors and eating their softer parts into disrepair.

The servant lurked often in the upper corridors these days, sometimes just watching her, and sometimes demanding, "Keys." He seemed disappointed whenever he peered at the small gold key.

Bluebeard might have meant the second floor alone to occupy Mollena for months – perhaps even until his return. Her search for Francine and Cecily, however, pressed her to explore more quickly than she otherwise would, spending days investigating rooms where she would have spent weeks.

When Mollena's explorations descended to the first floor, the old servant seemed ever at her elbow. He took to calling her, "Mistress of the House," the sarcasm dripping from his nearly nonexistent lips.

Mollena gritted her teeth through it and continued to explore. The first floor rooms seemed richer and better kept – perhaps presenting the trophies of the adventures of Bluebeard's younger days. One room was bare except for a large, stuffed tiger, the knife wound that had killed it still visible across its throat despite the taxidermist's skill. Another room held a full suit of primitive armor from a warrior chieftain, the breastplate and helmet covered with brilliant orange and yellow feathers arranged in swirling patterns. She gazed upon it briefly and backed away.

"The master will be sorry to hear how little of his collection excites your fascination," the servant said from far too close behind her. Mollena restrained her scream and turned with as much dignity as she could muster.

"It's all very lovely," she said sincerely.

"How can you know? You spend so little time in each room." His tongue darted from his mouth. "Unless you are looking for something?"

Mollena let the question hang, stepping around him and continuing down the hall.

She found stores of money and jewels, vivid dyes, precious metals, and bills of sale from seaports around the world. She'd known her husband was a rich man, but the weight of all that treasure brought it home to her in a way she hadn't realized before.

The weeks wore on. Cecily and Francine did not come to her bed. Even the servant seemed weary of tormenting her. The rooms went on endlessly. The memories of her night with Bluebeard softened. Could she truly not enjoy her time in the house? Would she let a dream take over her days, turning them urgent and fitful?

Mollena woke one morning and picked up her key ring. She searched for the brass key with the heart-shaped handle. Wonder budded in her breast as she opened the round, red door. A Paris stage! It might be childish, but she could pretend.

She darted in and hunted through the bits of satin, fur, and velvet, rubbing them against her skin and dressing herself in scandalous outfits. It made her giggle to see her simple body dressed in such fine things. She played in the room until long after dark, then slipped back to bed still wearing black lace underthings.

"I see you've finished exploring, beautiful." Cecily's lips brushed Mollena's ear as she spoke. "Have you forgotten us?" Mollena struggled up and opened her eyes. Francine sheltered a candle in a flower-covered dish, providing dim light to the room.

The women were both dressed as if they'd played in the dressing room with Mollena earlier that day. Cecily wore a dark green silk corset that pressed her small breasts up into full white globes, and an elegant waistcoat. Francine's bright pink nipples peeked through her short, sheer white shift.

Francine set down the candle and came over to straddle Mollena on the bed. Mollena reached up to hold the other woman around the waist, but Francine swatted her hands away and peered at her face. "She never searched for us in the first place."

"I did! I tried, but I didn't find you," Mollena said. She reached out now for Cecily, wanting to feel the comfort of flesh from at least one of the women.

Cecily obliged, taking Mollena's hand and idly stroking her neck and shoulders with it, guiding Mollena's fingers toward her cleavage.

"Listen," Cecily said. "We love you. Can you believe that?"

Mollena pulled her hand away from Cecily and tried to concentrate. "No one's ever touched me the way the two of you do."

"Not even your husband," Francine said in a satisfied tone.

"Of course he didn't," Cecily said. "He was interested only in his own pleasure. Making you learn the 'duties of a wife.'"

"Don't sound so bitter," Francine said. "Those aren't so bad."

"Hmmph," Cecily said. "I prefer when these things aren't done out of duty." She trailed a finger up Mollena's outer thigh. Her tongue followed her finger, licking first Mollena's thigh then Francine's. Mollena nearly went mad. Involuntarily, her hand went to the back of Cecily's head and her back arched, lifting Francine. The light woman laughed and pushed Cecily's head away. "Please concentrate."

Cecily rolled her eyes, then looked back at Mollena. "We love you," she said again, and the words sent a thrill through Mollena's body that ricocheted back and forth between her heart and the groove between her legs. "If you love us, too, you won't give up. And when you find us, you might learn about the terrible fate that awaits you in this house."

"Don't tell her to—"

"I'm warning her, Francine. I'm being fair."

"She shouldn't look for us," Francine said.

"Do you really think she's safer if she doesn't?"

Mollena sat all the way up, pushing both women off her. "Please don't fight. In the morning, I will continue. I promise."

Cecily smiled. "I know you will." She took Mollena's hand again, this time guiding it under her waistcoat. Mollena slid her hand in deeper, feeling the soft fur between Cecily's legs, and the warm, wet slit it covered. Cecily thrust her hips forward to open herself to Mollena. Her flesh parted, and Mollena blushed as her finger slipped inside the tight passage into her body. Cecily's flesh was almost uncomfortably hot. Despite her nervousness, Mollena could not help but probe Cecily, and the other woman gasped with every movement of Mollena's hand.

Idly, Francine reached under Mollena's lacy black petticoat and began to swirl her finger against the bare skin there, working her way between Mollena's legs. Francine mirrored the motions that Mollena took up with Cecily, trailing kisses up Mollena's neck as she did.

Mollena reached for Francine with her other hand. The red-haired woman pulled up her shift so that Mollena could reach her between her legs as well. Mollena pressed two fingers into the tight sheath there.

Cecily raised a sly eyebrow as Mollena began to move her hands rhythmically inside both of the women. Cecily crawled her hand across Mollena's belly and pulled her garments entirely out of the way. She tweaked Mollena's nipples and pushed her fingers into her mouth. Then, she brought her hand down to join Francine's at Mollena's entrance, working her fingers in beside the red-haired woman's and stretching Mollena wider than Bluebeard had done.

The stimulation made it impossible for Mollena to keep her fingers moving, but Francine and Cecily took over, rearranging themselves sinuously so they could rub themselves on Mollena's hands while retaining access to her body.

Cecily's hand moved sharply inside Mollena, her fingers thrusting in deep and hard. Francine was softer, cupping her mound gently, pressing against her inner wall with her fingers, and rubbing her thumb over the bud between her legs.

Mollena almost choked on her moans. Every muscle in her body tensed until it almost hurt. She forced her eyes open so she could see the two beautiful creatures that shared the bed with her. Cecily's black hair had come loose from her braids, tendrils sticking to her sweaty, pale forehead. Francine's blue eyes narrowed to slits as she rolled her hips on Mollena's hand at the same pace she used to stroke between Mollena's legs.

A long, low cry burst from Mollena's throat and coaxed the rest of her body to follow it. She felt herself rising above her body. Then her awareness snapped to the throbbing between her legs. She would have flailed, but the weight of the other women on her hands held her in place. Mollena screamed as the throbbing spread into a beautiful ache across her entire body.

And she understood when Cecily and Francine held her wrists firmly and brought themselves to join her in that state. They were all together there, safe in the pleasure of the dream. Mollena would have been perfectly content except for the lingering thought of her search, and fear of what secrets it would uncover.

Chapter 3

The Small Gold Key

Mollena slept almost until noon the next day, waking with a foul taste in her mouth and a foggy head. It had been a long time since her last meal and she was starving, but she rolled up and immediately reached for the key ring that Bluebeard had given her.

She sat cross-legged, sorting through the keys. She could avoid the truth no longer. The small gold key seemed sullen in her palm.

Mollena's heart pounded urgently. She could not be bold enough without help.

She put on a floor-length blue silk gown, arrayed her hair in an appealing cascade, and added a string of pearls and a pearl ring. She pretended to have Cecily's fire and Francine's sense of calm. She hung the keys at her waist and went downstairs for a quick meal.

As she ate, Mollena lifted the gold key and looked at it closely. The grooves along its sides held old, rust-colored stains. She recalled Bluebeard's voice, as clearly as if he stood beside her now: "If you use the small gold key, we'll both be sorry."

Mollena hardened her heart to her awe of Bluebeard's trove. She worked her way through the house faster now and more methodically, opening every door in case it hid further rooms or closets, sorting the keys she'd used from the ones she hadn't. She soon finished exploring every wing, nook, and alcove of the first and second floors. She hadn't found Francine and Cecily, but three unused keys remained on the ring Bluebeard had given her. There had to be three more doors somewhere in the house.

Mollena hesitated. There was no sign of the old servant. She heard nothing but her own breathing. The basement promised the only additional doors. She gathered her courage and descended.

She doubted anyone had disturbed it for years. She lifted her candle high and almost choked at the sight of the passage before her, clogged with gloom and spiderwebs.

Mollena stepped forward, waving her hand around her face and compulsively brushing filth off her hair and fine dress. The first door she tried opened onto darkness so thick that the candle's frail light didn't penetrate it. Mollena swallowed a nervous scream and stepped deeper into the room.

She tripped and scrabbled for something to hold, her hand finding and grasping a rusted iron bar. She forced herself to calm down and turned slowly, letting her eyes adjust to the dim light that began to penetrate the room's dark corridors. It was a wine cellar. Mollena almost cried with relief.

She returned to the passage. Her pulse didn't speed at all as she calmly opened the door to a storage space crammed with tools and broken furniture. This was simple, she thought. One door to go.

She continued down the passageway, looking for the final lock. Bluebeard couldn't possibly know that she had used this last key, she told herself. The servant, for all his threats, wouldn't be able to say for sure either. She could open that door, tell Francine and Cecily that she had looked for them without finding anything, then accept that they were figments of her imagination. She could enjoy the eroticism of the dreams, and set about accepting the realities of life with her husband. Perhaps things would be all right. He'd been cold and unsympathetic about the death of her father, but he was very rich and seemed resolved to leave her mostly to her own devices.

The floor of the passage changed from stone to dirt. Every trace of finish disappeared, and it turned and slanted deeper. The air chilled. Mollena began to wonder if the tunnel could collapse on her, or worse, behind her. She touched the golden key and could have sworn it felt hot in her hand.

The passage ended abruptly in a flimsy wooden door that didn't close all the way. A thick chain and a tiny padlock secured it. She didn't have to look at the key in her hand to know that it would fit.

Mollena glanced at her candle. She wasn't sure if she would be able to make it back to the stairs before it ran out. Her heart thudded in her chest.

Tentatively, she reached out to the door and tried to pull it open without opening the lock. She succeeded in getting a sliver of a view into whatever was beyond, but couldn't see into the darkness. A strange, sweet smell wafted from the door.

Mollena turned away and started back up the passage, but only made it a few steps before she stopped.

Deliberately, Mollena set the candle down in the earthen floor near the door and fitted the golden key into the padlock. It sprang open so violently it almost hit her in the face. She unwound the chain and pulled on the door.

She smelled sweet rot and iron. Mollena pulled her dress up to keep it from trailing on the ground and ducked a little to step inside the room. She recognized Francine and Cecily immediately, even considering their current state. Propped up against the opposite wall, their hair – one head black, one red – spread around their partially decomposed bodies. Francine seemed to have been there longer than Cecily, but the corpses had been stored the same way, well-preserved in the cool of the basement. Bluebeard must have killed them in this room – blood covered the floor.

Mollena jumped at a sound that turned out to be her own voice sobbing. She fell to her knees and heaved. She was light headed. Mollena passed out on the gruesome floor.

"Now she knows," Francine said grimly.

Mollena still lay on the floor of the basement room, but the red-haired woman smelled like sun again, and her flesh was whole and glowed with health. Mollena stood, wobbling a little, and reached for Francine's throat, feeling the unbroken skin there.

"What's going on?" Mollena said.

Two thin, strong hands gripped her shoulders and steadied her. Cecily.

"When you're unconscious, you see us as spirits, not bodies," Cecily said. "But there isn't time to be unconscious now. That old servant sees more than you think he does, and the signs that you've been here are all over you. You need to get up, go upstairs, and figure out how to escape this place."

"I can't leave the two of you like this," Mollena said. "You deserve a Christian burial, at the very least."

"Cecily's right," Francine said. "You should save yourself."

Mollena laughed in disbelief. "If that's how you feel, why did you bring me here in the first place? Why did you visit me at all?"

The other two looked ashamed. "We needed you to open the door," Francine said finally. "We wish to take our revenge."

"You are the only one who understands us," Cecily added. "We've shared pleasures with you that we never felt in life. You've shared our mortal peril."

"We love you," Francine whispered. "You are so alive."

"We mean to keep you that way," Cecily said firmly. "Listen to me now and get up. We'll be all right where we are."

Mollena felt hysterical. "No!" she said. "I swear to you, I'm not leaving without you. I promise I will make sure you both get a chance to rest in peace."

Francine cursed. "Bluebeard will be home soon, and his servant is watching you!"

Cecily's pale skin turned almost translucent. "Get up now, girl! Run upstairs! Run all the way up, to the widow's walk! At the very least, don't let him murder you in the darkness below. Fling yourself into the sea before he does!"

Francine slapped Cecily. "Don't tell her to throw herself into the sea! Run, Mollena, but we'll be with you. We'll help you escape. Don't let him take your life."

Francine's last word ended in a scream that shook the foundations of the house and shocked Mollena out of the dream.

Mollena jerked to a sitting position as if someone had pulled her up. The candle had gone out, and she was alone in the blackness with the corpses. The room's sour smell made her retch again. She felt around the filthy floor until she found the keys. Horribly, impossibly, the blood that stained it felt wet and sticky against her skin.

Putting out a hand, Mollena found the wall and guided herself to her feet and back to the passage. Once there, she walked as fast as she could without tripping in the dark. The stairs seemed farther than she remembered.

Mollena stopped at the base of the stairs to listen. She could catch no hint of what might be waiting for her above. As silently as she could, she crept to the top of the stairs and listened again at the door. Still hearing nothing, she pulled to ease the door open a crack. It wouldn't move.

She forced herself to stay calm and tried a second time. The door was shut and locked from the outside.

Harsh laughter reached her ears from the other side of the door. "You foolish girl," the servant said. "Did you think I had neglected my duty? You can wait there until the master returns."

Mollena gasped. "What? No! I'll die in here."

"Nonsense. You probably won't starve before his ship puts in."

Mollena pounded and screamed, but the door did not give way, and neither did he.

Mollena could not guess how long she sat huddled at the foot of the basement stairs, the corpses of her dream lovers decaying slowly just a short walk from her position. Without light or food, she lost all sense of time.

The light that flooded down the staircase could have been a hallucination, and so she did not lift her head when it touched her.

But with the light came a shadow. "Hello, wife," Bluebeard said. "My servant tells me you have been very much enjoying the run of the house."

Mollena tried not to whimper as she straightened up. She felt like a child before him, so much shorter and smaller and weaker. "Hello," she said. Her voice cracked.

"You look dusty and a bit the worse for wear," Bluebeard said. Mollena looked down and saw cobwebs and dust clinging to her arms and palms. She had been sick on her dress, and it was dirty and stained. "May I see the keys I gave you?" Bluebeard's tone rang sweeter than she had heard from him.

Mollena climbed the stairs to stand before him. Her hand trembled as she handed them over. She thought she could hear Cecily and Francine screaming about escape in her mind, but his big body blocked her way, and she couldn't think where or how to run.

Bluebeard gave a little cry and lifted the golden key apart from the rest. Sticky blood dulled its entire length. "I said we would both be sorry if you used this key," he murmured. He dropped the keys and settled his arms on the doorframe to either side of Mollena, stepping in so that his body pressed tight against hers. His member rose hard between them. Bluebeard kissed her neck. Mollena flinched. "I find I'm not sorry at all," he murmured into her hair. "Though I daresay you will be."

"What are you talking about?" Mollena said.

"You know now, my love. You know everything. We can have one last night together, and you can get to know me as I really am. No longer any reason to hide the truth." His rough hand cupped her throat gently but completely.

Mollena stiffened. Her mind raced. She could shove him, but he was stronger and well-placed to resist her. Desperately, Mollena tried the opposite. She pulled him toward her as hard as she could, winning a surprised grunt from him and upsetting his balance.

He grabbed a fistful of her dress and the fabric separated as neatly as if it had been cut. Mollena didn't stop to watch him fall. She broke free and darted toward the staircase. There was a thud behind her, and she ran for all she was worth.

She took the stairs two at a time, fear making her faster than she'd thought possible. Before long, she heard Bluebeard's heavy footsteps behind her. Mollena followed Cecily's instructions and made for the widow's walk.

She burst out onto it, shrieking as she grabbed at the outside of the house to stabilize herself. The sharp tang of the sea stung her nose as she fought for breath. The widow's walk stretched along the cliff side of the house, ending across from Mollena under a forgotten, tattered flag, where the structure faded into disrepair.

She looked over her shoulder. Bluebeard ran at her heels.

She darted away, but her foot slipped on a patch of damp, rotting wood and she caught at the side of the house for a dizzying second. The world spun, and the house seemed to stretch even higher above the cliffs. Mollena forced herself to keep moving, to edge out along the treacherous, narrow walk. The wood creaked beneath her feet. She was afraid to wait for Bluebeard, but also terrified to test the walkway any further.

"Run!" She heard Cecily and Francine shouting. She obeyed, forcing herself to trust her feet on the precarious surface.

"You won't get away, woman!" Bluebeard called. "There's nowhere to go!"

Looking ahead, Mollena couldn't help but agree. She was running out of walkway already, and as she approached the end, the structure grew even more rotten and unstable. Just behind her, it splintered under Bluebeard's heavy weight.

Soon, Mollena could go no further. She glanced at the foamy waves below. Cecily had said to fling herself onto the cliffs rather than allow Bluebeard to get her. Francine had said to throw him down instead. Mollena couldn't do either one. She held herself as tall as she could and turned to face Bluebeard.

He stopped his forward charge and stared at her. "Francine, Cecily, and Mollena. My three wives will all be together."

"You killed Francine and Cecily," she said, finding her voice

He produced a knife from his coat. Mollena shuddered, recalling the tiger and the bodies in the basement. Bluebeard shook his head. "I didn't kill them," he whispered furiously. "They chose to die. All of you chose not to obey me, as a good wife should. But I have been a faithful husband. I take time to visit them whenever I am at home. And I will keep you, too. I will provide a home for you so long as I live." He stepped closer, the walkway complaining beneath him.

Mollena didn't want to die. The ragged flag snapped above her head, and she glanced up at it. Bluebeard took another step, and the joins holding the widow's walk to the side of the house creaked loudly. She scrambled up onto the banister and grabbed the flagpole with both hands.

Clinging to the metal, she stomped as hard as she could on the rotten wood, hanging on for dear life when the walkway gave way beneath her feet.

Bluebeard fell with it, cursing her all the way down. The cliffs waited below, beaten by the violent ocean. Mollena swallowed hard.

It was a long time before Mollena got the courage to unwrap herself from the pole and ease her way back across what was left of the widow's walk. When she got back inside the house, she went straight to the bedroom, locked herself in, and collapsed under a weight of fear and exhaustion.

Cecily and Francine waited in the dream, sitting on the bed as if they'd been there all evening. Mollena blinked wearily, tired even in that other place. "I promise I will come to you just as soon as I can. I'm sorry I didn't have the strength to do it right away."

Cecily and Francine held hands. They both wore wedding gowns, Francine's light and frilly and Cecily's fitted and shimmering like a pearl. "We have special instructions," Cecily said. "Please don't bury us."

"What?"

"Throw our bodies into the sea," Francine said. "Our spirits can't find peace until we break our ties to Bluebeard. We want to go in after him, meet him underwater, and make him answer for his crimes."

Mollena felt a chill at the fierce expression on Francine's normally serene face. She put her hand on top of the other women's hands. "I will," she said. "I'll make sure to do it exactly as you wish."

The three looked at each other for a long time, and Mollena burst into tears.

Francine stroked her back. "What's the matter?"

"The two of you are the only friends I've had in so long," Mollena sobbed. "I'm so sorry for what happened to you, and I'm glad that you're going to find peace now, but I'm going to miss you so much. I don't know what I'll do without seeing you."

Francine pulled Mollena's face into her bosom, its sun-kissed scent igniting intense desire in her lover. Mollena reached around her back and tore open the buttons of her gown, pushing it down off Francine's shoulders and revealing her round, full breasts. Mollena threw herself on them, kissing, licking, stroking, and squeezing. She pinched both nipples and Francine gasped.

Cecily's full, throaty laugh filled the air behind Mollena. "You're not shy tonight, my dear heart," she said. "I'm glad." Cecily undid Mollena's nightgown and slipped it off without making her pull away from Francine for even a moment. Francine had begun to moan urgently under Mollena's attention to her breasts. Her hips bucked wildly, still tangled in the lower half of her nightgown. Cecily reached over and slid that off, too.

As soon as she did, Francine guided one of Mollena's hands down between her legs. Mollena couldn't believe how slick she was. She let her hand explore Francine idly, smiling at the desperation with which the red-haired woman ground and gyrated her hips.

Out of the corner of her eye, Mollena saw Cecily stand and peel off her own gown, tossing it on the floor. When she returned to the bed, her pale skin was so soft that Mollena groaned. "Let me show you something," Cecily murmured, the usual hint of ironic amusement in her voice.

She grasped the back of Mollena's head and guided her away from Francine's breasts and down to her belly. Francine panted and murmured incoherent words. "Don't stop yet, my sweet," Cecily said. She pushed Mollena's head down further, to the cleft between Francine's legs.

"Lick her," Cecily whispered.

Francine's moan had a sob in it the first time Mollena put out her tongue. She lapped tentatively against the other woman's sex, her hand still moving inside her. Between Francine's legs, Mollena tasted tang of summer ocean. She breathed deep, finding herself almost overwhelmingly aroused by the flavor. She licked up the slick wetness that covered every bit of the soft pink skin between Francine's nether lips.

"You're going to drive her mad," Cecily said. She pushed Mollena's head again, centering her on the hard bud of flesh at the top of Francine's cleft. "Suck on that."

Mollena did. Above her, Cecily kissed Francine, so that the sharp, desperate moans that Mollena unleashed from the red-haired woman were muffled by Cecily's mouth and tongue.

Francine's body tensed and bucked hard. Mollena slid a hand

around to her bottom and held tight, not letting up on sucking that bud of flesh. Mollena thrust her fingers in and out, sharply the way Cecily had done to her, then she and Cecily were both holding Francine as the red-haired woman writhed and wept in their grasp.

When Francine finally relaxed, Mollena let go and sat up, grinning at Cecily. The dark-haired woman kissed Mollena, her lips soft and lingering. Her rough tongue darted out to lick Francine's juices off Mollena's face.

Mollena moaned and pushed Cecily onto the bed on her back, spreading her legs around Cecily's thigh.

"You two look beautiful together," Francine said.

Mollena had never felt so beautiful. Her lifelong ideas of being plain disappeared in Cecily's arms. She buried herself in a kiss that felt as smooth as silver, rubbing against Cecily's thigh as she did. Soon, she felt Francine's hands, too, pinching her nipples, smoothing her hair, teasing her sex.

Mollena gasped and pressed harder against Cecily's thigh. "Wait," Francine whispered. She pulled Mollena away from Cecily a little and worked her way beneath her. Mollena shrieked as Francine arranged Mollena's thighs to either side of her head reached inside her with a soft, hot tongue.

Cecily smiled against Mollena's mouth and pulled away from their kiss, sliding her body up so that Mollena's mouth could easily reach her own slit. She pulled Mollena's head into her lap, murmuring, "You know what to do now, love."

Cecily petted Mollena's hair, spreading her legs and leaning back against the headboard.

At first, Mollena couldn't move her tongue. She was too caught in the pleasure of what Francine was doing between her legs. Then she forced her tongue out and tasted Cecily, sharper and sweeter than Francine had been. She closed her eyes and felt herself enveloped by the two women. She mimicked the movements of Francine's tongue and fingers, and soon they were all moaning.

Cecily grabbed the back of Mollena's head and pulled her in tight, groaning and thrusting her hips up. The feeling of Cecily shuddering against her face overwhelmed Mollena, who ground against Francine's face. Francine nipped her softly, and Mollena gasped into Cecily's body and shuddered with her. She couldn't have said where the pleasure started or ended, all she knew was that it passed so freely between them all.

Francine kept her tongue moving until Mollena was sobbing, her cheek resting against Cecily's thigh.

They eased away from each other, all breathing hard. Mollena studied the others, their shapes so dear and yet still so mysterious.

Cecily started to kiss her again, but Mollena stopped her. "I have to know what's going on."

"Well," Cecily said dryly. "For one thing, you're going to be very rich. I imagine you'll inherit Bluebeard's house and everything in it."

"Considering what he did to you, don't you think his wealth was ill-gotten? How could I keep it?"

Cecily's face hardened. "I paid with my blood," she said, "as did Francine. If there is any benefit to be had from his crimes, I demand that it go to you."

Mollena nodded slowly, trying to put on a brave face. Francine pressed her cheek against Mollena's stomach. "Do not worry," she said. "Do as we asked. Leave Bluebeard to us."

Francine and Cecily held her close until her exhausted mind slipped into a black sleep.

When Mollena woke, she went at once to the basement to take Francine and Cecily out of that horrible room.

She did this herself, despite how she struggled and retched, loading their corpses onto a cart and rolling them up to the staircase, then hauling each up the staircase, then loading them back onto the cart. It was noisy, rough work, and the old servant came in while she did this and stood watching her, his mouth working. "You can't unleash those demons on the world," he said finally.

Mollena could not help laughing. "Demons? Your master was the demon. These were victims."

"Hungry spirits. No revenge can satisfy them. They should be left where they lie, locked in forever."

"If you wanted me to believe you," Mollena grunted, resuming her work, "perhaps you should not have trapped me in the basement."

The servant dropped to his knees.

"What are you doing?" Mollena asked.

"I feared the master," the servant whimpered. "But do not let the spirits free."

"Are you afraid they'll take revenge on you, too?" Mollena stared him down, feeling powerful and pitiless. "Women," she said, "do not always obey." She pushed past him, calling over her shoulder, "You will need to find other employment, of course."

Mollena dragged the cart with the corpses out of the house and to the cliffs. She tried not to look at the bodies as she rolled them off the edge to fall a long way into the cold, green water. She wanted to remember Francine and Cecily as beautiful, warm, desirable women, not as these broken, brutalized shells.

She sat on the slimy rocks, looking out over the water. She wondered how many things it held in its unknown depths. She searched her memory for a prayer she could say to ease Francine and Cecily on their way, but words escaped her. At last, she made the sign of the cross and went inside.

It was her house now, and it was empty. She didn't like the idea of being alone here, without even Bluebeard's ghost wives for company. Mollena laid plans in her mind, resolving to send to town to hire on several servants to help her clean and put things in order.

That night, Mollena dreamed of Francine and Cecily, but their presence didn't feel real. Mollena's mind simply produced memories of their stroking hands and soft skin and warm mouths.

She pushed the visions away and searched for something true.

Screen Siren

Director Sam Raymond lacks the star power to work with living actresses—instead, the studio makes him stretch his rock-bottom budgets by casting the undead. By night, he labors at a screenplay for the actress he hopes to cast one day: the lovely Jessica Savage.

In cruel Hollywood, however, aging hopefuls sometimes arrange to die in order to have a chance of appearing in a casting call—what used to be called suicide has become a career move. Jessica succumbs to temptation and appears on Sam's lot as part of a zombie "meat pile. (M/F)

Chapter 1
Career Suicide

Every actress is dying at all times, fading and wilting before the camera. Her skin is wrinkling, her hair is whitening, and her teeth are falling out in an incremental process of decay that a good actress makes her audience subconsciously aware of at all times. The best actresses make you ache for them, not just sexually, but also in anticipation of their eventual deaths.

Good directors work quickly enough to capture the moment of the actress's beauty, and the best work slowly enough for the audience to see she is ephemeral, that she is dying.

Sam Raymond isn't a good director, so he doesn't get to work with living actresses. His screen sirens glow with the polyester perfection of stage makeup and careful refrigeration. Their change is less poignant, more primally repellent. They deliver their dialogue with necessarily stilted precision that lacks real passion or emotion. The studio delivers the "hopefuls" for his casting calls in big vans stacked high and squirming with what the industry likes to call "the meat pile."

He'd complain about the talent pool, but zombie actors and actresses come nearly free, and the studio isn't willing to spend more than nearly free on Sam. They barely tolerate paying basic expenses, particularly since his last couple features tanked at the box office.

He tells himself the dead aren't really different from the dying. Beauty slips away from the woman — semantic distinctions about whether the life in the actress is fading or rotting are really just technical points. The poetry of the experience is the same, really.

Besides, living actresses always look like death in historical pieces, like the ones the studio assigns to Sam. Living people with working pores can never stay fresh when the California sun pounds them through all those layers of period clothes and makeup.

Sam peers through the blinds over his trailer's single window at the latest meat pile van, delivering dark-haired, recently deceased and revived "beauties" suitable for the role of Greta, a self-absorbed debutante who will have her reputation ruined by an encounter with the rakish Rafe. The trailer's overworked, ancient air conditioner churns wetly, straining to achieve the thin hiss of chilled air it puts out across his workspace. He wipes sweat from his palms onto the expensive pair of pants he bought from Banana Republic. The pants have so far failed to be worth the investment — Sam still gets mistaken for crew all the fucking time.

He comes out of the trailer clapping his hands, pausing to be sure the delivery guys see him framed in the doorway beside the nameplate proclaiming him the director. His posturing would go more smoothly if he didn't double over the moment the stench from the van hit his nostrils.

He can never get used to the smell of the undead, and when you unload a whole pile of them onto noonday asphalt, they just *bake*.

Sam collects himself.

"Let's line them up and start evaluating," he calls out to the crew. "Check their mouths while we get set up for a screen test. My leading lady has to have all her teeth this time."

His assistant director appears at his elbow, neck flushed red and sweaty from ears to collar. She's been arguing with someone again.

"What is it now, Deborah?" Sam asks.

"We've fallen even further in the studio's estimation," she says, slipping into the strangely formal sentence structure she uses when she's fuming. "The actresses they've shipped today lack the benefit of full screening and quality control."

"I'm tired. Speak English."

"They sent them straight from the morgues. These honeys haven't even been checked for full brain death. I'm not sure why the studio thinks this is a cost-saving measure, since our insurance premiums are about to go through the roof."

"Did you tell Tommy and Dave?"

"Those trigger-happy sons of bitches? They're excited. They think they've got this under control. They don't seem to understand that if your security guard has to shoot your lead actress because she's awakened and hungry for brains, things aren't looking good for your movie or your paycheck."

Sam sighs. "I've got a lot of experience with zombies. I know the signs of potential awakening. I'll handle this."

"Be careful, Sam. These might even bite. I want your job, but not yet."

He flashes a grin at her. "You'll want to wait for a better script." They slept together once, and he's still amazed it wasn't awkward. They've slipped into easy camaraderie since then.

Sam approaches the assembled line of female zombies, constricting the back of his nasal passage and letting his mouth hang slightly open so his breath can bypass his nose. An assistant runs behind him, taking notes.

"She looks wrong. Her neck wounds are too visible. Shoot that one. Now. *Now.* She's about to attack." Gunfire stutters beside him, but he's used to it and doesn't even flinch. "She's too ugly. She looks too much like the girl in Carl's last movie."

The first time he did this, he thought about the death, but zombies were news then. Everyone was still getting over losing family members and friends, or recovering from spending days holed up in a broom closet aching for water and listening for screams. It was weird at first to accept that the monsters had been mostly domesticated, to sit calmly at a restaurant while undead horrors delivered refreshments rather than leaping towards the living with their dirty, bloody teeth bared.

The official explanation makes sense whenever Sam thinks about it—most zombies do as they're told. If the living command them, then no harm will be done. The danger comes when a person doesn't undergo full brain death, when he or she awakens into undeath with intelligence and personality intact, feeling hungry for living flesh, surrounded by a sea of mindless monsters just waiting for commands. Not all these "true resurrections" come back evil, but the ones that do—well, that's what took out most of Asia.

Sam was a little shocked when the surviving nations switched from working to eradicate zombies to deliberately creating them to use as cheap labor. Despite a variety of checks and procedures designed to separate the docile zombies from the ones likely to think for themselves, the idea never seemed quite safe to him. But he comes from a family of migrant workers and knows very well the lengths people will go to avoid paying a decent wage. More importantly, since his career as a director required working with zombies, he'd forced himself to adjust.

He moves efficiently down the row, faintly relieved he doesn't have to worry about sparing anyone's feelings. He recognizes quite a few of the offered creatures—in California, aspiring actors and actresses sometimes opt to die while they're still young and attractive in return for the promise that their zombie selves will be sent to a casting call before being hired out as day laborers. This used to be called "suicide," but now it's considered a career move.

Sam has rejected nearly every female specimen. He is only so critical when he's in a bad mood—when he feels overlooked. He looks to see what options are left and stops, mouth open all the way now.

How many times has he dreamt of being face to face with *her*? How many times has he had the shameful, clichéd fantasy about her and the casting couch? How many times has he envisioned her sharp and delicate face upturned and eager to please? He once went to see her in a play and spent the entire two hours staring at a bruise on the inside of her right elbow, wishing he too could mark her flesh, even if only for a day.

Deborah is beside him again.

"That one looks live, doesn't she? I'll give Tommy the signal."

"No!" Sam nearly shouts. "I want her for my lead." Jessica Savage. For a feverish four-year period, Sam had written a screenplay for her once every three months—though no one ever saw them. More recently, he's pounded away at a single effort, revising ad nauseam, hoping to find some way to make it less awful and more worthy of her.

"Are you sure?" Deborah's voice is skeptical. "She has that look, don't you think? Her eyes seem too aware. I think we should shoot her."

Deborah is probably right. She is more than competent as an assistant director. If the world were fair, Sam would be working for her. And Jessica's pale, rigid face does seem a little sly. If this weren't Jessica, he would shoot her rather than take the risk. Zombies, after all, are the ultimate disposables.

Sam cannot bring himself to pass up what will certainly be his last chance to work with Jessica, even if she appears now in this much-changed form.

"Let me get a closer look," he murmurs to Deborah. "Have someone hold the others back, will you?"

He steps closer. The allure of his mental image of her is so strong he forgets the stench and takes a deep breath. He expects the cayenne chocolate smell she has in his fantasies — particularly in the one where he takes her to his mother's house and they all cook molé together before Sam and Jessica have wild, chocolate-smeared sex in his childhood bedroom.

She does not smell like molé, or any food Sam would like to eat. He gags a little, but Hollywood has taught him to swallow his disappointments. He takes her hand in the gentlemanly way he always imagined. She surrenders it to him nervelessly. Flipping over her forearm, he checks her, finding the thick, perfectly round hole through her veins that is typical of a broker deal. She died for this casting call, for this moment with Sam, here and now. The idea warms him. She chose him, even if she did not know exactly what she would get.

Sam peers into her dark, empty eyes. He agrees with Deborah that there is more to them than there ought to be. Jessica Savage might be in there somewhere. His hand tightens around hers.

The rational part of Sam's mind knows this means he ought to step away and signal Tommy and Dave to riddle her with bullets. But the likelihood she is somehow still Jessica — even if this version of Jessica would tear him limb from limb with her molars if given the chance — appeals deeply to the part of Sam that has longed for Jessica Savage since he came to Hollywood, the part that made an obscure aspiring actress into a private obsession and deeply held fantasy.

Hollywood has taught Sam one thing: You can't have what you want, so you take as much as you can.

"She's fine," he calls in a steady voice. "She's our lead."

Sam hovers over the makeup artist.

"She still looks dead."

Kyle turns and glares at him, his mascara and eyeliner making the expression suitably dramatic. "She *is* dead."

"Can't you put more color in her face?" He peers at Jessica. She has always been pale, but he worries audiences will see her as putrid. She has always been a little bony, a little hard. He used to see her as something breakable. Now he worries flesh will hang from her face, loosening from her bones and weakening the lines of her profile.

Kyle grunts and picks up his powdered blush.

"You know who really looks like death warmed over? That actress Simone Burns. I worked with her six months ago. She has acne scars, her skin tone is washed out, and she's getting some serious laugh lines. She should have retired years ago. A woman these days can't get away with working in the industry when she's pushing 30."

"I don't care about Simone Burns," Sam says.

"Your girl here was getting old, too. Probably figured this would be her last chance before she started having to play stepmothers and bitter old ladies."

"I would have cast her as lead anytime, even when she was alive."

"At the rates you pay, SAG would never let you have a living actress." Gingerly, Kyle pulls Jessica's lips back from her teeth, checking them for smudges of lipstick.

"Seems like a shame, doesn't it?"

"Only if you want to deal with the pain in the ass that is a real leading lady. Simone Burns wouldn't come to work unless the director himself delivered coffee to her trailer. You should be glad for what you have."

"I told you I don't care about Simone Burns."

"Right." He makes a final adjustment to Jessica's lip liner. "What do you think?"

"It'll do."

"I'm working miracles here and that's all you're giving me?"

"I said it'll do. I just wish you could have gotten her face to have that sort of glow."

"The glow that comes from being alive?" Kyle rolls his eyes and pushes back his chair. "Since you're so interested in her, how about *you* get her set up for the camera? I'm going to get a coffee."

Sam brushes the hair back from Jessica's face. Before he can think too much about it, he holds his breath, leans in and gives her a quick kiss on the temple. It makes him feel dirty to use her body in any way when her mind is not there.

"Listen," he tells her, "if you wake up, I'm not going to just shoot you. I want to talk to you."

Sam takes the camera from the director of photography.

"Let me show you how I want this shot to go."

The DP argues, his eyes small and angry behind the round lenses of his glasses.

"What you're asking for is not good technique. When you're shooting undead, you don't want the camera to linger. It will break the illusion. You're going to make the audience think about how she's dead."

Sam swings the camera's bulk into position, right where it belongs, caressing the planes and curves of Jessica's face and body. He runs it from hair to high-heeled foot, touching down and pausing from time to time on her dress, but also emphasizing the negative shapes created by the naturally sexy pose of her body. He is going to make people see what he sees. If the camera is any sort of useful tool, it will cooperate.

Jessica Savage is not gone yet. Sam searches for every sign of life—an ironic curve to her cheek, the knowing position of her fingers on her hip—and holds the camera on each one.

Sam should be asleep in his trailer, but instead stands in the shadows at the edge of the lot, watching the crew cautiously approach the zombies' holding pen to feed them. For once, he's glad people never recognize him as the director. There's enough talk going around the set about his unhealthy obsession with Jessica as it is.

The rot of the creatures' bodies is more visible than usual. They've been stripped to save the costumes from being soiled by the necessary gore of feeding.

Sam makes himself watch the creatures slaver and groan as the crew scoops calf brains from a vat and tosses them onto the asphalt at the center of the pen. Evening has cooled the pavement, but the meat still sizzles when it hits the blackened surface.

Sam knows seeing Jessica feed will force him to remember she isn't human. He hopes subjecting himself to this stomach-turning sight will bring him back to reality, give him the relief he needs from the feverish pitch his fantasies have developed since casting her.

The monsters pile onto the calf brains as their caretakers shudder and turn away.

Sam swallows and shoves his hands deep in his pockets. He shakes a bit from the effort of keeping his gorge down. It helps to keep his eyes a little unfocused.

He has lost Jessica in the press of bodies. He takes a steadying breath and searches for her.

Alarm pounds through him for a moment when he can't see her. He's heard of zombies getting caught up in their feeding and eating each other, in addition to other available food.

A careful scan of the pen tells a different story. Jessica sits entirely apart from the press of creatures around the pile of calf brains, seemingly uninterested in the food, her arms wrapped around her trembling body.

Sam stares a beat before the truth dawns on him. Then he is running for the pen, hoping he's the only one to notice she has awakened.

Chapter 2
Last Chance Sex

"Why the hell would you sit here alone with me?" Jessica asks, staring at Sam. She also says she's cold, so he has wrapped her with all four of the blankets he keeps in his trailer, and is only a little worried about never being able to wash out the smell.

Sam is not entirely stupid, so he trains a pistol on her and keeps his distance, sitting cross-legged in a chair as far across the room as he can get. He lowers the gun slightly before he speaks. "You don't seem dangerous right now. Do you have an overwhelming urge to eat my brains?"

She lifts her head and fixes him with her dead and strangely animated eyes. His bravado quails.

"As a matter of fact," Jessica says, "I do." Her voice is thicker than he remembers it, as though her tongue has swollen. Sam supposes he doesn't know what several days of rot will do to a person's vocal cords.

"Do I *need* to shoot you?"

"Well, now that you haven't for a while, I really don't want you to." She wraps her arms around her knees. "Shit."

"Can you control yourself?"

"Yes! Jesus! If not, I'd have jumped on you by now, and you'd have shot me already! Right?"

"Sorry."

She shakes her head, a hint of the fragility he likes returning to her posture.

"This is just not something I expected to happen when I, you know, signed up for this."

"I wish you hadn't signed up for it," Sam says softly. And confesses. "I was writing a screenplay for you. Working on getting a better contract with the studio."

"I can't believe you even knew who I was."

"I can't believe you weren't getting offers every day."

"I can't afford to think about this. I'm already dead." Jessica stares at her hands, prodding at the neat hole in her veins, and shudders. "Show me this screenplay."

She skims the pages he hands her, then wrinkles her nose.

"It's bad. It smells worse than me."

He hangs his head in shame.

"I know."

"Anyway, I assume there's some point to this? You didn't just bring me in here to tell me I could have gotten a job when I was alive if only I'd known to come to you?"

Sam stands and takes a couple steps closer, watching her carefully. Almost afraid to blink, he sets the pistol on a shelf, making sure she sees him let go of it.

"I want to make a deal with you," he says.

She nods slowly, her eyes so vulnerable he wants to take a picture of her. Sam restrains the urge. She has already slipped away, he tells himself. No camera would be fast enough to catch what he's seeing, because he's really looking at the ghost of his desire.

"I don't want anyone to know you've awakened," he tells her. "I'll keep it quiet. I want to finish this movie. And I also want to spend some time with you. After the movie is over, I probably *will* have to shoot you, but I want things to be as nice as possible until then. I want us to try to pretend you're still alive."

"What the hell kind of deal is that? There's nothing in it for me."

"You don't get shot right now. You get a lead role in a movie— that's what you died for, isn't it? We just started shooting. I could still swap you out if I had to."

"Fine. Then what's in it for you?"

Sam takes a deep breath and closes the rest of the distance between them. He runs one hand down the side of her face, breathing through his mouth so he can imagine she *does* smell like cayenne and chocolate, watching her teeth and muscles for any sign of attack. She stares at him wide-eyed.

"Are you serious?"

"For more than five years, you were all I wanted," Sam tells her.

"And you never managed to talk to me after a play? Give me a little hope? Or ask me out for a drink like a normal person?"

He pulls back and nearly forgets to keep watching her.

"It's creepy, I know," he says.

Jessica's hands feel very hot when she places them on Sam's shoulders. She leans toward him, and he trusts her enough to close his eyes. His sense of self-preservation makes his skin twitch as he awaits her touch. When it comes, super-heated lips brushing softly against his, he groans and throws caution to the wind, tangling himself in her body, pushing her back on his couch and only then realizing his clichéd fantasy is coming true.

"I would have thought you were cute," Jessica whispers. "It makes me sad."

"We've got to take what we can get," Sam says. In his ardor, he makes the mistake of parting his lips, pressing his tongue into her mouth. The resulting gagging fit propels him off her body and onto the floor, ruining the moment utterly. He rolls and spits while she watches him with a pained expression.

When he gets hold of himself, Jessica has rearranged his blankets around her body, drawn her spine straight in a pathetic imitation of dignity.

"Maybe you should just shoot me," she says.

Sam shakes his head. He refuses to let this last chance pass him by.

"I still want you," he pants. "I'll just have to be careful."

She whistles, awkwardly because her facial muscles don't seem as elastic as before. "If I'd been with you, I'd never have had to worry about gaining weight. That would have been nothing compared to this."

Sam manages to smile. He takes a deep breath, shielding his nose with his hand, and closes his eyes again. He is tempted to resort to memory, to summon the images of her that have heated his nights for years. He resists the urge. He can fantasize about what she was for years to come. The only point of going through with this, of trying to be with her even as a zombie, is to feel what she is apart from fantasy.

"Please touch me," he says.

"Aren't you afraid I'll start tearing you apart? I'm supposed to be the ultimate evil, right? The awakened monster that destroyed most of the world?"

He shrugs.

"I'm sure there's some truth to that story, but who knows what it was before the government and the media got hold of it. I've talked to you long enough that I just don't see you turning on me like that."

Her fingers skim the bottom of his V-neck shirt, lifting it enough for her heated flesh to play over his skin just above the waist of those expensive pants. He forces away his desire to protect himself, tensing his abs to hold himself in place. If they'd been together when she was alive, Sam thinks, he'd probably have tensed his abs in an effort to look fit. He tries to tell himself it amounts to the same thing, and has to fight down a flood of bitterness.

"I think the hunger will get stronger," she murmurs. "It's already pretty bad. I don't think I'll hurt you now, but in a couple of hours it might feel different inside my mind. I might not be able to be this close to you without losing control."

"That would have been such a hot thing for you to say a few weeks ago," Sam says, trying to laugh at the situation.

"Stop reminding me, okay?" Jessica's voice is plaintive. "Just stop."

He opens his eyes to find her face inches from his. He doesn't think her tear ducts work anymore—if they did, her eyes would probably be shining now. Even without that signal, Sam recognizes the intense insecurity so common to actresses.

"You're the most beautiful woman in the world to me," he tells her. "I swear. I promise." He kisses her hairline, careful this time to keep his mouth closed. He's glad she can't see the expression on his face—his lips have pursed as if he's sucking on a lemon, and he knows the sight would give the lie to his words.

His deception works, and Jessica is emboldened. She sweeps his clothes off. The fact of her touch, more impossible than ever, takes him back to an ecstasy he can't distinguish from fantasy. Maybe those images he's carried for so long are all he ever could have felt of her, Sam thinks. If the living Jessica had touched him, he doubts he could have taken it for what it was. Surely, he would have larded that with just as much expectation. Disappointment would still have threatened to bubble through his facade.

He gives in and pretends her hands are soft and warm — instead of too soft and too warm. Sam tries his best to imagine there's a future or a purpose to the feeling of Jessica peeling away his T-shirt, sliding his pants over his hips, or freeing his cock. He tries to summon a sense of eagerness for the possibility of being, at last, inside her.

She lets him undress her, and to his surprise this is easier. Her body is still fresh, still ripe, still what he dreamt it would be. When Sam holds his breath, he can forget himself. He can run reverent fingers over the swell of her breasts, down the long, taut muscles of her stomach, and over the soft flesh of her inner thighs. He can touch the subtle angles he's watched from the audience so many times. In a moment of nostalgia for what could have been, he touches his fingertip to her right elbow, where that bruise once was, and presses gently.

He thinks of the camera, and now he does retrieve one and take pictures, trying to save whatever of her life he still can. Her beauty slices into his chest, probably because this time they have together is worse than borrowed.

The woman of his dreams smiles at him and positions herself the way he asks her to, and Sam tries to tell himself this, too, could satisfy him, just having this record of her welcoming him. He takes pictures as long as he dares, but he knows this is his only chance to touch her, and though part of him desperately does not want to touch her anymore, he can't bring himself to give up on what he wanted for so long.

He's as accustomed as possible to what she is by this point and is able to breathe through his nose. He mentally scrolls through the things he's imagined doing with her — slipping his hand inside her bra while looking out over the water, holding the back of her head as her lips part over his cock for the very first time, going down on her until she giggles and screams. His dick knows no better than to get hard and strain toward her.

Jessica runs her fingers over it and cocks her head. "Do you want to put it inside me?"

Sam hesitates, thinking of her unnatural heat, and her dryness. He doesn't want to hurt her—or himself—and squeamish, libido killing questions pop into his mind. He could use lube, but he's not sure he could stay hard through the effort.

He strokes her hair and asks, "Can you feel when I touch you?"

"Sort of. It's not what it would have been."

He plays his fingers over the curve of her hip. "I want to make you feel good."

Jessica laughs in his face. "Are you asking what I think you are? You couldn't even kiss me."

Determination fills Sam. He is not going to let this situation stop him. Seeing Jessica Savage as a zombie forced him to recognize many things he would rather have ignored—chief among them that his life is never going to become what he once hoped it would, that he is never going to enjoy the reputation and the love he once wished for. He clenches his jaw, coaxes her down again, and spreads her legs, as if this act of ultimate sexual penance can set everything right again.

Sam lowers his face to her sex. Jessica lies back and sighs, one hand gripping Sam's upper arm. He can tell immediately that she won't come, but she seems to want him to do this anyway. He wonders if she will feel physical pleasure, or simply emotional pleasure, at what he's trying to prove.

He knows better than to take a deep breath. With a supreme act of will, he pushes his tongue out of his mouth and touches it to her clit. It tastes wrong—Jessica was supposed to pour forth arousal with the flavor of salty caramel, and she was supposed to be responsive beneath him, twitching to the rhythm of his slightest touch. Sam was supposed to be able to show her the special swirl with the tongue that makes a woman groan from deep in the back of her throat and clench her fists. She was supposed to grab him by the hair and pull him tight against her crotch, and he was supposed to bury himself deep in her scent and love every minute of it.

In real life, it's a hard thing to get through. Sam has never wondered what death tastes like, but now he knows. It is meat gone sour, nerves gone dead, old scents that never quite washed away. Deborah once called him selfish for saying he'd never go down on a woman on her period, and he gets the wild, inappropriate urge to laugh at what she might say if she saw him now. He wants to gag, and he clenches the muscles of his throat with all of his power to make damned sure he does not.

He can wet Jessica with his saliva, but she is not wet for him. He can spread her stiffening labia apart to let him deeper, but he has no real wish to do so, no rush of excitement as he approaches her now-putrid cunt.

Sam wishes he could lose himself in fantasy, but the reality of her new existence is too awful to be ignored. Here and now, with his face far too close to her dead sex, Sam is with Jessica as she truly is, his view at last unfiltered by his dreams and desires.

He forces himself through the act for her. He'd been foolish to imagine he could make her feel beautiful—surely, his disgust and strain are obvious. Still, he wants her to know with every fiber of her being the full strength of his desire. He wants to leave no doubt. He has so little time to claim her for his own. Her zombie skin can no longer bruise. This is the only way to show her.

He licks her until he can't stand it, then he licks her some more.

When his tongue hurts from the exercise, he sits back on his heels, knees tingling. He kisses her once on the inner thigh and lets a long breath out. Powerful sadness constricts his chest.

"Sam," Jessica says, sitting up slowly. "Come here."

When he does, she kisses the head of his cock and wets her hand from her now soaking cunt.

"You don't have to do that."

"You deserve it."

Her hand, slick with his saliva, travels up and down his cock, teasing and tickling at first, then gripping firmly and really stroking it. Sam looks down at her. She can still act. She seems fervent and fertile sitting on his couch. She is good enough to make him imagine this won't be the only time.

He finds, however, that he doesn't need an act anymore. He has licked cruel reality, and this is what is left for him. He stares unflinchingly at the hole on the underside of her wrist as she strokes him. He is getting what he wanted, even from beyond the grave. Even if it takes a horrible shape.

She traces a finger of her free hand along the underside of his balls. Sam shivers and comes with a ragged exhalation. Jessica lifts a come-covered hand to her lips, licks at it with her dull-colored tongue.

"I knew you would taste good," she breathes, and the hunger in her expression makes Sam stumble backward and reach for his clothes.

"This can't happen again," he tells her, in what he is sure is their last private conversation, and the last time he will dare to be close to her without a gun in his hand.

"The role?"

"The sex."

"I thought you said it was good."

"It was. But," he shudders, "I just can't."

"Admit it," Jessica says. "It's not what you wanted."

He clenches his fist.

"It has to be enough. It just has to be, because that's all there is."

She pulls his body onto the couch beside her and curls against him.

"Let's lie like this for a minute, but make sure you don't fall asleep. I'm starting to get really hungry, and it might not be safe."

"I won't forget," Sam says. He snakes one arm over her chest and cups a breast. It's another thing he has fantasized about, and he doesn't know how he feels anymore about satisfying these fantasies.

She is burning hot, and he immediately starts to sweat everywhere he touches her.

"Is it all a lie?" she asks. "Hollywood? Is it all this disappointing?"

"Maybe not to the people watching," Sam says. "I hope not to them. I hope we make this look better than it is."

"My parents wanted me to forget about being an actress and come home, but I just couldn't."

"You still have parents?" He is faintly shocked, both by her family's luck with survival and by her willingness to throw it away.

She shifts in his arms, creating a bit of distance between them.

"You should take me back to the pen. I'm really hungry."

"Wow. Okay." Sam trembles as he gets away from her and dresses, his stomach turning.

She stops him one last time before they exit the trailer.

"Sam," she says, "I'm sorry I'm dead."

"Me, too," Sam says. "Me, too."

If you enjoyed this story, you can sign up for a free membership at
ForbiddenFiction and discuss it with other readers
and the author at the *Screen Siren* story page
at http://forbiddenfiction.com/library/story/AL1-1.000221.

The Miracles of Dorothea of Andrine

In 1794, at Little Flowers Convent in a remote village, the sisters have begun to teach about the ecstatic pleasure of the womb and claim to possess the power of the milk that fed the Savior. The memory of the late Reverend Mother Dorothea of Andrine has inspired worshippers to great fervor amid reports of miracles of healing. Besieged with requests to beatify the holy woman who started this movement, the Church dispatches the Right Reverend Louis Montblanc, Bishop of Andrine, to investigate the cult of Dorothea. (M/F, F/F, M/F/F)

Chapter 1

The Condemnation

Letter from the Right Reverend Louis Montblanc, Bishop of Andrine, to His Eminence, The Most Reverend Cardinal Clement Barth, Vice-Postulator for the investigation of Dorothea of Andrine:

Written on the seventeenth day of August in the year of our Lord one thousand seven hundred and ninety-four.

The Office of the Bishop, Cathedral of St. Paul, Royan, Andrine

Your Eminence:

In previous communication, I have made you aware of my deep misgivings regarding the case of the proposed beatification of the late Reverend Mother Dorothea, of the Little Flowers Convent in Andrine. To reiterate briefly, as bishop of the diocese in which her ministry took place, I found her to be a divisive figure given to erratic behavior and borderline heretical statements. Had Little Flowers Convent not been so far removed from the center of diocesan life, I might have found it necessary to investigate the Reverend Mother for misconduct—not as a candidate for sainthood! As it stands, I am sure I erred in judgment. I should never have allowed her ministry to continue unmolested in the face of the scandalous rumors that reached my office.

It disappoints me that a beatification investigation has indeed been opened, and this sentiment is not mitigated in the least by the numerous letters and petitions from laypeople requesting such action. To my mind, this is a perfect example of why the ministers of the church are entrusted with the spiritual life of the people. Without spiritual fortification, men are easily led astray by the pretty words of a charismatic (and physically attractive) woman.

My objections notwithstanding, you have entrusted me with the execution of the processes de non cultu, and I will faithfully carry out this commission. Especially in an irregular case such as this, it is imperative to ensure that the people living near the Little Flowers Convent obey the decree issued by the wisdom of His Holiness, Pope Urban VIII, which prohibits the public worship of servants of God before beatification has been discerned and recognized.

Since your letter of assignment arrived, I have done the utmost possible to gather reports of the activity around Little Flowers Convent. My office is several days' ride from that location, and that has regrettably limited my efforts. I write today, however, to inform Your Eminence that my initial research has led me to believe that an extended in-person investigation is not only desirable but of the utmost necessity.

Addressing this duty must needs deprive the diocese of my ordinary services, but I believe that once I have laid out the case for this action, you will agree that I should go forthwith and discreetly. It is too dangerous to the reputation of the Church to allow the information I have uncovered to spread at all, even to trusted servants of God. I, of course, except Your Eminence from these concerns, and pray most sincerely that you will find your bearings in this strange case more readily than I myself have done.

I beg that you will reconcile my superiors to this absence, and that you will take these initial causes for concern strongly into account in your consideration of the proposed beatification of the Reverend Mother.

I have heard rumors of unusual statements made by the Reverend Mother in her personal writing—I received several letters from her myself that boasted questionable theological lineage. Similarly, I strenuously object to the form and manner of her alleged posthumous miracles. Despite strong personal feelings, I leave those matters outside my purview to Your Eminence's learned discretion. In what follows, I will focus on the cult of Dorothea of Andrine, which appears to have developed in a most improper direction.

Now I come to the crux of the matter: the evidence. I have sent this letter by a mute and trustworthy messenger specifically because of the highly inflammatory material it contains. I would never ordinarily subject Your Eminence to the frank language to be found in the account transcribed below, except that I believe that in their verbatim form they support my chosen course of action most clearly.

My first awareness of the cult of Dorothea of Andrine (beyond what is to be had from rumor) came from one Henri Delauney, a traveling merchant who on several occasions attended the Liturgy of the Hours at Little Flowers Convent. He seems an honest man, though not overly educated in either letters or religion. I had been able to trace several rumors in my own city back to him, and so began my investigation with an extended interview of this good tradesman.

I transcribed the interview myself, unwilling to entrust even my excellent clerk with these sensitive matters.

Monsieur Delauney appeared most agitated to have been summoned to my presence. He mopped his forehead though the day was not particularly hot, and begged my blessing in an overly pious fashion which did not suit him. He is a relatively young man, fine of feature though somewhat portly. He dresses a la mode, but without the unfortunate air of foppishness that often attends those who care for style. That day, his flesh appeared quite pale, particularly in contrast to the blackness of his hair.

I attempted to set him at ease with a brief discussion of matters of trade and assurances of the love and attention of our Lord. When he remained anxious as to the purpose of our interview, I did not hold him in suspense, explaining that I wished to learn what he had observed of the local veneration of Dorothea of Andrine.

As soon as I uttered the name, he colored purple from the top of his shirt collar to the tips of his ears. "I am a good Christian, Your Excellency," he said. "I go every Sunday to Mass, and often during the week. I confess my sins and contribute my tithe."

I allowed that he sounded most faithful and asked him to explain why such a thing would be in doubt.

"The nuns at the convent seemed to believe I did not understand the full teaching of the Church."

"In what sense?"

"I attended Terce several times at Little Flowers, having traveled to Andrine for an extended period. Right away, I thought I had never seen Terce done quite that way before. They said some prayers and psalms I did not recognize, and the sisters' gestural devotions did not look entirely proper."

I could not decide which alarmed me more: the idea of unfamiliar prayers and psalms or the phrase "gestural devotions." I asked first about the psalms.

"Your Excellency, I do not speak Latin, and I have not memorized the psalter, so at first I thought I lacked the learning to recognize these. But then I heard them say, 'Dorothea,' several times, and not only as part of the collects. I knew she used to be the Reverend Mother there, but it seemed they had added her name to the Apostles' Creed and the Glory Be. They kept repeating something like 'in utero voluptatem excessu.' I apologize, Your Excellency, because I am sure I have got that wrong, but I have never heard that refrain before—certainly never so often."

Your Eminence can imagine my concern, given that this unlettered merchant seemed to be attempting to put together a Latin phrase about the ecstatic pleasure of the womb. I betrayed no disapproval in my countenance, simply nodding and directing him to explicate the gestural devotions to which he had previously referred.

"They did not cross themselves the way I was taught with my catechism. Each sister held either a crucifix or an icon of Reverend Mother Dorothea. They began by touching their foreheads, which is what I do, but then they touched much lower than I learned to." At this point in his narrative, his blush deepened, and he ceased his conversation.

"Please go on. Perhaps you could demonstrate."

Monsieur Delauney rose from his chair, stammering, "I beg pardon from Your Excellency." He touched his forehead, but instead of then touching his fingers to his lower chest or navel, he reached much lower, to the groin, and rolled his hand there for a lengthy period, transforming a holy gesture into a most obscene and forbidden act.

He resumed speaking, his voice hoarse. "The sisters would do it like this, Your Excellency, and groan and pray to the Holy Ghost while they did." His hips gyrated, and I had to look away.

"I'm sure that is quite enough," I told Monsieur Delauney.

"There was more," he said.

I sighed and fixed my gaze on him again. He finished this supposed cross not by touching the left then right shoulders, but by pinching and plucking the left and right nipples! I am sure such a blasphemous and indecent performance could not be found in the lowest houses of vice in this city. I gestured that he should resume his seat, and turned my most fearsome scowl upon him.

"Monsieur, I hope I do not need to impress upon you the gravity of this investigation. This is no time for clowning, and you are in the presence of a bishop of the Church. If you do not respect me as an individual, you must at least respect my office."

The good man blanched. "I swear, Your Excellency, that is how the sisters did it in Terce. I was afraid, seeing it. It distracted me, Your Excellency. The devil leapt up on my shoulder and gave me terrible thoughts, seeing twelve sisters crossing themselves that way."

My own pulse raced imagining it, and I crossed myself three times the proper way. Much as I may have wished to leave the matter there, I felt a duty to carry on with my questioning of Monsieur Delauney. Next, I turned my attention to his claim that the nuns believed he needed further religious instruction.

"They said they included devotions to the late Reverend Mother as part of their Liturgy of the Hours, due to her great saintliness and wisdom. They said I must learn these devotions in addition to my daily prayers."

"What were these devotions?"

"Two sisters took me aside. They were named Sister Claire and Sister Therese."

He paused a long time in his account, and I was forced to press him.

"Your Excellency, may I speak as to a confessor?"

"I must transcribe your words for the benefit of the holy men investigating the Late Reverend Mother Dorothea of Andrine, but be assured your account will go no farther. If it would comfort you, I will perform the Rite of Penitence directly following this interview."

"That would be a great relief, Your Excellency. A great relief." He visibly gathered himself, adjusting his cravat and making the sign of the cross over his lips with his thumb. I believed his piety and concern for his mortal soul to be quite sincere. He began speaking again, haltingly. "The sisters—Sister Claire and Sister Therese—they were young and beautiful. Sister Claire's lips were plump as berries, and just as red, and Sister Therese, well, her bosoms—"

Here, I interrupted him. "I understand that the sisters' unusual manner of crossing distracted you, Monsieur, but some secrets may still remain between you and our Lord until we get to the matter of your confession."

"I apologize, Your Excellency, because it relates to what you asked me to explain. I was looking at the sisters, though I knew I should not have carnal thoughts about servants of the Lord. The sisters noticed, and they giggled together and asked if I enjoyed their God-given beauty. I nodded and cleared my throat. I could not come up with anything proper to say. Sister Therese took both my hands and placed them on her bosoms. She told me to squeeze them as I would a pair of apples."

"Shocking!"

"I was certainly shocked, Your Excellency. I asked what this had to do with devotions to the late Reverend Mother, and Sister Therese implored me to touch her first, having faith that she would explain all directly. I confess I obeyed most enthusiastically after that. I explored the flesh she offered me for quite some time, manipulating it with my fingers and palms. They wept some fluid, but I did not think much about that at the time. After a while passed, Sister Therese opened her habit, and I was quite overcome by the unconcealed splendor of her bosoms. Milk-white skin, she had, with little pink nipples like hard candies. There was a smell, ambrosial but salty, that rose up from her naked flesh—"

"Monsieur!"

I must report that Monsieur Delauney paused to adjust his breeches before continuing his tale. "In any case, these bosoms banished my powers of speech. Upon her invitation to resume my ministrations, I dove in with lips and tongue and tasted of them as if of the ripest apples..."

"And the devotions, Monsieur?"

"I quite forgot them for the better part of an hour, licking the entirety of the surface of her bosoms, and lifting them to taste the sweat below. It was Sister Therese who reminded me. I would have given suck to her nipples, but she smiled down at me kneeling before her and curled her fingers in my hair. Gently, lovingly, she pried me from her sweet, delicious breast. 'What do you think of them, Monsieur?' she asked. I did not know how to reply. It did not seem my place to judge such natural wonders, and I said as much.

" 'You are as kind as you are pious,' she replied, but then leaned forward and whispered in my ear. 'Would you say that they are ripe?'

" 'Indeed, lady, you are in the prime of maidenhood,' I responded.

" 'I tell you this next, Monsieur, as witness to a miracle that I hope will inspire your devotion. I am a maiden, but through my devotion to the late Reverend Mother Dorothea, who taught that God holds all women in high esteem, the Lord has given me a portion of the favor he showed to the Blessed Virgin Mother Mary. Do you believe?'

"Still faced as I was with her bosoms, I could not but believe. I stammered my wonder and appreciation of God's miracles. She went on a while about the blessed nectar that fed our Lord when he was but a babe, then she knelt along with me, returning my hands to her bosoms. This time, she did not allow me to explore them, but held them in place reverently, so that I could feel the heat of her skin.

" 'Will you drink, then, of the milk given to the Gate of Heaven and Star of Ocean, which flows through myself and Sister Claire just as it did through the Blessed Virgin Mother Mary?'

"I did not understand what she meant. I could only nod. Sister Therese guided my head to her breast and fed me her nipple. Then I knew she meant me to suckle as a babe, and I did. I drank of her, and it may be blasphemy, but I believed at that moment with all my heart. I have never tasted the like. I thought I would never want for food again, and the liquid satisfied my palate completely. The flavor escapes simple description—rich yet sweet, salty yet clear, thick and white like milk, yet far more refreshing. Upon reaching my gut, it produced a curious, clarifying sensation quite the opposite of the fog instilled by wine. I knew my actions would ordinarily be considered carnal, but, though my member ached within my breeches, I felt great reverence, and trusted that this divine drink truly came to me by the power of the Holy Ghost.

"I drank her dry and sat back on my heels gasping, only to find that Sister Claire knelt beside Sister Therese, crossing herself in that distracting fashion. As soon as she saw me disengage from Sister Therese, Sister Claire unveiled her own bosoms. They were not as much to my liking as the generous weights offered by Sister Therese, but the nipples covered half their surface, cherry-red as her lips, and — "

Again, I saw fit to interrupt, for the sake of both our souls. "I assume Sister Claire also offered you drink."

"Heavenly drink, in great measure. But by this time, I confess, my thoughts had grown more carnal, and I reached into Sister Claire's tunic to caress her. She, too, smelled delicious, and she allowed me to explore the curves of her hips and thighs, though Sister Therese pulled my hands away each time I reached for her most intimate flesh.

"When Sister Claire's supply of holy milk was also exhausted, I dropped to the floor and panted. Sister Therese at this point reminded me of the devotions. I did not know if I had the strength for anything more. I struggled up to my knees, knelt, and waited.

"Both sisters began to touch me, freeing me of my clothes, and stroking me everywhere. Sister Therese whispered in my ear, 'Do you still care to learn our devotions?'

"I told them I would learn anything they wished. Sister Therese smiled and kissed my forehead. Her fingers closed around my member, while Sister Claire hefted my sack.

" 'You have struggled with disease, have you not?' Sister Therese touched me pointedly, and I could not mistake her meaning. As I have confessed to my parish priest, as the result of an unfortunate indiscretion in my youth with a prostitute, sores typically defile my member. 'Look,' she said. Glancing down, I saw myself as pure as a boy. She would not let me speak my questions.

" 'You must thank the Reverend Mother for what she has done for you,' said Sister Claire. 'Venerate her now. Call on her name.' Both sisters squeezed and caressed my private parts. I had begun to think our interaction sinful, but upon the sight of my purified member, I reconsidered. Pleasure filled me, but not only in the obvious places. Satisfaction, comfort, and bliss penetrated to my very soul as the sisters laid hands on me, and I could very well believe it the work of the Holy Ghost or the Blessed Virgin or Dorothea of Andrine or whomever they wished I credit. I groaned their saint's name, and the sisters tugged my member. They were slow, patient, and very compelling.

"Before long, I spent myself all over their fingers and the floor before me. Shame returned to me, and I glanced from one to the other in alarm. But Sister Therese only brought her hand to her mouth and licked my seed, closing her eyes and crossing herself as she did. 'You have been blessed by Dorothea of Andrine and by the Holy Ghost,' said Sister Claire, mimicking the gesture. I murmured my confusion, and she made me do as they had done. I hesitated to touch tongue to my own emission, but their meaning became clear as soon as I obeyed them. My seed had transformed into the same fluid as their milk.

" 'Blessed Dorothea commands two practices of devotion,' Sister Claire told me. 'Each day, after Terce, Sext, and Vespers, you must call on her and venerate her as we have shown you, offering this purest sacrifice. The second devotion requires that you share the healing with which she has favored you. All who drink of your milk in faith will be healed. But you must not allow the ungodly to taste of the divine liquid with which our Lord was fed by his most holy Mother. If you do these things, you will enjoy the blessing of Dorothea all the days of your life.'"

By this point in Monsieur Delauney's narration, I was quite beside myself. It took several moments of silence for me to bestir myself to answer him, and I began with a brief prayer for the intervention of the Blessed Virgin, followed by the collect for protection. Monsieur Delauney waited anxiously for my response, and I made him squirm and wait longer than strictly necessary, for by then I felt less kindly disposed toward the merchant than before.

"Have you practiced these so-called devotions?" I asked finally.

"I have, Your Excellency."

"And yet you say you are relieved when I offer the Rite of Penitence. You must have been aware of your most grievous sin."

"Your Excellency, I feel her presence. And I have healed both men and women —"

"Women and *men*! Men, also, have drunk of this blasphemous seed of yours! You have behaved as a Sodomite!" I upbraided him further for quite some time, then did perform the Rite of Penitence. He left my office a most contrite man, and I believe his burden of sin had been eased.

For my part, as Your Eminence may imagine, disturbance hung most heavily upon me. I will leave aside the matter of these blasphemous miracles, which can be the work of none other than the devil himself. These are outside the sphere of my investigation, though I beg Your Eminence to set the appropriate parties to study these events and return to you with full and accurate reports. Confining myself within the scope of my duties, I was able to obtain several accounts corroborating the testimony of Henri Delauney.

The sisters at Little Flowers Convent have indeed been instructing the faithful in sinful practices, under the guise of teaching devotion and piety. The Church must act in response to these most evil acts performed in the name of the cult of Dorothea of Andrine. I trust Your Eminence will agree. With Your Eminence's blessing, I will travel to Little Flowers, where I intend to put a stop to the irregular worship that has arisen in the name of the late Reverend Mother. Sisters Therese and Claire, whose names appeared in many of my interviews, must be tried for witchcraft. I will apprehend them and submit them to the judgment of the broader Church.

I will set out the moment I receive word of Your Eminence's approval.

Faithfully,

Louis Montblanc, Bishop of Andrine

Chapter 2
Innocence Corrupted

Letter from the Right Reverend Louis Montblanc, Bishop of Andrine, to His Eminence, The Most Reverend Cardinal Clement Barth, Vice-Postulator for the investigation of Dorothea of Andrine:
Written on the twenty-sixth day of January in the year of our Lord one thousand seven hundred and ninety five.
Auberge de la Croix, Forges-les-Eaux, Andrine

Your Eminence:

Delays of post and travel being what they are, it has taken far longer for me to arrive at Little Flowers Convent than I should have liked. Unfortunately, Your Eminence's reply to my previous letter did not arrive at my office until after the start of Advent. With that season of joy and anticipation hard upon me, and the corresponding expansion of my duties, I deemed myself unable to carry out my mission to Little Flowers until after the feast of the Epiphany.

Having executed my obligations to the diocese, I made haste for Forges-les-Eaux, well aware of the urgency of my charge on behalf of the broader Church. I arrived yesterday afternoon, and found a situation even more dire than that described by Henri Delauney. I am sure another missive will follow shortly, but such is my horror at the initial picture I have formed that my concerns must spill onto the page this very moment, denying all efforts to contain them until such time as I can report on action in addition to observation.

Certainly, I will endeavor to suppress and contain the widespread blasphemy and heresy being carried out in the dubious name of the late Reverend Mother Dorothea of Andrine, but before I can again be capable of sober logic, I must turn to Your Eminence as a brother in Christ and beg for your prayers and consideration before God. I have thus far avoided sin, but I am also convinced that my soul has been in great peril since the moment I arrived in this accursed place and found myself among adherents to the cult of Dorothea. If a devoted servant of Christ such as myself has come to such dire straits, how much more must the temptations here affect the laity! Your Eminence would do this place a great kindness by remembering us all in your devotions, particularly when calling upon the Holy Mother of Our Lord, who must surely be appalled at the perversions performed in her name at Little Flowers Convent.

Please forgive the extremes of my despair. As you peruse my account of what has transpired over the past hours, Your Eminence will see these are not mere histrionics.

When I arrived at Forges-les-Eaux, I wore the dress of an impoverished holy man, not the insignia of my office. The laity here are pious, and a local innkeeper immediately offered me a room free of charge, as a gift to the greater glory of God. I thanked him sincerely, for the road had wearied me, and went up to sleep.

Shortly before vespers, the innkeeper's daughter knocked at the door. I roused myself and let her in, expecting her to perform cleaning duties or to offer me bread and scraps as a monk's dinner. Instead, she displayed a silver dish and prostrated herself before me. "Child?" I do not experience many temptations to misconduct, but the devil drew my attention at once to the strawberry-blonde hair escaping the back of her cap. I believe Monsieur Delauney's story had primed me to seek an occasion of sin. I stumbled back from her lovely form.

"Please, Father. Allow me to assist with your Vespers devotion."

"I hardly need assistance to say the prayers that are my duty, my dear."

"Blessed Dorothea taught that the beauty of a woman can always assist in the contemplation of the holy." She loosened her bodice, and the merchant's story sprang afresh to my mind.

Wicked thoughts lay thick upon me. Already, I craned my neck for a better view of the imminent display of her bare bosoms.

"I would collect your holy seed and keep it for my own purification later," she said, dropping the garment and lifting the silver dish. I would have cursed her as a harlot, except for the sweet and utter innocence that radiated from her face. Observing her, great sorrow pierced my heart at how the late Reverend Mother and her corrupted sisters had spread their twisted doctrine among good, gentle, and god-fearing people.

I turned away and asked protection for all of our souls. When the Holy Ghost gave me strength to do so, I dismissed her. She departed upon my request, but in a state of great consternation and contrition. She expressed concern that I would not be able to say Vespers without a companion, and offered the names of a variety of women who could serve in her stead, in each case commending them as great examples of religious devotion and loveliness. With difficulty, I convinced her that my spiritual exercises required me to offer my devotions in utmost privacy, but this statement only increased her fascination with me. Before she left the room, she begged to be allowed to return later in the evening to lick up any holy remnants of my Office from the floorboards.

The images this young woman conjured through her entreaties disturbed me mightily, and after she departed at long last, I was forced to spend the remainder of the evening in strenuous prayer. I resolved to mortify my flesh for good measure, and partook of no food or water from that moment until the present. By the time night fell, I knew God had given me the duty of stopping the activity of this blasphemous cult.

In the morning, I visited Little Flowers for Terce and found all as Monsieur Delauney had described. The twelve sisters cut figures more appropriate to houses of loose women than to the holy places of a nunnery. Their habits hugged their curves most scandalously, and some wore black lace where a thicker fabric would have been proper. They did not all wear wimples, and those that did allowed loose locks to fall brazenly free of the fabric. Pride in their feminine beauty seemed to have guided them to retain long, lustrous hair rather than submitting to the blessed humiliation of shorter cuts.

Each sister ground her body suggestively against an icon or crucifix in exactly the manner the merchant demonstrated to me. A few provided particularly egregious examples. One, a red-headed vixen I

later identified as Sister Therese, slipped her crucifix under her habit
and pumped her body up and down. To complete her obscene act of
supposed devotion, she produced the defiled holy object, the Savior's
poor figure glistening with the evidence of her sin, and brought it to
her lips, where she licked it clean. She lingered over Our Lord's intimate areas with a lascivious intention that would have been clear to
any observer.

It dismays me to report that this was not the most shocking display. Sister Claire is a dark-haired slip of a woman whose apparent
innocence masks an incredible capacity for depravity. Attached to her
kneeler was a large crucifix, carved from thick, dark wood. At first,
I could not understand how the kneeler could still be used considering the obstruction this crucifix would present. Then Sister Claire
stood above it and threw her skirts over the wooden object. She knelt
slowly, her fingers trembling as they clutched her prayer book, and
her face transported with an ecstasy that I knew could not be holy.
She moved with care, almost as if she struggled with pain. I could not
stop myself from thinking of the size of that crucifix and wondering
how such a small woman could manage to enthrone it in the intimate
place where it surely lodged.

Sister Claire bent her head, her forehead wrinkling with effort.
She recited her psalms all the while without stumbling over a single
word. At last, her downward progress ceased, and the devil tempted
me with speculation as to how deeply she had seated that crucifix. As
if she could hear my wicked thought, Sister Claire lifted her head and
fixed her gaze on mine. From there, she began to rock and pray, her
body working itself yet lower as she did.

This evil display so transfixed me that only then did I realize that
Sister Claire's recitation came from no psalter I had ever heard. Perhaps it bore slight resemblance to the Alma Redemptoris Mater, or
other Marian hymns, except that the wonders of nature to which it
attested were not the familiar miracles of bearing our Creator and remaining ever virgin. Instead, in flawless church Latin, Sister Claire and
the other nuns present extolled the joys of the spasms of the womb,
which their verses said would bring forth the power of the triune God
into the world if induced once for the Father, once for the Son, and
once for the Holy Ghost. Incredibly, that was the mere beginning of

their blasphemy, for what followed amounted to a detailed description of ways to induce such paroxysms, and of the character of spasms best suited to honor each member of the Trinity.

Though the meaning of the words themselves must have been lost to all those not fluent in the lingua franca of the Church, the sisters' movements left little to the imagination. Monsieur Delauney had seemed forthright in his descriptions, but I wondered if that good man had still seen fit to hold back some of what he had experienced for fear of my judgment. Any witness to a service such as the one I observed should have fled the building long before the sisters had the chance to offer their twisted corrections to his devotional practices. If their antics have instead increased since Monsieur Delauney's last visit to Little Flowers, then I fear the rate of acceleration of their devious blasphemy.

In short, the sisters illustrated their psalms by abusing themselves in a shocking public manner. I debated whether it was proper for me to remain as an observer. It might have been better for my soul to perform an immediate *exeunt*. Had I put a stop to the proceedings at once, I might have educated those in attendance. Ultimately, I decided that the greatest value lay in my ability to record the habits of the cult of Dorothea for Your Eminence's benefit. This cannot have been the only such event, and I could not justify preserving the dignity of my own soul while perhaps failing to gather the information needed to end the activities of the cult altogether.

Please know that the complete account I will make is not intended to arouse prurient interest, and stems from no such motives on my part. Rather, I hope to arm Your Eminence with every weapon necessary to force the immediate cessation of all efforts to submit the late Reverend Mother Dorothea of Andrine to the process of beatification.

The paroxysms of the Father, the sisters chanted, should represent the glory of creation and should stem from the seat of creation itself—the womb. The liturgy of the sisters' worship demanded that they approach that most holy place as closely as possible, which meant that all twelve sisters began to imitate the supposed pieties of Sister Claire. As I watched in horror, the women leading the service inserted various objects to truly improbable depths. While Sister Claire chose a crucifix for her exercises, others used candlesticks or other household items.

Sister Therese chose to demonstrate her devotion in an even more dramatic fashion. She stepped out from behind her kneeler, where she was joined by an elderly craftsman who must be a resident of Forges-les-Eaux. This man knelt and presented a piece of wood as an offering. It was larger than Sister Claire's crucifix and ornately carved.

I would have found it beautiful had it not been intended for such an unholy purpose. Though I could not see its full detail from a distance, scenes carved on its sides depicted the division of the heavens from the earth, the creation of the animals, and other stories from the first eleven chapters of the book of Genesis. Since the object was as thick as the craftsman's arm, I, at first, believed its blasphemous use would be symbolic. Sister Therese, however, does not appear to be a woman who settles for less than physical extremes. She performed the sign of the cross over the craftsman, then repeated the gesture three times over the carved wood. Then she threw her skirts over both man and object, and sunk several inches in stature as she widened her stance around him.

Within moments, the perversions being performed beneath her habit became clear. Her skirts draped his head, but did not hide its bobbing movements. The craftsman's broad shoulder moved rapidly, at first causing me to think that Sister Therese's body had absorbed that monstrous object with horrifying ease. Then the woman shuddered, took the name of our Lord in vain, and clutched the craftsman's skull through her garment. He froze, and her face took on the same expression of concentration that I had seen on Sister Claire.

Sister Therese cried out, panting and moaning as if possessed by a demon. At one point, she even whispered, "No." The craftsman ceased his ministrations at that, but she caressed the back of his head and urged him on. "I sacrifice myself in the name of the Lord and the Blessed Mother!" she shrieked. She could have been referring either to the Holy Mother of God or to the disturbed former leader of that defiled convent.

She followed this with a truly incredible effort, screwing her face up with strain, and grunting like the lowest animal. The object the craftsman held had seemed so large when he displayed it that I could not help but feel sympathetic pain watching her. This act of self-abuse clearly took its inspiration from other practices of mortification, for she could not have felt much pleasure when speared by such a terrible thing.

Sister Therese breathed rapidly from her exertions. The craftsman's head moved. The sister raked her hands all over her body and jerked as if in the throes of a seizure. He must have supported her, since I could not see how she could otherwise remain standing while having such a fit.

Sister Therese threw back her head, screamed out the "Glory Be," and collapsed to the chapel floor, taking the craftsman with her. For one chaotic moment, as the two struggled in her skirts, I thought I would witness an act of fornication in the house of the Lord himself. Then the craftsman worked his way clear of her, in disarray but still clothed. His chin and upper lip glistened and his eyes had taken on a heavy, dissolute expression. Before he could rejoin the worshippers in the pews, Sister Therese worked her way up to her knees and ran a finger through the sinful juices that covered his face. This she brought to her lips, closing her eyes as if she tasted the sweetest nectar.

"You are healed, good sir," she told the craftsman. "Go in peace."

No one explained what had ailed the man, but the joy and awe that crossed his face suggested a serious malady. The crowd rejoiced, but I fisted my hands in my garments and gritted my teeth, for I knew from the Latin that two more such displays would yet come to tempt my mortal soul.

Sister Therese rejoined her sisters, her steps jerky and strange. I realized that the craftsman's offering had not resurfaced from beneath her skirts along with its maker, and shuddered, concluding that it remained seated in the blasphemous woman's apparently ample depths.

The chant transformed, and I learned that, according to this profane liturgy, the paroxysms of the Son should represent his role as divine mediator. The wicked atmosphere had quite shaken me by then, and I confess that my sinful mind offered up a number of fantastic and unholy possibilities for how such an homage could be accomplished. Would a woman acting as mediator transmit the knowledge of a man to one of the supposedly maidenly nuns? Would Sister Therese share the object lodged within her with the other eleven sisters? I tried to tear these wicked thoughts from my mind with little success, and again, Your Eminence, I must suggest that the sisters' activities must have a powerful corrupting effect on the people of Forges-les-Eaux.

A new sister stepped to the front of the group, and had I not known the evil of that place, I would have thought her a simple farm girl. A lock of pale blonde hair escaped her wimple, its golden tones contrasting with the ruddiness of her skin. Her cheeks glowed with the appearance of health and good eating, and I could not stop myself from contemplating the perversions that lay in store for her. My flesh stirred, and I removed a fountain pen nib from my pouch and pressed it into my palm, hoping that the pain there would remind me of our Lord's stigmata and what he suffered for the sake of our sin.

This sister, I later learned, is Jeanne. She called forward a young woman kneeling in one of the front pews, who clasped hands with a young man I presumed to be her husband. That fellow leaned over and kissed his wife's forehead, then helped her to her feet and assisted her in walking to Sister Jeanne.

The young woman limped and leaned heavily on the man beside her. She was dark and lovely, with the curves of the Madonna and a few curls escaping the hat perched on her head.

At the sister's direction, the man held the woman from behind, supporting her weight, while the sister raised the woman's skirts, revealing that her left leg ended in a tangle, her foot hanging uselessly from the end of the limb. A large bloody spot marred her stocking just above the ankle. The evidence of her injury cooled my ardor somewhat, allowing my body to relax.

Sister Jeanne, however, did not stop lifting the wife's skirts. She handed the man folds of cloth to hold as she peeled up skirts and underskirts to expose the woman from the waist down, with nothing remaining to protect her modesty but her free-hanging pockets, the bottoms of her stays, her stockings, and her garters! My gaze focused on the dark space between her legs and the mysterious shapes just visible beneath her thick, curled hair. Perhaps you will think me naive, but I have known myself destined to be a man of the cloth since a young age, and have always kept myself pure. This frank sight had heretofore been hidden from me. Even my brushes with temptation had not taken me so far.

Far from being outraged by the indignity being visited upon his wife, the man simply held the skirts Sister Jeanne gave him, smiling as the congregation feasted its eyes upon her most intimate parts.

The chant rose to a crescendo — I no longer listened to the Latin closely enough to provide a translation — and Sister Jeanne leaned forward and whispered something to the woman and her husband. The husband shifted his grip on his wife's garments, so that he held them in place with only one hand. Then Sister Jeanne grasped his free wrist and guided his hand between his wife's legs. At the same time, the nun took one of the wife's hands as well, leading it to join her husband's.

Sister Jeanne moved with comfort and expertise that no nun should have possessed. She made the man slip his fingers inside the woman, then smoothed the woman's concealing hair and spread her open. She directed the woman to place her fingers over a nub of flesh she revealed at the top of her split, demonstrating a rolling movement that caused the woman to gasp and fall back against her husband.

I could hardly breathe by then, and the devil's influence over my flesh made my body ache all over. Sister Jeanne remained confident and firm, seemingly unaffected by the tableau she created for the congregation. She pulled the man's fingers in and out of his wife's body in a smooth, steady rhythm, and encouraged the wife to continue toying with that bit of flesh.

Before long, both the woman's legs lifted off the floor, flailing and kicking to either side of Sister Jeanne. Her body rolled and strained and went stiff in places. Her face began to sweat, and she leaned her cheek against the outside of her husband's arm and panted through parted lips. She struggled for a second with Sister Jeanne — I thought perhaps she meant to pull her hand away from where the nun directed her to such insistent ministrations. Sister Jeanne prevailed, however, and the young wife gave a desperate, mournful cry and went limp, though neither her husband nor Sister Jeanne allowed her relief even at this development.

So caught was I in sinful lust that it was not until Sister Jeanne peeled off the young wife's stocking that I realized that both it and her leg were clean of blood, and her foot whole and useful again. The congregation nearly shouted the words of the "Glory Be," and some broke out into song. The sisters attempted to contain the people as the husband led his wife back to their pew, but the crowd would not be silenced. With joy radiating from nearly every countenance, they burst into the Ave Maria, drowning out what must surely have been blasphemous instructions about the paroxysms of the Holy Ghost in the sisters' own chant.

I cannot say what the unholy psalms instructed the worshippers to do. I only know that suddenly every person in that chapel excepting myself grasped themselves in the most intimate places. A matron not two feet from me, who until that time had seemed restrained and very nearly respectful, planted one hand over the juncture of her legs and the other over her left breast and began forcefully abusing herself. She doubled over the pew, grunting as her hands worked. Her gown bunched around the violent motions of her fingers.

I knitted my own hands together, attempting to protect myself from unconsciously mirroring the sin of those around me.

The matron rocked her hips and screamed, and suddenly wetness burst forth, soaking the fabric of her gown at both crotch and nipples. I blinked, uncertain of the cause of the dampness. A quick glance around the building, however, revealed that all but I had experienced the same phenomenon at the same moment. Damp stains adorned the front of each man's pantaloons, and the women suffered the release of fluid from both breasts as well as from the womb.

The sisters broke forth into a chorus of "Sanctus, sanctus, sanctus." I thought they might come to me as they had to Monsieur Delauney, seeking to instruct me in devotions. I did not trust myself to so much as speak to them. Despite my resolve to observe and report to Your Eminence, I could not have withstood another moment in that evil chapel. It smelled not of holy incense but of bodies and all forbidden pleasures of the flesh.

I fled before the sisters could tempt me further, and contented myself with asking a few questions of a man outside, who told me the sisters' names and maintained that such "miracles" and blasphemous practices occur several times a day at Little Flowers Convent. (My shock and outrage were evident, but this good man showed no shame at all, instead attempting to reassure me that the ways of the Lord and His servants can be mysterious.)

Your Eminence, I have done no wrong. I have not sinned. Once I have collected myself, I will set about putting a stop to these activities forthwith. You have nothing to fear, for my faith is unshaken. I will not allow the devil to profane our Holy Church, and most especially not through the cult of the accursed Reverend Mother Dorothea.

I must spend this day in prayer, but it has strengthened my spiritual resolve to write these words to you. I beg you to pray for me and for Forges-les-Eaux as frequently as possible until these horrors have been cut off at the root. I shall write again very soon to tell you that the Lord's will has been accomplished here.

Supported by faith, as always,

Louis Montblanc, Bishop of Andrine

Chapter 3
Corruption Unsuppressed

Letter from the Right Reverend Louis Montblanc, Bishop of Andrine, to His Eminence, The Most Reverend Cardinal Clement Barth, Vice-Postulator for the investigation of Dorothea of Andrine:

Written on the twenty-seventh day of January in the year of our Lord one thousand seven hundred and ninety five.

Little Flowers Convent, Forges-les-Eaux, Andrine

Your Eminence:

It with the utmost chagrin that I follow my confident letter of yesterday with a new missive begging for whatever assistance you can see fit to provide. In particular, I now believe it may be necessary to perform exorcisms on Sisters Therese and Claire, and perhaps on all twelve of the nuns in residence. I need reliable, steadfast, and stolid clergymen to help with this endeavor, for, I am embarrassed to say, I have found I cannot manage it on my own.

As Bishop of Andrine, I should be more than qualified to perform these exorcisms myself, and indeed to take all actions necessary to shut down the dangerous cult of the late Reverend Mother, but I, at this point, lack the requisite spiritual energy. I have taken residence at Little Flowers, having commandeered the late Reverend Mother's office, but I cannot guarantee how long I can remain in control of the situation and of myself.

If Your Eminence understands nothing else from this correspondence, please know that this convent will certainly go to the devil without immediate intervention from Rome, and it seems quite likely that it will take Forges-les-Eaux and perhaps all of Andrine with it.

I will strive to continue reporting the acts that I have observed since my last communication, but I must warn Your Eminence that the resulting account must needs contain acts of such perversion that I quail at the sin of writing it down. In addition, I fear that my own perspective has been corrupted (as you will soon see when I explain what has befallen me). I can only hope that the holiness of Rome can cleanse these pages and the place that produced them, though I very much worry that my words could fall into the wrong hands and inadvertently promulgate the blasphemous teachings of this evil cult.

Directly after posting my previous letter, I shut myself into my room at Auberge de la Croix to pray and meditate. I forbade the innkeeper from allowing any person to disturb me for any reason, knowing that I could not then have resisted the temptations of his daughter. The rest of the day passed uneventfully, aside from the torment in my soul. I continued to refrain from food, and chose to spend the night in recitation of the psalter rather than asleep in my bed. In truth, this last was to prevent the occasion of sin that my own flesh presented.

As the sun rose, I traversed the road to Little Flowers Convent, noting the unusual amount of foot traffic en route to dawn prayer. While I, of course, support increased lay attendance at services of the hours, it seemed certain that the sisters of Little Flowers had inspired devotion through lust rather than faith.

I arrived at the Convent well before the sisters began another of their blasphemous services. At that point, I revealed myself in the fullness of my rank and placed Sisters Therese and Claire under arrest in basement cells. Considering the chaos and disrespect I had witnessed the previous day, I was surprised at how compliant the sisters were. None fought or argued, and the sisters I arrested did nothing more than bow their heads and retire to their respective confinements.

Foolishly encouraged by this show of obedience, I allowed myself to feel hope. I presided over dawn prayer myself, and despite the great distance the sisters had drifted in their observances, they demonstrated facility with the rites approved by the Mother Church.

Believing myself just a few days away from a favorable report to Your Eminence, I instructed the sisters to use appropriate rites for the remainder of the day's services, and went to examine the late Reverend Mother's office. This space has been used by Sister Therese in the time since the accursed Dorothea's death. From what I gather, Sister Therese would have been elected the next abbess had she not refused the position, arguing that the Reverend Mother is still present and watching over her flock.

I collected a number of inappropriate writings, which I am forwarding along with this letter, in hopes that they will be of use to those responsible for other aspects of this investigation. After occupying myself in that way for several hours, I gathered up a quill and scroll and headed down to the basement to interrogate Sister Therese and Sister Claire.

I had not been so foolish as to allow the sisters to incarcerate the two main offenders without inspecting their accommodations myself. When I had them placed in their cells in the morning, all seemed in order. Each sister had a small cot, a pitcher of water and a chamberpot, and a kneeler which I hoped would serve as a reminder to seek forgiveness through prayer. They resided in consecutive cells, but each was made of stone, with no break in that material save the locked door through which they had entered and a tiny window at the top of each cell to allow some slight fresh air to those within.

Imagine my surprise when I later visited the basement and found nothing at all separating Sister Therese from Sister Claire — not stone, not walls, and not clothing. The feminine moaning that greeted me as I approached from the hallway should have alerted me to the activity going on within the cell. I may perhaps be forgiven, however, for trusting in the integrity of stone and presuming the noises to come from self-abuse and nothing more.

Stepping up to the small window in the door to Sister Therese's cell, I was alarmed to witness a tangle of naked female flesh that my eye could not immediately decode. Only when I realized that I beheld two bodies entwined could I comprehend the vision before me. On the floor in the center of the cell, Sister Therese straddled the thigh of Sister Claire, and allowed her own thigh to be mounted in turn. The two women rocked and jerked together, while each caressed the breasts of the other. They passed tender kisses from one to the other as if sharing a treasured object.

I am aware of the perversion of lesbianism, but never expected to see such a brazen example of it. I stared for several minutes, too much in awe of the extent of the sisters' transgression and sin to take any action.

As I watched, Sister Claire freed her lips from those of Sister Therese, then extended her tongue, as long and pink and wicked as a cat's. She licked a line from Sister Therese's temple, down the side of her face and neck, then to the base of her throat. Sister Therese groaned and lolled her head back, bringing her hands to her own breasts and offering them to her debased colleague. Sister Claire accepted this obscene gift and bent her head to the full bosoms that had featured so prominently in Monsieur Delauney's tale. She suckled there, while Sister Therese writhed. When she lifted her head, her lips carried traces of fresh white milk.

Sister Therese did not content herself with milk from the breast of her partner in perversion. She disentangled herself and spread Sister Claire's legs so wide that I saw even more of the female anatomy than I did when Sister Jeanne exposed the young wife during yesterday's service. She proceeded to insert fingers into Sister Claire's channel and rub her bared flesh until thick, white honey flowed onto her hands. Sister Claire rolled her head from side to side as if possessed by the devil himself.

By this time, I realized that for the sake of my own soul, I must leave off my observation and take action. Still, I hesitated, long enough that I saw Sister Therese lift her fingers to her mouth and suckle them with the relish of a person savoring the finest delicacy. Then she returned her dampened fingers to Sister Claire's split and ran them lightly and quickly through every fold. The two women grinned at each other like girls at play, and set to giggling.

Sister Therese dipped her head low and licked at Sister Claire's honey directly, and from the way she moaned her appreciation, it must have tasted very fine indeed. I must confess that at this moment I noticed that my hands had strayed without my permission to the front of my cassock, and that I ground one fist against my hardened member. I recognized also that my thoughts tended toward wickedness.

Ordinarily, Your Eminence, I would save such revelations for my personal confessions if I did not believe them to have bearing on the strange occurrences that were to follow. I beg your forgiveness and indulgence, and deeply regret having to burden you with such filth.

In any case, a great struggle began within me. I sought to regain control of my offending digits, but, like St. Paul before me, soon found that "For that which I do I allow not: for what I would, that do I not; but what I hate, that do I." Though I loathed myself for it, my hand did not quit my member. Instead, it grasped it and began an enticing squeeze, even as I continued to drink in the site of the two nuns engaged in their perverted game.

After all that I had seen since I arrived in Forges-les-Eaux, it seemed the slightest touch could cause my own eruption, but I resisted granting myself this sinful relief. I toyed at the edge of sin as the scent of Sister Claire's body filled the cell and poured out the little window through which I watched her. Almost, I could taste her honey in my own mouth, so powerful and compelling was that aroma. She rolled her hips upward, laughed delightedly, and pounded her fists against the stone floor, and it seemed as if I were the prisoner, not she, for did not the bars of the prison shut me out of the joy which was all too clearly hers?

My breaths came in short bursts, in time with hers. I wanted to lift my voice and cry out with her. The little window at the top of the cell illuminated her naked body so that it shone with the pale glory of a halo, and so that Sister Therese's hair, draped over Sister Claire's thighs and the tiny round bulge of her belly, crackled and flamed. I felt caught up in holy ecstasy, and for a few seconds, lost my own knowledge of the evil in the act I witnessed. As light bathed the two nuns, I saw their pleasure as beautiful and sacred, and the blasphemous words of their strange Latin liturgy ran through my mind.

I pulled up my cassock, seeking to touch my member more directly. When I caught it in my hand, I found it weeping. The appreciative moans of Sister Therese came to mind, and I lifted a drop of that fluid to my lips, expecting sweetness and life such as Monsieur Delauney described. Instead, I tasted the bitter salt of tears, and the sourness of old cheese.

The unpleasant flavors of my flesh returned me to myself. I coughed, even as my face heated with shame. I returned my cassock to its proper position, but the sisters had noticed me by then. Sister

Therese left off her efforts between Sister Claire's legs and turned toward the cell door with a knowing smile.

"Our good and holy bishop has been enjoying our devotions, it seems," said Sister Therese. Her vixen's voice made me flush deeper. She spoke with the insolence of a common tart, and the vision in which I had indulged myself seemed like the tawdry romantic fantasy of a client at a brothel.

She stood, making her breasts bounce as she did, and wiped the back of her hand across her face. Then she crossed the small room in two quick steps and thrust her hand out through the window in the cell door. "Do you want to taste it, Your Excellency? You will find that, by the grace of our Reverend Mother, it has been transformed. It will taste sweeter than communion wine."

I shuddered with both desire and revulsion. "Return your hand to your side and clothe yourself," I ordered. Only then did my addled brain consider the improbable facts of what I had seen. "I enclosed you in separate cells," I said, peering into the room.

Sister Therese smiled as she helped Sister Claire up off the floor. "His Excellency wants us to get dressed, my love," she said, as if Sister Claire had not heard my words herself. She tossed me another brazen grin and strode through the space where there had been a wall earlier that day. From what had been Sister Claire's cell, Sister Therese said, "The Reverend Mother Dorothea taught that the faithful cannot ever be separated from one another. We are all one in the body of Christ."

"Wickedness!" I spat.

"That's what you came down here for, isn't it, Louis?" Sister Claire said, looking me in the eye for the first time since this strange interview had begun. Hearing my Christian name fall from her lips affected me more than I would like to admit, startling me so much that I first reacted as a man to a woman rather than as a bishop being treated with shocking insolence.

I rebuked her, but she thanked me for it as if I had paid her a compliment. She stepped closer to me, and I wished against my will that the cell door did not separate us.

"You don't have to hold yourself apart from us, Louis," Sister Claire said, her voice soft, gentle, and more persuasive than the devil's. "You've always put so much pressure on yourself, haven't you? To be better than a man. To be free from sin. You cry out about wickedness, but what you really want from us is permission." She pressed her body against the cell door and settled her face against the window.

I stumbled back, terribly afraid of how my body reacted to hers. Beneath my cassock, my member strained. I wanted to press myself against the wall, to turn the barrier between us into the thing that joined us. I knew my thinking had succumbed to the sisters' blasphemy, but still I resisted.

"You are a man," Sister Claire murmured, though the shape of her lips reminded me of the fact more than her words. "Our Lord made you so. He will not begrudge you the acts of a man. The Reverend Mother Dorothea taught that God created pleasure as well as pain, and yet you seek out pain and deprivation, and deny yourself the fullness of the experience of the world."

I lifted my hand, I knew not what for. Sister Claire seemed unutterably beautiful to me, her delicate features causing exquisite pain in my chest. In her dark eyes, I saw the compassion of the Holy Virgin herself, and the jut of her chin seemed brave and fragile.

"Touch me," she said, her voice trembling with divine longing. My fingers approached her lips. My eyes began to close, as if they refused to watch this act of surrender. "Touch me in the name of Dorothea."

At this accursed name, my mind cleared just enough. My eyes snapped open and my hand froze in place, though it trembled as if pulled to Sister Claire's face by a lodestone. I hung in the balance, listening to my heart beat and feeling my breath catch in my throat. At last, I located my voice. "I will find a way to help you, Sister. I will not defile you."

I turned and ran, knowing that I could not interrogate the women then or perhaps ever. The sound of hymns from the chapel found and followed me, and in my state of confusion I could not have said whether they spoke of holiness or blasphemy. In great fear for my soul, I made my way to the late Reverend Mother's office with single-minded purpose, where I immediately shut and barred the door behind me. If I could have barred it from the outside, I would have, for the memory of Sister Claire's face—and of her nakedness—still compelled me.

Once inside and safe for the moment, I fell to my knees, ignoring the pain of the stone floor's sharp edges. I prayed and cried out for my savior, and soon wept with shame, loss, and the thwarted but still-present desire to sin. Hours passed as I begged for forgiveness, and entreated our Lord to show me the way forward.

Some time after I began to pray, comfort flooded my chest like a physical force, and my sobs quieted as if of their own volition. A distant memory of my mother tickled the edges of my mind, and I remembered laying my cheek against her breast and twirling a lock of her hair around my finger.

A warm, maternal voice spoke to me then. "Louis," it told me. "You may not need healing for your body, but you need it for your soul. You are a broken man. Come to me, and I will return you to yourself."

The voice heartened me at first, but by the end of that speech my blood ran cold, for I could see I was to be tested by yet another assault from the demons that possess this place. I whispered a prayer for protection and raised my head. "Show yourself, Satan," I commanded.

There was no answer for a long time, but I knew I was not alone. Finally, the voice spoke again. "Louis, I am not your adversary."

This time, I pinpointed the origin of the voice — a small bust of the Reverend Mother that resided in a place of honor in the corner of the room. I wondered if the demon-infested object had often spoken to Sister Therese. Slowly, I rose to my feet, attempting to find the spiritual strength to meet the challenge before me. What I had to do must be done quickly, I knew, before the forces of evil here twisted and confused me again.

I lunged toward the statue, prepared to sweep it from its shelf with one quick motion and dash it to the floor. Before I could accomplish this, however, I noticed that its cheeks were wet. My traitorous hand refused to obey me for what felt like the hundredth time that day.

I examined the statue more closely and found thick, white fluid running from both its nipples, as well as from its eyes. Picking it up, I could not find a connection to any source of liquid, and an examination of the area that ensconced it turned up no telltale damp patches.

As I handled the statue, I inadvertently cupped one of its breasts. Though I was alone and the action had been innocent, shame pierced me. I snatched back my hand and stared at the rivulet of milk running down my palm.

It could not be what it seemed to be, I told myself, and yet I had to know. I lifted my hand to my lips and tasted of the milk of Dorothea of Andrine for the first time. Those few drops of fluid burst across my tongue with revelatory sweetness that—God help me—far surpassed any religious ecstasy I had felt when partaking of the Blessed Host. Even that small amount satisfied the hunger that had gnawed at me since I had begun my penitent fast, and the aches and sandy sensations of the sleepless night faded as well. My entire body, or perhaps my entire being, warmed and glowed with it, and I wanted to fall to my knees all over again. This time, however, the urge was not to cry and beg but to sing praises. Monsieur Delauney's account returned to my mind, and I understood the feelings he described having while drinking of this milk.

I could have fallen completely then. Certainly, I wanted to bow down before the blasphemous Reverend Mother and drink until she would provide no more. I still possessed some slight remainder of the old discipline, however, and so before I could lose myself completely, I snatched up the statue and threw it out the window. It dropped against the stones below, and may have shattered.

Wonderings as to its fate have intruded many times as I write to you, but I dare not look. If I see it whole I may yet humiliate myself before it.

My sins are many, though my mind is so clouded I am not sure how to label them. Lust? Idolatry? Pride?

Pride.

I will claim the sin of pride for thinking myself able enough to combat the evil here without assistance. Your Eminence, please send help. The devil scratches at the door of my soul.

With humble faith,

Louis Montblanc, Bishop of Andrine

Chapter 4
Abuse of Power

Letter from the sinner Louis Montblanc to His Eminence, The Most Reverend Cardinal Clement Barth, Vice-Postulator for the investigation of Dorothea of Andrine:

Written on the twenty-ninth day of January in the year of our Lord one thousand seven hundred and ninety five.

Little Flowers Convent, Forges-les-Eaux, Andrine

Your Eminence:

I must tender my immediate resignation from my position in the Church. Frankly, your humble correspondent is no longer worthy of calling himself a servant of our Lord. Were I in your presence, I would weep over your feet and bathe them in ointment as the sinful woman did for our savior.

My member stirs as I write these words, and I know my fall from grace is complete. Your Eminence, I have given in to my basest desires, and I cannot repent them enough to make myself desist from them.

I fear for affairs at the Cathedral in Royan, but am now so utterly unfit for my position that I fear that returning to set my office in order would only spread the corruption to which I am now subject. If my word still carries any weight with you, I hold up the Reverend Guillaume Béringer for your consideration as my successor. He has always been a man of devotion and holiness, and might well have handled the processes de non cultu for Dorothea of Andrine with more steadfast faith than I have done.

I beg you to block any and all further consideration of the late Reverend Mother for beatification. I, for one, am damned to hell because of her.

In shame,

Louis Montblanc

Letter from the sinner Louis Montblanc to His Eminence, The Most Reverend Cardinal Clement Barth, Vice-Postulator for the investigation of Dorothea of Andrine:

Written on the thirtieth day of January in the year of our Lord one thousand seven hundred and ninety five.

Little Flowers Convent, Forges-les-Eaux, Andrine

Your Eminence:

It occurs to me that you may attempt to convince me that all is not lost. I kept my communication yesterday short because I did not think it seemly to detail my sins to Your Eminence. A man of holiness such as yourself should not have to endure the lurid facts of my ill-advised and perverted actions.

Upon further consideration, I do find it necessary to subject you to the specifics, both so that there can be no doubt that it is appropriate for me to immediately vacate the position in which I had served, and to contribute one last body of evidence against the proposed beatification. All along, I have not spared you exposure to the obscenities practiced here because I believed it important that you understand their full extent. I fear that in this case I wished to hold back in order to protect what remains of my dignity. A sinner such as myself has no dignity left to preserve. I shall instead swallow my pride and confess to Your Eminence all that I have done.

I locked myself in the late Reverend Mother's office for two full days, afraid to venture out and meet with further temptation. After my taste of the milk of Dorothea, I felt no further hunger or fatigue until the second morning. I occupied myself with constant recitation of the psalter, and by regular readings of the Reconciliation of a Penitent, but I did not forget the irony that these devotions were made possible by the unholy fluid I had allowed to pass through my lips.

No one disturbed me at all, and soon I became overwhelmingly curious as to the status of services at Little Flowers. Had the sisters continued to perform the Rites approved by the Church? Had they maintained the incarceration of Sister Therese and Sister Claire? God help me, I also wondered if those latter two women still occupied themselves with their incredible perversions.

I considered waiting to hear from Your Eminence, but that would likely have meant remaining in confinement for months. It would have been unconscionable, I thought, to neglect diocesan affairs for so long. Another irony, I suppose, in the growing catalog of my hypocrisy.

At last, I emerged and explored the convent. All seemed to be running happily and tidily. The sisters had returned to the ordinary rites, and lay attendance had fallen off accordingly. Sister Jeanne informed me that Sister Therese and Sister Claire remained below, in the separate cells that had been assigned to them, and that besides seeing to their basic needs, everyone awaited my instruction as to what should be done with them. Everything seemed so normal and quotidian that I questioned my memory of what I had witnessed before.

Planning to solve this puzzle, I asked Sister Jeanne to come to the office. Shutting us in, and ignoring the rather pungent scent that had arisen there during my time of sequestration, I inquired about the extent of the changes at Little Flowers.

Sister Jeanne blinked innocently and allowed that perhaps the services there had drifted over the years. She reminded me that Forges-les-Eaux is a rather provincial place. She thanked me for having set the sisters on the proper path again, and commented that the late Reverend Mother would never have wanted Little Flowers to go against the instructions of Rome.

Her contrite humility surprised and pleased me, but I recalled the seemingly agreeable way with which the two vixens in the basement had gone to their imprisonment. I knew I would never forget the intensity of the temptation to which they had subjected me. I maintained a suspicion that you will agree was quite justified, and let her feel a bit of the anger that had built up within me since I'd arrived at that town.

"Sister Jeanne, we're not speaking here about garbling the words of the Our Father. I saw you—" Here, words failed me, and I found I could not look at her soft, honest face and pronounce the ugly facts of what I had seen her do to the young wife.

Sister Jeanne dipped her head. "You don't have to spare my feelings, Your Excellency," she said. "Whatever you saw me do, you should correct it so that I may better serve our Lord."

I stared at her. Had she been Sister Claire, I would have judged these sentences to be another evil test. For all her apparent innocence, Sister Claire knew what she was doing. Faced with the guileless Sister Jeanne, however, I questioned myself even more, and wondered if perhaps Sister Jeanne had fallen prey to the machinations of her worldlier and more blasphemous sisters.

When I spoke, my words came out more gently than I had intended. "There was a woman at services a few days ago, with a damaged leg."

Sister Jeanne's eyes sparked, and she nodded quickly. "I remember her."

"Well, the things you did to her—" Again, I could not continue.

"Healing her?" I wondered if she was deliberately baiting me, but could see no option besides persistence.

"The way you touched her."

"The laying on of hands?"

"Sister Jeanne, surely you cannot truly be so naïve. The woman's leg was damaged, and yet that was not where you touched her."

"Must I lay hands directly on the wound, and on no other place?"

This was the moment that grievous sin took hold of me. I closed the distance between us, my mind on fire with the memory of the scent of Sister Claire's naked body, the sight of the woman Sister Jeanne had exposed, and the many other acts I had witnessed over the past several days. Gripping Sister Jeanne by both wrists, I hauled her up out of the chair in which she had seated herself and pulled her tightly against my body. She did not resist me. At once, my member responded, hardening and straining under my cassock. She must have felt it, but I still could not be sure if she knew it for what it was.

Mimicking her treatment of the young wife, I pulled the skirts of her habit up until the lower half of her body had been bared to my scrutiny. The wiry hair between her legs waved gently, as if moving to a breeze I could not feel in that overheated room. The smell of woman assaulted my nostrils and half-maddened me.

Words churned in my throat, but I could not yet release them. Instead, I wrenched Sister Jeanne's hand into place between her legs, spreading open her split and forcing her to touch the nub of flesh where she had directed the attentions of the young wife.

Seemingly unaware of the wickedness of the act, Sister Jeanne merely uttered a brief prayer and began to rub herself, allowing her head to fall back against my shoulder.

This was not the reaction I had expected, but now I found myself torn between berating her for submitting to perversion so easily and seeing how far she would continue it. Suddenly, I wanted to take advantage of her apparent credulity, to see how much I could get away with doing.

As our Lord warns in the gospel of Matthew, thought proved as good as action. As soon as I envisioned what I wished to do to Sister Jeanne, my hand carried out my imagining. My fingers followed Sister Jeanne's, and for the first time in my life, I felt the thick honey that can pour from a woman's slit. My sinful fingers bathed in the wet heat of her, and traced a path through her folds and deeper into her body. Sister Jeanne sighed and spread her legs wider, and the aroma of her fluids went to my head like strong wine.

In that moment, I knew she would taste of the milk of Dorothea, and this last bit of understanding pushed me beyond any good intentions I may have had until then. After two days of wanting that miraculous and unholy liquid, I could not now resist the opportunity to drink of it. Without a doubt, I planned to drain her dry.

My fingers speared into the space between Sister Jeanne's legs. "This is sinful, whore, not holy," I said between gritted teeth, attempting to convince myself as much as to shame her. "Only a loose woman gives in to this. A woman of God does not spread her legs for a man. She does not display her intimate places, she does not pleasure herself, and she certainly does not do both at once."

To be honest, I did not give her much chance to respond. A few times, she began a word, but my hand worked at her so furiously that she could get out no more than the first few sounds of it. I walked us both to the late Reverend Mother's writing desk — the very place from which I now write these words — and pushed her onto it. Fear flickered through her eyes, but trust rapidly replaced it. I should have felt shame, but by then my frenzy of need did not allow it. I yanked her habit up over her head, hiding her face from my view, and took what her body offered me.

Dropping onto the desk above her, I took up one breast and found it heavy and full. I squeezed the nipple, and gasped with desire when the milk of Dorothea trickled out. I pinned the unresisting Sister Jeanne's arms to the desk and drank my fill.

That liquid filled me like everything I had ever needed or wanted. I thought I would never be hungry again, would never again be lost or confused, would never again have to endure uncertainty or pain. I emptied her left breast before I realized what had happened, and for several minutes, I continued to suckle at her empty teat like a demanding babe while she emitted pathetic little groans beneath me. So desperate was I for that strange spiritual food that I began to chew on her nipple as if that might release more of the milk.

Finally, rational thought returned to me enough that I understood why I no longer received sustenance from Sister Jeanne, and I was able to switch breasts. Another period of bliss followed. She was warm and soft beneath me, and I loved her intensely until the milk on that side, too, ran out.

Then need returned to me. Whereas the tiny taste I'd had from the statue had been enough to erase my hunger and keep me sated for more than a day thereafter, it seemed that the more I drank from Sister Jeanne, the more I thirsted. I wrenched her legs apart and buried my face between them, knowing only that I still needed.

I suppose the perversion I performed is ordinarily done to achieve some sort of pleasure, but no finer sensibility drove me. Hunger, pure and simple, guided my tongue to Sister Jeanne's opening and forced it inside. She tasted good there, though that honey did not flow so freely as the milk. I pushed my fingers inside her to scoop it out and into my waiting mouth.

From beneath the habit that sheltered her, Sister Jeanne prayed for me. Her words slowly penetrated my depraved mind until my sense of shame returned to me. My chest seized, and I stumbled back from her, falling to the floor beside the desk. Burying my face in my hands, I let out a howl of despair, for even as I realized what I had done, I still wished to taste of her.

"Sister, I have wronged you," I said, sobbing.

Her hand brushed my shoulder. Her habit made a soft thump as she removed it completely and cast it to the floor. Her face, revealed again, smiled with all the benevolence of a saint in an icon. She held my gaze and, still lying on the desk, spread her legs wider.

"The Reverend Mother would want me to give you everything you need," she said, her voice trembling, and my member surged with understanding and desire.

If I had made love to her as she invited me to, it would still have been a sin. Your Eminence understands that as well as I. And yet, how much more I sinned in truth when I rose shakily to my feet and turned the full force of my anger upon her!

I can offer no good explanation for why her selflessness so enraged me, only that it struck me as yet another temptation, another test that would find me wanting. If she had cried, if she had begged me for mercy, then sanity might have returned to me. I might have found my restraint again. Instead, she offered me something I could not help but take.

I flung myself onto her, still hungry for something I was not getting. Monsieur Delauney's story now became a mocking memory. I felt nothing of the grace he described. No healing or transformation came upon me, only this sinful, endless need.

My teeth sunk into her flesh. I grasped her hips and squeezed until the pain showed on her face. She lifted her hips to meet me, and I tried to drive into her, but my member only battered clumsily against her nether regions. Never having been with a woman before, I had no lover's finesse.

As rough as I was with her, Sister Jeanne continued to give herself to me. She took me in her hand and guided me to her entrance, which gripped me with a slick, welcoming heat that made the moment even more of a cruel parody. She whimpered as I found that place, and I did not know if the noise was one of pleasure or pain.

I didn't want her to enjoy it. I didn't want myself to enjoy it either. I thrust forward with blind, blunt meanness. She screamed, and the shock of the sound froze us both for a moment. Then she gave me another of those gentle smiles, and I couldn't look at her. I buried my face in her hair and rutted with her. She continued to pray, something from that vulgar ritual of Dorothea's. She tried to slide a hand between our bodies, and I thought that might lead to a kind of joy. I snatched her hand away and held her down to the desk, spearing her with mechanical single-mindedness.

Something gathered in my loins. I might have found release if I had continued what I was doing, but instead I tore myself away. There was nothing virtuous about the interruption, though. I bore no illusion that I had avoided sin in so doing. Instead, I wanted to feel the sin in all its ugly emptiness. The milk of Dorothea had left me thirsty, and I wanted no other satisfaction.

Sister Jeanne lay on the desk, her jaw hanging open, her hands moving feverishly now that I had released her, as if they could not find a place to rest. Only then did she understand that nothing she had done would save me. Tears collected in her eyes, but I was too mean and small to attend to her.

"Leave me," I commanded. She nodded quickly and moved to reclaim her habit. That, too, I did not want to allow her. I pushed her naked out of the office door, and locked it behind her.

Her habit lies now in a heap in the corner, reproaching me. I smell her body on my skin, and taste the sour remnants of her milk in my mouth. I deserve nothing, not even my own life. Monsieur Delauney claimed that the milk of Dorothea performed miracles, but it has done no such thing for me.

Your Eminence, strike my name from every book. Forget me.

A Sinner

Chapter 5

Irregular Reconciliation

Letter from the Right Reverend Louis Montblanc, Father Superior of the Society of Dorothea, to His Excellency, The Right Reverend Guillaume Béringer, Bishop of Andrine

Written on the sixteenth day of June in the year of our Lord one thousand seven hundred and ninety five.

Little Flowers Convent, Forges-les-Eaux, Andrine

Your Excellency:

Please forgive the delay of my response. As you can imagine, Holy Week festivities wore all of us out, and I now find myself well into Pentecost, with a large pile of correspondence awaiting attention. Before I proceed to the matter of your inquiry, please allow me to congratulate you on your appointment to my former post. You always exemplified holiness and devotion, and I am touched that, even in my ignominy, my recommendation did not harm your candidacy.

I understand your confusion as to my current role as Father Superior, given the desperate tone of my previous correspondence. The only true response is to invite you to attend services here in Forges-les-Eaux, where the power of the Blessed Reverend Mother can touch you most potently. Through Holy Dorothea, I believe you will be led to a deeper relationship with Mary, Star of Ocean, than you ever thought possible. These divine women can guide you into intimate communion with Our Lord and, indeed, every member of the Trinity.

I also suspect you will be amazed by the miracles of healing that are nearly commonplace in our humble convent—and, though the restoration of my own soul is far from the greatest of these accomplishments, it certainly counts among their number.

Since that is the question that I suspect interests you most, and also abundantly illustrates the mercy of the late Reverend Mother, I hope you will indulge my narrative.

If His Eminence the vice-postulator informed you of the details of our correspondence, you will know that when last I wrote, I held myself to be the lowest of sinners. Indeed, I had nearly resolved to throw myself out the window directly after posting my letter.

I did, however, feel a duty to see that my letter made its way to His Eminence, so all I had endured would not be entirely in vain. In pursuit of this goal, I eventually emerged from sequestration. A part of me expected to be instantly accosted by sisters and laypeople defending the erstwhile virtue of my poor abused Sister Jeanne. I would have accepted such an assault as my due, and only begged that my letter be conveyed to His Eminence before they did as they would with me.

Instead of an angry mob, however, I found myself awaited by Sister Claire, whose elaborate installation in the hallway outside the office suggested that she had set herself there for quite some time, expressly for my sake. I cannot say I was surprised to see her out of her cell — on the contrary, the sisters had followed my instructions beyond my expectations. She wore her habit, and sat with hands folded on her lap, every line of her body stern and lovely. Her forehead wrinkled just slightly, and I could not decide whether the lines indicated concern or disapproval.

"Your Excellency," she said when I showed my face. Then, softer, "Louis."

I swallowed hard, and could not find my voice. I wanted to go to her for comfort, but also to hide from her scrutiny.

"Louis. Come here." She patted her lap like a woman calling a pet. I stepped closer, uncertain as to exactly what she expected me to do. When I came within her reach, she caught me by a fold of my cassock and drew me onto the floor beside her, guiding my head onto her thighs. I thought I smelled that strange milk faintly on her habit, and terrifying hunger stirred in me again. I may have whimpered, so frightened was I of repeating my previous shameful actions.

Sister Claire showed no fear, stroking my hair with cool fingers instead. "Sister Jeanne is well. She has forgiven you. God will forgive you if only you ask through the mercy of our Lord. I am here to help you. I have been praying for you, along with the Blessed Mother and Holy Dorothea."

Tears heated my eyes, and I dampened the fabric of her habit beneath my face. "I do not deserve your prayers."

"Your Excellency, you know as well as I that prayer has nothing to do with deserving."

I choked. Anger stirred in my chest, but now the sin of that place seemed lodged within me rather than within Sister Claire or the late Reverend Mother or any of the other nuns. What they had done, right or wrong, had been done with joy and in love. My own acts had been base, shabby, and willfully set against all I held dear.

Still, I knew she spoke the truth. I had been so caught in accusations of blasphemy that I had allowed myself to stray from the path of love. She had never left it. I lifted my head, still wanting her as a man wants a woman, but also as a congregant wants a priest and as every person wants and needs our Lord Himself.

Even humbled as I was, I could not entirely abandon my former condemnation. "How did you get out of the cell in the basement?"

"You know that Sister Therese and I were only imprisoned because we allowed ourselves to be."

"How can I trust you after all the things I've seen and heard here? You've taken my soul to the devil."

She cocked her head, her frown deepening. "Louis, I offered you grace through the Holy Mother, and my own love as a Christian and as a woman. If you examine your conscience, I think you'll see that the acts you're ashamed of did not come from taking what was freely given. You tried to take something else, and you tried to punish Sister Jeanne by inflicting your own pain on her."

The tears streaming down my face blinded me to the sight of her. She knew my soul even better than I knew it myself, and yet I resisted seeing things as she did. "How could I have done otherwise? If I had given in to you, I would have given in to wickedness!"

"Louis, you drowned yourself in wickedness. If you had opened yourself to the Holy Mother, as I hoped you would, you would have seen that nothing here at Little Flowers is based on wickedness."

I would have protested more, but she pulled me up onto her lap and pressed my head against her breast. The small lump nestled against my cheek, and I could not help tonguing at it through her habit. "The milk did not heal me," I whispered.

"If a wicked man stole holy oil from the sacristy and anointed himself with it, would you expect God to grace him with the true healing of the Holy Ghost?"

"Sister Jeanne did not protest."

"She tried to give to you, but you did not accept. You wanted to take." Her soft, pitying tone filled me with shame all over again. I turned my face in toward her chest like a child. "Louis, you can have what you need. You just have to ask, and accept what is given as grace."

Her nipple stood out tautly through the habit, and I understood then that Sister Claire's offer stood, that it had never been withdrawn, even when I had behaved abominably. Especially when I behaved abominably. It was so like the grace of our Lord, and it dawned on me that I still judged, even as a sinner who knew no grace himself. If the grace I experienced at Little Flowers Convent was so like the grace of our Lord, how could I be sure it was not His very grace, even as the sisters claimed it to be?

True humility blessed me like cool water on a hot, sleepless night. I slid off Sister Claire's lap and knelt before her, taking her hand and kissing the fingertips.

I did not understand most of what I'd seen since coming to Little Flowers. It still sounded like blasphemy to me. The scriptures, however, say, "Ye shall know them by their fruits." Sister Claire and Sister Therese led a convent that I had witnessed producing grapes and figs, while in my own soul, I had discovered nothing but thistles and thorns. The Pharisees of old must have heard our Lord's teaching as blasphemy, and yet there were many who still managed to open their hearts and ears to His message.

I bowed my head. "Please. I am not worthy that thou shouldest come under my roof: but speak the world only, and my soul shall be healed."

With her first finger, Sister Claire lifted my chin until I looked into her dark eyes and found only compassion in their depths. She stood and pulled her habit off over her head, revealing her holy nakedness to me.

I looked at her with eyes that were already beginning to be transformed by forgiveness and redemption. I saw that Sister Claire had no reason to feel ashamed. All the shame I had felt lay in my own breast, in my own conception of what it meant to see her unclothed.

As a bride of God, Sister Claire had given our Creator many reasons to take pride in her. Her modest, womanly beauty shone forth even when I would previously have called her nudity indecent. Her nipples were just as Monsieur Delauney had described them, I thought, cherry-red as her lips, and covering half the surface of her breasts. That good man, who had been so often in my thoughts those last days, struck me now as much more virtuous than myself. In his simple devotion, he had accepted the gifts of Little Flowers and used them to spread healing throughout Andrine. I had done so much less with so much more on offer.

I would have dipped my head in shame again, except that Sister Claire knelt on the stone floor before me and offered me her breast. By then, I knew the healing it contained, and I wanted it, but I almost gave in to temptation again and took her mouth instead. I wanted her for myself, on my own terms, and I understand now that this selfishness is where I went astray before.

Our Lord would share his bride with me, and grant grace to me through her, but not if I made a whore of her.

By grace, I did not violate this. I allowed Sister Claire to lead my mouth to her nipple, where she gave me suck.

This time, the milk was different, more like that first taste I had from the statue of Holy Dorothea. It flowed forth from the breast of Sister Claire and settled deep in my stomach, then deeper still, down to the bottom of my soul. There, it satisfied an ancient craving that must have traveled with me since the moment I first opened my eyes as a babe. To know that mother-love, given as freely as to an infant, but received with the understanding of a man, is to see something of God that is never otherwise revealed. It is to see what the Garden of Eden was meant to be, to understand what Holy Mary knew from the moment of her own birth, to be connected to the Creator through our

Lord as all clergy have preached and heard preached for many years.

I was not greedy. In fact, I would have released her nipple if Sister Claire had not pushed it toward me. "Drink a little more than you can stand," she whispered, for that, also, is the way of our Lord God.

I took what she offered, this time with the proper humility. Afterward, I submitted to her when she lifted my cassock away from my body and revealed my own nakedness. She bent and gave me a holy kiss on the forehead, sealed with the sign of the cross. This, I knew, would be the most she would acknowledge my desire for her as a woman, for her pledge to our Lord was true, and this was already more than I deserved.

"Please forgive me, Sister."

"Shush. All is forgiven. You'll see."

She took me in her hand. I tried to see her as the medium through which I was touched by our Savior, or by the Blessed Mother, but sinful man that I am, part of me still could not forget that this hand belonged to Claire. She stroked me to life, whispering that everything would be all right. I could not help but believe her.

No person has ever touched me the way that Sister Claire did. I do not mean to refer to the delicacy of the body parts she rubbed and cupped. I mean that she touched me as if she knew me better than I did myself. If she had wished to make me spend in mere seconds, she could have. Instead, she held me on the edge, forcing me to endure pleasure. I understood that this was part of the lesson she had to teach me, and I tried to learn from it, as uncomfortable as it made me.

Your Excellency, I was not then used to enjoying experiences without guilt, though now I know that God intended His creation to include much pleasure for His children. I sobbed and begged for mercy, leaning my forehead against Sister Claire's arm.

She soothed me, somehow knowing that I needed succor at a time when most men would have felt no pain. While one hand worked my member, the other cupped my sack and traced the sign of the cross on the insides of my thighs. In obedience to her own sense of timing, Sister Claire began to speed her movements. I knew I was about to find release, and protested weakly, "Please, Sister. I have no right to —"

"Relax, Louis." She gave me her mouth then, as part of the incalculable generosity of our Savior. Her lips opened the gates to life itself. I pressed my tongue into her mouth and she accepted me. Can you understand what I mean when I say "accepted," Your Excellency? This woman knew every detail of my darkest hour, and yet showed me nothing but the purest, God-given love.

I poured myself into that kiss. I let her bring my member to release. I spilled my seed onto her fingers. When she lifted it to my mouth, I feared I would find bitterness, but instead, just as Monsieur Delauney had explained, I tasted the milk of Dorothea, thick and life-giving. Sister Claire and I shared these first fruits of mine, lapping it off her hand, then kissing again and allowing it to pass from her mouth to mine and back again.

If I had given in to my human desire, I would have demanded more than I was given. I would have taken her there on the hard stone floor. Sister Claire had changed me, though. My years of theological study did not teach me as much about what it is to be transformed by forgiveness as she did then.

We knelt together and prayed, and I joined Sister Claire in requesting that Holy Dorothea pray for my soul.

In the days that followed, I had many conversations with Sister Claire and Sister Therese, and even Sister Jeanne.

When His Eminence sent investigators to assist me, Holy Dorothea worked another miracle, and they chose to remain at Little Flowers Convent as well. We have a lovely community of faith here, and we have ministered very effectively to Forges-les-Eaux and other surrounding townships.

After a few months had passed, Sister Therese suggested I take on the role of Father Superior. I was stunned, since I did not see myself as a worthy candidate for such a position. Sister Therese and Sister Claire, however, believed it important for a man to participate in the leadership of our ministry, so that the veneration of Holy Dorothea is not seen as a cult of hysterical women. In truth, the women here have taught me more about our Lord than I had ever hoped to learn, but I understand the reason for their concern, having been afflicted by similar misjudgment in my early days here.

In light of this explanation, I hope you will understand that I cannot desist from my activities here. To do so would be to betray the power of love and forgiveness that has redeemed my soul.

Send investigators if you wish, or come yourself. I am confident that any who witness the miracles of Dorothea of Andrine will see the holiness that I have seen, and will not wish to deny the healing she so freely gives.

Faithfully,

Louis Montblanc, Fr. Superior of the Society of Dorothea

If you enjoyed this story, you can sign up for a free membership at ForbiddenFiction and discuss it with other readers and the author at *The Miracles of Dorothea of Andrine* story page at http://forbiddenfiction.com/library/story/AL1-1.000200.

The Snake and the Lyre

Eurydice longs to marry Orpheus, but his self-centered love for his music blinds him to her sensuality. A cruel Naiad seduces and kills Eurydice, unleashing the full hunger of her desire. When Orpheus braves the Underworld to save his lost Eurydice, can he pull his bride away from its depraved pleasures? (F/F)

The Snake and the Lyre

Eurydice rested her cheek against Orpheus's thigh. His rich voice tingled in her ears, its timbre sweet as a persimmon. His foot tapped slowly as he plucked his lyre, rocking Eurydice's head with the ancient rhythm of the ocean.

The strings of the lyre—they trembled and thrilled beneath his fingertips. They exulted and crooned. Eurydice would have responded just that way had he thought to draw his music from her body rather than the instrument.

She didn't mind the rocks on the hill where they sat, and yet she recrossed her ankles under her body, fidgeting. Her heel pressed between her legs, sinking slightly into her cunt. Safely hidden by her skirt, Eurydice rocked on it in time with Orpheus's song.

She closed her eyes and pretended that the notes slipping into the wind around them were his hands slipping into her clothes. Her inner thighs shivered. His tongue could leave wet trails there. He could find his way to the juncture of her legs and sing only to her, his full lips and white teeth forming private poetry. Eurydice imagined his eyes, the shade of grapes in the vineyard, gazing up along her belly and between the peaks of her breasts. She would grip hunks of his black hair and pull his face tight to her. She would lock her ankles at the base of his spine and refuse to let go until she tired of finding release against his beautiful mouth.

"My love?" Orpheus's song had ended. He stroked her hair—too gently. "Eurydice, my love? What did you think of that Hypophrygian setting? I might compose in that mode for our wedding. It speaks so delicately, expressing the yearning of youth joined with the peaceable accord of family life."

Eurydice made the effort to smile. She kissed the top of his thigh through his tunic. "Your music would make the gods ache. It will be lovely." She inhaled his sharp, male scent, lifted from his body by the heat of the day. She pressed her lips to his leg again, a little higher up.

Orpheus frowned, adjusting his grip on his lyre. "The Lydian mode might be more traditionally appropriate. Simple happiness — that's a good atmosphere for a wedding." He scratched absently behind Eurydice's ear. "I think I can transpose this, so you can hear them one after the other."

She sighed and touched his ankle, just above the strap of his sandal. She angled her body to emphasize the swell of her breasts and lifted her eyes to his through the veil of her curling dark hair. "Orpheus...."

"Yes, love?"

"Perhaps you could lay aside the lyre for a little while?" Eurydice moved her hand up past the hem of his tunic. The muscles of his thigh twitched as she approached his cock.

Orpheus's indulgent smile dashed her hopes against the rocks of his perfect cheekbones. He retrieved her hand from beneath his clothes and returned it to her. "The wedding will come before you know it, my dear. We'll spend all night making love and singing to the stars."

Eurydice folded her hands in her lap, unable to resist pressing them against her crotch. "Of course," she said. "You want to try the Lydian mode, you said?"

"Go down and bathe in the spring below the juniper tree," whispered Eurydice's friend Apollonia on the day of the wedding. "Invite the Naiads to come and dance to your betrothed's lyre."

Eurydice giggled. "Does he need more recognition? The sun stands still in the sky to listen to him."

"You'll be the only woman in Thrace to have Naiads honor your wedding."

"Aren't they dangerous?"

"Playful," Apollonia said. "Beautiful. Sensual. People will talk about your wedding for years. It will be worth it."

Light splashed onto the hills like the water of the clearest stream. Apollonia grinned and waggled her eyebrows. Drunk on the promise of the day, Eurydice allowed her friend to coax her out of her clothes and point her toward the juniper.

Warm mud caressed her bare feet and tickled her naked calves. Eurydice ran her hands down the sides of her body. Now, the breeze teased her nipples. Tonight, it would be handsome Orpheus, her husband at last.

Eurydice dipped a foot into the sun-warm spring. "Sweet ladies of the water," she called. "Would you like to dance at my wedding? Silver-tongued Orpheus will play and sing for his esteemed guests."

"Or-phe-us," the water sighed, its surface rippling. The silt at the bottom bubbled. A pale arm emerged, as strong and slender as a young tree.

"Yes, Orpheus! He will be my husband!" Eurydice dove eagerly into the water and took hold of the hand, helping the Naiad out of the sucking sand.

The nymph clasped the offered hand and crawled up Eurydice, her skin cold and slippery. She darted between Eurydice's legs, her moss-green hair tickling her thighs. She wrapped her arms around the young woman's stomach and surged up to break the surface, her pebbled nipples scraping Eurydice's.

Eurydice gasped, her lungs suddenly tight.

"The wife of Orpheus," the Naiad purred. "We have heard him sing. Is his tongue worth the silver of its sound?" She winked. A clever hand darted between Eurydice's legs, parted her folds.

Eurydice jumped back, covering her cunt protectively. The nymph laughed, the water of the spring quivering with her merriment. "So shy." She placed a hand on Eurydice's waist and idly dragged a lily pad toward them. "Tell me, how does he play his instrument?"

The Naiad's lips nuzzled the young woman's ear. "Does godlike Orpheus know where to place his hands along the neck to draw the loveliest tunes?"

Eurydice realized with a shock that the Naiad's fingers followed her words, caressing up and down her throat. She knew she should make her excuses and escape the spring, but the thought of Orpheus's hands doing the same held her in place. The calluses from playing the lyre would feel rough against her skin. He could reach into her cunt and strum to his heart's content.

The Naiad pressed her slick lips to the base of Eurydice's throat. The young woman moaned. "Does Apollo's favorite musician know which touches produce which notes?" She nipped the same spot with her teeth, eliciting a shriek, then licked with her rough tongue, making Eurydice sigh.

"I long to know," the Naiad whispered. "Does our handsome player prefer his rhythms fast or slow?" Her hand returned to Eurydice's cunt, and this time the woman did not resist or pull away. The nymph's finger wriggled inside. Eurydice unconsciously spread her legs wider to accommodate the invasion. The finger stroked lazily at first, then accelerated to a pounding crescendo that made the young woman lose her feet and fall into the water, still wound around the nymph.

They floated there, Eurydice staring nervously into eyes the pale gray of river stones. "Speak, girl," the nymph demanded.

"Orpheus," she began, then trailed off and cleared her throat. Her pulse pounded everywhere the Naiad had touched her, but most strongly between her legs. She tried to disguise her longing. "Orpheus plays on his instrument, not his betrothed."

"Ah. Not a very giving lover, then, if he's left you virgin."

Eurydice bit her lip. She didn't wish to speak ill of her future husband. "He wants to share his love with me when the time is right. He says it's worth waiting for the perfect night."

"And what do you say?" The Naiad cupped Eurydice's breast, rolling her nipple between her long fingers. "Do you cherish a little girl's romantic dreams? Or a woman's desires?" At this last, she pulled Eurydice onto her thigh, driving hard against the center of her need. "I think you need more than Orpheus can offer you," said the nymph.

A whimper escaped Eurydice. She rode the nymph's leg helplessly, their hands tightly clasped together. The Naiad guided Eurydice's arms back so that her breasts thrust forward. She lifted her head from the water and flicked her tongue up and down on Eurydice's nipples.

Orpheus's bride-to-be arched into the nymph's mouth, her hips rocking in the water. She strained and reached for the pleasure that seemed just a breath away, thinking still of Orpheus's strong jaw and knowing fingers. She paid no attention to the water lapping first at her armpits, then just below her chin.

Eyes squeezed shut, Eurydice came against the Naiad's leg, the name of her betrothed on her lips. The word trailed off in a gurgle, triggering a panicked attempt to breathe.

Eurydice thrashed in the water, but the nymph's grip had tightened like a noose. She could not lift her head to the air above.

Through the wavering depths of the Naiad's spring, Eurydice saw a collection of water snakes swimming toward them, their bodies writhing and twisting. Her attempt to scream filled her lungs with water. The Naiad smiled and made a pacifying gesture.

The first snake coiled around Eurydice's ankle, weighing her down even more, holding her to the bottom of the spring. She struggled to shake it off, but before she could make headway, another twined itself around her breast. Its body squeezed the sensitive flesh, and then its head drew back. Eurydice watched in horror as its mouth opened wide enough to span a man's thigh. It's thin, sharp fangs embedded themselves in her breast, above and below the nipple.

The nymph held Eurydice in place, stroking the viper's head affectionately. The bite hurt less than Eurydice expected. Ecstatic warmth spread through her body, starting at her nipple but quickly rushing down to her cunt and up to her head.

Looking down her body, Eurydice saw another viper wending its way up her thigh. Its head probed between her legs. She would have panted if she'd been able to breathe. The snake penetrated her just as another bit her neck where it joined her shoulder.

Eurydice's body shuddered, tensing and relaxing while blackness bubbled in her mind. Would her husband have felt like this inside her? "Orpheus," she whispered, slipping entirely into the vipers' underwater nest.

Vipers wrapped Eurydice's neck and filled her mouth, smooth muscles pressing against the insides of her cheeks. Aching pressure between her legs revealed their presence there as well. Snakes around her ankles held her legs apart. Others stroked her nether lips with their bodies as they squirmed into her cunt, traveled deep inside, then out again.

Sensual heat enveloped her, sliding over, around, above, and below her. She lay comfortably, her body held and supported. Silky scales rasped gently over her skin, leaving her shivering in their wake.

Eurydice trembled. The water had gone. Instead, she and the snakes occupied a dark room, its features difficult to determine. She could not have guessed how long she had lain that way, her body being plundered by the snakes. She slid her hands carefully down her body, avoiding contact with the vipers.

Sticky residue covered her inner thighs. It felt like her own dried juices. How many times had she come? Eurydice tried to get to her feet, but the snakes resisted, suddenly binding where they had caressed.

They held her in place at dozens of points—her neck, her shoulders, her elbows, her wrists, her waist, her knees, her ankles. From the press of them, one viper rose, its body twice as thick as any of the others. Eurydice whimpered into the mass of snakes that filled her mouth.

A snake slithered out of her cunt, followed by another and then another. She wondered how many had been inside her. The massive viper found her opening and easily slid its head inside. It struggled to get in deeper, its muscles whipping its body back and forth between her thighs.

The snakes must have broken through her hymen while she'd lain unconscious. Her body slowly stretched open to allow the enormous viper room within her. The pressure of the snake's diamond-shaped head against the walls of her cunt matched a building inner tension.

Another viper, still slick with the juices of her cunt, worked its way between the cheeks of her buttocks and prodded at her other hole. Eurydice shook and poured herself into muffled screaming.

She didn't think she could come. Her body felt too full to ripple and spasm. And yet, as the thin viper pushed tentatively into her ass,

Eurydice's cunt clenched almost unbearably around the thick snake inside it. Sweat trickled between her breasts. Her hips worked uncontrollably. Her tongue worked against the vipers in her mouth.

She could have remained in that blissful oblivion forever except that familiar tones came faintly to her ears, echoing strangely as if traveling a great distance. That cursed Hypophrygian mode—she heard it clearly. *Orpheus?* Now frantic, Eurydice struggled against the vipers, shame replacing her pleasure.

A heavy foot trod outside the room where she lay. She could already envision the disappointment and contempt in Orpheus's violet eyes when he looked upon her, writhing and spreading herself like a whore. Her face and neck burned.

But the man who appeared in the doorway seemed neither surprised nor disdainful. His thick, black eyebrows knitted as he studied her. He had a broad face, as ominous as storm clouds. "Eurydice," he said slowly. "Your husband is here for you."

The man clearly expected a reply. The vipers seemed to understand. They removed themselves from her mouth. Her distended cheeks relaxed. Eurydice sighed with animal relief before she could summon words for the man. When she did, her voice did not sound like her own. "Who are you? Where am I?"

"I am Hades," he replied. "You are in my domain."

Eurydice shuddered. Dead on her wedding day, bitten by a viper while held in a Naiad's embrace. What must Orpheus think of her? "Please don't let him see me," she whispered. She smelled her sex heavy on the air.

"He has convinced me to release you to the land of the living. I came to bring you out to him."

A viper slid over her belly, and Eurydice could not suppress a moan. Could she truly return to Orpheus? Would he want her if she did? Her body now seemed a mockery to his love of beauty, his perfect intentions. She hesitated.

Hades smiled kindly, holding out a hand. Eurydice managed to stand and go to him, her knees still weak from her long stretch of rapture. "Child, don't look so fearful," said the Lord of the Underworld. "This place differs from the land under the sun. We do not flinch from our desires here, but we keep our secrets with the most sacred respect."

He tugged her to the door. When Eurydice still resisted, he sighed. "If Demeter saw the forms her daughter Persephone takes with me in this place, she would blight the earth in eternal cold fury. What you have found here will await your return, and no living soul shall learn of it."

Eurydice swallowed. "Please, Lord. Swear that Orpheus will not see me until we return to the world above."

Orpheus and his ever-present lyre walked ten steps before Eurydice. She sighed with longing. Every line of his body spoke of perfection. She admired his powerful calves, tight buttocks, strong shoulders. She wished she could see his face, but she still stumbled naked and shamed through the halls of the Underworld. Eurydice could not bear the thought of meeting his gaze while in this place, the truth of her desires crusted on her thighs for all to see.

What other man would brave the Underworld and drag his love from the grip of Lord Hades himself? Eurydice's breath caught at the romance of it all.

"My love, are you still behind me?" Orpheus said, his voice low and anxious.

"I'm here, my Lord," Eurydice replied. Creatures of the Underworld lined the passage where they walked on either side, their forms grotesque and suggestive. She tore her eyes from a woman with a face between her legs, and then from a man who opened his mouth to reveal three flicking tongues.

"How do I know you are not an apparition of my Eurydice, meant to deceive me into leaving this place without my wife?"

Eurydice swallowed. "Test me, my Lord." A snake dropped from the stone ceiling of the passageway. She jumped to avoid it, but could not help wondering if this was one of the snakes that had been inside her.

"Sing me our wedding song in the Aeolian mode."

"The mode of mourning, my Lord?"

"Indeed, this is the way I sang it when I found my love had

drowned in the spring at the base of the juniper."

Eurydice thought hard. He had made her listen to this composition in so many different forms, indifferent all the while to her panting after his body. Hesitantly, Eurydice sang the first notes.

Before she found her footing in the melody, Orpheus took over, accompanying himself with his lyre and improvising dramatic variations that made her lose her place in the song. Eurydice frowned, struggling to pass her test while also keeping up the pace through the passageway.

A man with a thick horn in the middle of his forehead threw a handful of snakes at her. One landed in her hair, slithered down her throat, and fastened its fangs around her still-bare nipple, suckling at her like a babe. Eurydice gasped at the sexual surge that passed through her body, faltering.

"Eurydice?" Orpheus asked, halting his steps. "Are you quite well?"

"Yes, my Lord." Another viper copied the first, so that a snake hung from each of her nipples. Eurydice ached between her legs, their poison making her limbs languorous and slow.

"Please continue the song. I need to know you're still following me."

Eurydice closed her eyes. She felt feverish. She struggled to force notes past her thickening tongue. Vipers crawled over the stone floor toward her in an undulating wave. They wound over her feet and worked their way up her body.

A snake with the thickest body she'd seen lifted its patterned coral head, separating itself from the others on the floor. Eurydice's body remembered the ache of the vipers' insertion and longed for it. She wanted to pierce herself on that hard, triangular head.

"My love? Will you sing?"

Eurydice managed a few half-hearted notes, but desire for the viper dominated her attention. Up ahead, Orpheus sighed and stopped walking.

"Eurydice, please."

She stole toward the snake. It knew what she wanted, arching its body up to her and shaping itself into the most pleasing curve. Eurydice stood above it, her legs spread wide. She tugged on the snakes at her breasts, her cunt clenching tightly in response to the sharp sensation. She leaned down and stroked the snake's head, then guided it toward her trembling cunt.

"My love? Did I lose you?"

The viper's forked tongue flicked over her cunt, raking over her bud just before it buried its head inside her. Eurydice sucked her breath in through her teeth and plunged onto it. The flood of vipers wrapped her and pulled her flat on the floor, but she felt held, not restrained. Eurydice worked her hips wildly, trying to force the thick viper deeper inside her. She groaned in a voice not her own.

"Eurydice? What have they done to you?"

Too late, she realized what would happen, but she could not extricate herself from the vipers before Orpheus turned. They engulfed her flailing body, but the ecstatic motion of her fingers against her cunt left no doubt of her feelings about the situation.

Orpheus's handsome face contorted with disgust and horror. "Eurydice? No! It can't be!"

She wanted to respond to him, to explain herself, but when she opened her mouth, a mess of snakes slipped in. She closed her eyes, another orgasm beginning to take her over.

Orpheus's wails shattered the passageway, but the vipers covered Eurydice's ears as they dragged her back into their underground nest forever.

If you enjoyed this story, you can sign up for a free membership at ForbiddenFiction and discuss it with other readers and the author at *The Snake and the Lyre* story page at http://forbiddenfiction.com/library/story/AL1-1.000052.

Andromache's Prize

When Briseis belonged to noble Achilles, she had been better able to bear slavery. Now, though, the heroes have all sailed away home, leaving baser men to strip the carcass of Troy. Briseis has been given into the hands of cruel Calygdus, and nightly she suffers for his every shame and weakness. Until the night that Andromache and the women of Troy fall upon the Greek camp, slaying the men and releasing the women slaves, promising them freedom in the City of Women. Freedom, and love. (M/F, F/F)

Chapter 1

Remembering Achilles

The men came back from raiding too loud, too drunk, with sheepish grins on their faces. Briseis sat outside the tent she shared with Calygdus, repairing the bronze belt that Achilles had given her when she had still been innocent enough to love a man.

The day faded. That's what things did in Briseis' world. Once, there had been glory in this place — the great city of Troy, and the great army of the Achaians. Once, there had been Achilles, and Hector, and good, sweet Patroclus — heroes worthy of the name. Now, the city had fallen, the heroes had died, and yet she remained, drinking up the bitter dregs of war in the chariot-rutted meadow where she had lived ever since being taken from her home. The fight had finished, and yet people could not seem to leave. She sometimes thought nothing remained in the world but this.

The beauty of her face had faded, the strength of her passion had faded. Hope had faded.

She sighed at the men's unsteady gait across the worn and trampled meadow. Calygdus, to whom she now belonged, was impotent, a fact for which she thanked Zeus every day. Tonight he would at least want to pretend. If he was drunk enough, he might want to actually try.

Maybe tonight she could finally stab him in the heart and run away. She did want to be free. And failing that, she could stab herself in the heart, if she had the courage.

Courage, unfortunately, was what she had always lacked. Briseis never had a fighter's spirit. She was cursed with the gift of making do.

Briseis ducked into the tent and put away the belt, combed out her long, fair hair, and changed into clothes she didn't care about. The men's conversation came closer and wafted through the thin material of the tent.

"Can you believe what that bitch said to me?" Calygdus' voice would have stood out anywhere, high and nasal, trailing off into a gurgle when he paused. His voice went even higher as he mimicked a woman: "'Watch your backs tonight, boys. We'll be coming for your women.' She couldn't really have been Andromache. I'd think Hector would have married a bitch with at least a few of Aphrodite's blessings. Still..."

He must have gestured, because a moment later a round of raucous laughter burst from the men. After the laughter subsided, a young man's voice spoke up. "Why didn't you take her and her band right there in the road?"

Briseis rolled her eyes and stepped out of the tent, in time to get a good view of Calygdus' jaw working as he tried to come up with a response. A cruel light came into his eyes when he saw her. He reached for her hair and jerked Briseis to her knees on the ground beside him. He pulled her face against his crotch, and she knew to kiss at the limp mass under his tunic. Shame still stabbed through her heart at the act, though Calygdus had shown her off this way ever since he'd captured her. Achilles had never used her so callously, and before being taken by that powerful warrior, she had been the daughter of a king.

"Take this one," Calygdus said. "She's getting a little ugly now that she's used up and worn, but you can still see what Achilles must have liked about her. Look at those lips. And it doesn't hurt to know you're plowing the field in the footsteps of a great man."

Briseis bit back her retorts and kept her eyes on the ground. The gods had always hated her, and Calygdus was her latest proof. She had dared to attempt escape from the Achaians, but instead of finding a way to sail home, she found this oaf and his degradations.

"What's all this?" The old man joined their group. He'd once been a warrior among the Achaians, but the departing kings had sailed away in their treasure-laden black ships, leaving him behind with the rest of the dross.

Briseis liked him. He called himself No Name, did not delight in telling endless stories of his past exploits, and participated in the looting and general mayhem as little as possible. He remained at the tents with the women often, and she talked with him sometimes. He favored grim pronouncements about the end of the world and the sad state of the race of men, but this echoed the thoughts in her own head. She didn't mind.

"Stay to your knitting, old man," Calygdus said, to a reward of guffaws.

"Andromache says she's coming for your women? How can that be? Neoptolemus, son of god-like Achilles, made her his concubine during the sacking of Troy." Confusion trembled on the old man's lips. Despite her own humiliation, still trapped against the stinking balls of Calygdus, Briseis pitied No Name.

"Your stories are out of date, old man," Calygdus sneered. "The whore shanked Achilles' whelp in the thigh with his own weapon, dove out of his ship, and swam back to Troy, screaming about her dead son the whole way. Crazy bitch. What's she looking for back here? She'd have been better off laying back and taking it like a good slut should."

Briseis' heart pounded. Achilles had spoken often of the nobility of Andromache, and there could be no better proof of it. Andromache must possess honor and dignity that Briseis could only imagine. "Maybe she didn't want to leave her home," Briseis whispered, too moved to remember to keep her mouth shut.

Calygdus dropped a thudding blow on her ear. "Don't you have enough work for that mouth?" He lifted his tunic and pulled her under it more completely, yanking her hair until she opened her lips and took in one of his balls.

No Name's confusion persisted. "Andromache says she's coming for your women?"

"It's not going to happen," Calygdus laughed. "If Andromache tries anything, she'll be warming my bed tonight. If she displeases me, perhaps I'll send her to warm yours!"

The old man shook his head, not seeming to hear the bursts of laughter from the others. "She should be the wife of Neoptolemus, or ruling in Epirus beside Helenus. She should not be free."

"No, the bitch should not be free! What do you think I'm trying to say?" Calygdus released his grip on Briseis to make shooing gestures at the old man. She seized the opportunity to get away from him.

Briseis leapt to her feet and ran to No Name's side. "Old man," she said kindly, taking his arm. "Let me show you back to your tent."

Her grandfather had been confused this way before the end of his life. No Name's features resembled a child's, his skin too soft for the harsh winds that buffeted the ruins of Troy. His eyes, pale as the sky, watered and wavered when he tried to fix them on her.

"Wash off that old man's come before you crawl back to my bed, whore," Calygdus mocked Briseis. She ignored him and coaxed No Name to walk with her.

"You shouldn't be here either, girl," he said, shaking his head. "This has gone all wrong."

"Did he fuck you?" Calygdus growled when Briseis returned to him. He rubbed a meaty hand through his loose, greasy hair.

"Of course not." She would have found something to do on the opposite side of the tent, but he grabbed her by the wrist and yanked her to the ground beside him. She planted one shoulder hard in the dirt, grunting at the shock to her bones.

"Don't tell me you're not getting it from somewhere. A beautiful little thing like you." He traced the line of her cheekbone. His finger dug into her flesh. Briseis closed her eyes and turned her head away. He gripped her chin and forced her to face him.

Her heart pounded with the habit of fear, but more than that, Briseis felt tired of him. "What do you want?" The words came out with a sigh.

Calygdus buried his face in Briseis' hair. He rolled onto her, crushing her with his weight. Rancid smells left over from dinner stung her nose. She wanted to get this over with. If it went on too long, she might have to feel a bit of the old pain.

He stroked one of her breasts with ominous reverence and kissed the side of her face. "Tell me you want me."

"Please," Briseis said. "I want you." Acting came easily with long practice. She moaned when he undid the laces on her dress. She forced herself to purr and arch toward him when his hand slipped under the material, squeezing and groping at her bare flesh. She even spread for him when he reached between her legs.

"Say it again."

"I want you," she repeated, her nervousness increasing. The bruises from the last time he'd tried to take her and been unable had lingered.

He forced his body between her thighs. She closed her legs around his waist obediently, as if she wanted him, her stomach turning at the idea even as she stretched her face into a smile for him.

Calygdus fumbled, lining his half-hard cock up with her cunt.

"I want you," Briseis said again, hoping to encourage the reluctant tool as he worked to stuff it into her. She rolled her hips and tugged at her nipples. He'd forced her to put on lewd shows for him in the past. She forced down her pride and performed for him voluntarily, still looking to make the night pass more easily.

Calygdus groaned. "That's the way. Show me what you want." His fingers groped between her legs, blunt and blind.

She tried to remember Achilles' face. She used to get wet for him. Sometimes, she would come around his cock the moment he shoved it into her. That had happened the first time, despite her terror and her efforts to fight him off.

Heat flushed through her at the memory, and she moaned sincerely. "That's the way," Calygdus said. But his cock did not cooperate. It slipped to one side or another, soft and shrinking now. He growled with frustration and banged his pelvis against hers like a little boy having a temper tantrum.

"Fucking slut," he said. He slapped Briseis' face. She yelped with shock and outrage, then bit her lip and forced the sound down. Now, he would spend the night beating her. She'd taken it before, and she could do it again. She did her best to meet his eyes as the blows continued. Her lip split and filled her mouth with the flavor of metal. She retreated into her mind.

"Who is it?" he demanded. He'd been asking for a while, she realized. She just hadn't heard him.

"What are you talking about?"

"A hot slut like you can't live without it. I know it. Someone is spearing you."

"No!" Briseis said, truthfully, not liking the direction his drunken suspicions were heading.

He shoved one finger into her cunt, but wasted no time escalating it to three. Her memories of Achilles had not aroused her enough to prepare her for this. Briseis winced and tried to squirm away. He pinned her by sinking a knee deep into the flesh of her thigh. Briseis shoved at the limb helplessly, but his weight easily overmatched her attempt. He slammed his hand in and out of her until she cried out from the pain of it.

"If it's not me," Calygdus spat, "it's got to be someone. Who is it? Who is it?" Blows rained down on her face in time with the fingers driving into her cunt.

Briseis raised her arms to shield her face. This was routine, she told herself, not even worth noticing. Still, she trembled violently.

After a few minutes, she realized that the sounds of his flesh crashing against her body weren't the only noises breaking the night. The thunder of horses' hooves shook the ground. A woman's voice rose in a wild whoop unlike any sound Briseis had ever heard.

A piece of her heart followed the sound. Joy rose in her chest as long as the noise lasted, and the feeling made Calygdus fade.

Calygdus stiffened above her, something like shame flickering across his cruel features. "Andromache."

"You're afraid," Briseis murmured, in wonderment. What would it be like to be a woman and yet wield such power over men?

He looked down at her, curling his lip. "She's just a woman," he said. "If she hasn't had enough of war, I'll remind her of its ways."

He eased himself off her, joints cracking. He armed himself and slipped outside. Briseis hauled herself upright. She'd ache something awful in the morning, but the pain hadn't really set in yet. She'd had enough of war, long ago, even if it seemed no one else ever tired of it. She struggled to her feet, found her dagger, and stepped outside the tent in time to see a woman bury a spear between Calygdus's ribs.

The woman jerked her spear free and kicked the man away. Briseis stared at her. She held the reigns of a lovely black horse. The animal dwarfed her, but her small stature didn't lessen the power of her stance. All over the camp, women swooped down on fast horses, torching tents and leaving carnage in their wake.

The woman before Briseis tossed her hair back, fires from behind her giving the brown mass of curls a bright red corona. She wore very little—her breasts were bound tightly against her chest with strips of cloth and a garment around her waist seemed more a place to attach her weapons and tools than an effort to cover the cleft between her legs. An improbably large bronze shield was strapped to her left forearm, but she showed no strain from holding it.

"Andromache?" Briseis said, awed. This was the first time since the death of Achilles that a warrior's ferocity had stirred her.

The woman grinned. Even her teeth seemed sharp. "Daughter of Lyrnessus," she said, "what a shame it is that weak men continue to hold you by the chains the mighty used to bind you." She stowed her spear across her back and held out her hand. "Come with me. We'll travel together to build the City of Women."

"The City of Women?"

"We will carve out a place in this broken world. We need somewhere to start again, a place where the war stops outside the walls. Come, sister, and I will show you."

Briseis took Andromache's hand. Her bones were delicate, made for sewing tapestries, but calluses studded the skin of her palm. Briseis shivered and let Andromache lift her onto the horse.

Her brain pounded with one thought: *Not since Achilles.*

But before the warrior queen could race them both out of the ruined camp, she thought of No Name. "There's one other who shouldn't be put to the spear," Briseis said. "An old man. He's confused. Even if your women don't kill him, I don't think he can survive on his own."

Andromache fixed her with darkly burning eyes. Finally, she nodded, and they went into the camp together to retrieve him.

Chapter 2

The City of Women

Briseis' hands were torn and bleeding, and she didn't think she could lift her arms to pull her hair out of her eyes, much less to drive a spear into a wooden target. "Andromache," she said. "You've got to have mercy. I'll train again tomorrow."

The warrior woman turned, scowling. "Is mercy what you've been getting out of life, Briseis? Did your Calygdus have mercy on you? Did Agamemnon, King of the Greeks, when he stole you to his bed just to make a point? How about great Achilles, murderer of my husband and killer of your father and brothers?"

Briseis threw down her spear and put both hands on her hips. "No, Andromache, they didn't have mercy on me. But I'm not here to live the same life I had with them. You told me we're headed for a city that stops war outside its walls. I'll believe it when I see it, and when I meet someone who's not completely addled by battle lust and bloody honor."

A heavy silence surrounded her. Briseis glanced around and saw the other women in the camp watching her and Andromache with a combination of fear and envy. She ignored them and turned back to the fiery woman. Briseis displayed her bloody palms. "I'm going to go and wrap these in leather. I'll train again with you tomorrow, and I'll give you everything I've got but no more. I'm done giving more than that."

She turned her back and stalked away; half fearing that Andromache would cut her down for her insolence. When no one stopped her, she walked to the outskirts of the camp, where No Name had his tent.

The old man sat in the brittle grass just outside it. "Hello, Grandfather," Briseis said.

He looked up at her, his face at first suspicious, then changing to warm. "It's easy to see why Achilles loved you."

Briseis stopped, taken by a wave of bitterness. "And how do you know that he loved me? He never told me so himself."

"He defied the Atreidai for your sake. He punished Agamemnon with his bitter refusal. He stood aside from battle, heartbroken by the loss of you."

"That was about glory, old man. I was only an excuse."

No Name caught a flea with his thumbnail against the skin of his arm. "Not even the architects of this world could have suspected what you would become."

"A whore?"

He shook his head gravely and touched the side of her face. "You will bring the end of war."

Briseis laughed. "Are you a prophet now? Has Apollo visited you?"

"I am old. I am allowed to make no sense." They both cracked smiles at that one.

Briseis pressed his hand and left him. Soon, she strolled beyond the perimeter of the camp, sniffing at the few flowers that remained, splashing through the big puddles left in the chariot-rutted ground. When she tired of moving, she found a place to lie on the earth. She stared up at the sky and thought about how the soil beneath her had soaked up the blood of so many men and women. She supposed she could remember a time before the war, before the pillaging, before she was taken for the first time, but those few images of her family and home seemed colorless as a stone carving.

A footfall in the grass a short distance away brought her rolling to her feet.

"Your instincts are good, anyway," Andromache said. A sheen of sweat covered her bronzed skin and her hair was tangled from training. Every time she saw Hector's former bride, Briseis could barely breathe from awe at her strength. How could a woman transform herself so thoroughly, going from helpless prize of war to living imitation of Athena?

"Why are you looking at me like that?" Andromache asked.

"You don't look like a woman who ever belonged to a man."

"I never did," Andromache said, tossing her head. "Hector was my lover, my friend, my husband, the father of my poor lost child. He never owned me."

Briseis bowed her head.

"Daughter of Lyrnessus," Andromache said. "I am no better than you. I came to say that you were right."

"About what?"

"If we can't be different from the rest of them, what's the point of fighting them at all? You know that better than me."

Briseis smiled gratefully, and Andromache stepped closer. "What I learned," Briseis said, "is that you can always make your own life, no matter what's happening to you. There's a corner of your mind that belongs only to you. I didn't know that when Achilles first took me, and so I fell in love with him. But after that, I walled off a part of myself, and I always knew that I didn't have to open the gates to that place to anyone."

Andromache reached for her hand and guided them both down to sit in the weeds. "That's what I hope the City of Women is like," she said quietly. "That's what I want it to be. I've heard about a clutch of ships Achilles' Myrmidons left behind. We will go to them, kill any men who defend them, and sail over the ocean to find a place for ourselves."

"Andromache, how did you become this way? I don't imagine Hector taught you to fight, and yet you saved yourself. You didn't let yourself become a thing like..."

"Like you? You're not a thing."

"How did you find the courage to fight?"

Andromache was silent for a long time. She sat close enough that their bodies pressed together, and Briseis could feel her blood pounding through her veins and her breath coming fast and hard. "I used to be just a woman," Andromache said finally. "I loved my husband. I raised my son." Her hand squeezed Briseis' hard enough to grind the bones together. "When Achilles cut down my dear husband and the men brought his body back to me, something died inside me forever. Then, Troy fell. Neoptolemus flung my son Astyanax over the city wall, then raped me. A dark and terrible thing grew in me then. It replaced my love for Hector, for my home, and for my son. It makes me strong, and I can pretend the joy I feel at pressing a spear into a man's breast resembles the joy I used to feel at pressing my breast to Astyanax's lips to feed him my milk. Zeus has turned me to stone."

"I pray to Hera, and she has taught me the way of being softer than water," Briseis said.

"Show me," Andromache murmured.

Briseis lowered her eyes from the other woman's fiery gaze and pressed her mouth forward. The famed "white-armed Andromache" had been baked dark by sun and hardship, but her skin smelled fresh.

Their lips met. Andromache's wind-chapped mouth scraped against Briseis'. Briseis embraced her, finding her body taut everywhere except for the soft, tender skin of her scars. Briseis slipped her hand under Andromache's leather shirt and felt her breasts, fascinated by the pliant, supple flesh surrounded by so much muscle. Briseis continued her exploration by running her hands down Andromache's sides. For all her strength, she had a woman's shape—a narrow waist and generous hips. Briseis stroked them, then worked around to Andromache's lower belly. She found the signs of her pregnancy there, differently textured skin streaked like the marks of a tiger's claws.

The honor of a noble husband's children had never come to Briseis, and she had been spared the shame of bearing the whelp of an unworthy man. She caressed Andromache's scars with delicate fingertips.

The other woman moaned and seized Briseis, rolling her onto her back in the weeds. Briseis yielded, opening her mouth to Andromache's tongue. A thousand differences made themselves known to her. Andromache held herself over Briseis lightly even as she asserted dominance. Rather than forcing a path to Briseis' center, Andromache's legs found a comfortable, intimate way to entwine. She forced nothing, kissing patiently until Briseis parted her legs and clasped the back of her neck with both hands.

It felt strange for the gestures of desire to be true, but Briseis' body had never lied to her. Her cunt moistened, her nipples hardened, and her thighs trembled. She wanted Andromache, even if she could not be sure what that would mean. She wanted this for herself. "Undress me," she whispered.

Andromache undid Brises' robes as efficiently as if she had sliced them off with a knife. Briseis' stomach looked pale, weak, and soft beside Andromache's tan, muscled skin. She flushed with shame.

"This is the beauty they always spoke of," Andromache breathed. "You and Helen. The kind of women who could start wars between kings."

Andromache's admiration only increased her discomfort. "Please don't compare me to Helen," Briseis said. "Any woman has been cursed by Aphrodite—me, you, or the old woman who carries water. Besides that, I'm nothing like Helen." She did not know, but she hoped. Briseis could not stand the idea that Andromache had once looked at Helen with this same expression of lust and wonder.

Andromache shook her head. "Of course you're right. Feeling a man's desire seems to have changed my eyesight as well."

"A good man appreciates each woman for what she is." Achilles had. Briseis bit back the comparison.

Andromache pressed a kiss of apology to the side of Briseis' face. "Helen used her beauty as a weapon. She did not wear it so well as you. And she had long, dark hair, which she curled each morning."

This speech did not help Briseis' rising irritation. "No more about Helen."

Andromache laughed, wrinkling her nose. "I have no skill at this, I fear. It makes me feel pity for poor Hector, when he fumbled with his tongue in our youth."

Briseis cupped the side of Andromache's face, fingers gripping harder than she intended. She had never felt this way before, but more than that, she had never been free to feel this way. "I don't want to think about the past."

Andromache's eyes slipped down Briseis' body, her expression carrying more meaning than her words had managed. "I swear by Athena, the past is not what commands my attention at the moment."

Briseis relaxed. Her grip became a caress. Andromache's eyes searched hers for a long moment, then she, too, loosened her posture. She joined Briseis in a kiss that began slow but built again into the fire of genuine desire.

Andromache lowered her lips to Briseis' right breast. She bit the nipple lightly, then sucked. Her lips nursed softly at first, then grew harder. Briseis spread her legs and arched her back. "Please," she said. "Make me come for real. It's been so long."

She found Andromache's hand and guided it between her legs. Still suckling, Andromache slipped a finger into Briseis' cunt, stroking the inside wall in a way that made ticklish shivers spasm up and down Briseis' body.

Andromache's finger teased and slid through Briseis' growing wetness. She moved her mouth to the cleft between Briseis' legs. Her tongue could have been a sword that pierced Briseis through. Briseis cried out and grabbed Andromache by the hair, pulling her tight against her body. She spasmed under that tongue, around Andromache's finger. The sensation felt too strong, but she couldn't let go of Andromache, and the other woman's tongue never stopped moving.

Finally, Andromache released Briseis. The fair-haired woman lay gasping, color-spots obscuring her vision of her new warrior lover. "If we're cursed by Aphrodite," Andromache said, "it's past time we learned to make our own luck."

"Which of the gods is responsible for this ruined place?" No Name wailed. Briseis walked beside the horse he rode, holding its lead and paying only half her attention to him. She glanced at Andromache, at the head of the party, her body thrilling at the memory of the other woman's touch and tongue.

"Do you hear me?" the old man demanded.

Briseis glanced up at his face, blinking in the noon light. She surveyed the blasted, war-torn landscape. "Whichever it is," she said finally, "is not doing a very good job."

"The ships of the Myrmidons will be just ahead," Andromache cried to the group. The mass of women behind her could have been those great warriors themselves, resplendent in gleaming bronze armor. "Beyond that hill!" called the warrior woman. "My sisters, we will sail away from this place and be free."

No Name shook his head. He whispered to Briseis. "Child, there will be no ships beyond the hill. There's no grace in this world anymore. There can be no hope. No City of Women. It's just a story Andromache likes to tell."

Briseis expelled an exasperated breath. "Who do you think you are, old man? I've had it with your drivel."

"There will be no City of Women. The only things beyond that hill are a twisted olive tree and a dying stream."

Briseis' heart felt cold in her chest. "You're not Zeus," she said.

They went on in silence toward the crest of the hill, Briseis stumbling occasionally on the pitted earth. Her heart pounded harder the closer they got, and it irritated her that part of her believed the old man's prophecy.

Andromache was first to reach the place from which the Myrmidons' ships should have been visible. She approached with a triumphant gait, but froze. Briseis could tell from the way she held the muscles of her back that all was not as it should be.

She avoided No Name's eyes until they got close enough that she could see for herself. When they stepped forward and she saw the tree and the trickle of water just as he had described, she couldn't help glancing up at him. He shrugged apologetically, just as Andromache's shoulders shook and the warrior woman began to cry.

Briseis slipped into Andromache's tent through one of the back flaps, after managing to avoid the guards posted on each side. In the center of the tent, she saw a lump wrapped in blankets and heard breathy, voiceless sobs. "Andromache," she murmured.

"By Ares, Eris, and Hades, woman. Leave me alone."

Briseis moved closer, easing herself down to the earth beside Andromache's shivering body, which seemed even smaller than usual now. Briseis didn't know what to say, and so she just reached inside the pile of blankets and stroked her hand down Andromache's back. The other woman sobbed harder, and Briseis' heart hurt for her.

Briseis had seen Achilles, too, mourning and aching and crying, but he had never let her close to him when he was in such a state.

Andromache's wordless acceptance of Briseis left her uncertain. How could she behave as a person, rather than as a possession? What would she do for Andromache if left free to decide?

She worked her way into the blankets beside Andromache and clasped the warrior woman to her chest. "Softer than water," she murmured, and Andromache's body slackened in her arms, surrendering to her touch.

Briseis petted Andromache's hair, then loosened the leather shirt she still wore and pulled it away from her. She undressed Andromache completely, slowly, shadows flickering over the other woman's skin. Fierce enjoyment bloomed in Briseis' heart. This body belonged to her, as much as hers belonged to Andromache. Perhaps this went even beyond bodies, to the hearts within.

Then, because she still hadn't found the right words, she trailed her fingers up and down Andromache's body — over her breasts, still full and motherly; over her scarred and well-muscled arms; over her taut belly and the shiny stretch marks there left by the birth of Astyanax; over her short, thick thighs; and over her surprisingly delicate feet.

Andromache started to say something, but Briseis laid a finger over her lips. She let her mouth follow where her fingers had been, until Andromache's sobs turned to soft moans. Briseis rubbed at the tears at the corners of Andromache's eyes. Finally, she knew what she wanted to express. "You don't have to be so hard," she said. "You have me now, and I'll never leave you. Mourn for Troy and Hector and Astyanax and all of us, and I can take it in for you and keep it somewhere safe."

She guided Andromache's hand between her legs, and slipped her own fingers inside the warrior woman's cunt. Andromache snorted. "Is that what it's for?" she said. "To take in all the pain in the world?"

Briseis colored in embarrassment. She had thought of it that way sometimes while she lay beneath Achilles. Naive girl that she had been, she had thought that his joy in being between her legs might take away the pain of his dark fate, might make him love her the way that she loved him. Now, she arranged her fingers in the shape of a spear and stabbed them into Andromache so they would hurt a little.

The other woman grunted and arched her back, moving her fingers inside Briseis as well. "Maybe we turn pain to pleasure," Briseis ventured.

Andromache's juices soaked Briseis's hand. She began to give quick little gasps, which Briseis drowned in a deep kiss. The scent of their arousal rose sharp and pungent, filling the tent. Their tongues did battle. Briseis encouraged Andromache to ride her hand, to use it for her pleasure, but she also did not stint from doing the same in return. Briseis worked her fingers deeper and deeper into Andromache, the flesh she found seeming ever softer, smoother, and wetter. She wanted to get even deeper. For the first time, she understood the desire of a man.

Sweeping Andromache's hand out of her own cunt, Briseis knelt between the other woman's legs. She retreated her fingers and set about opening Andromache afresh. She wanted to possess her more thoroughly than any other, even Hector.

She began with patient licks to Andromache's bud, but soon her tongue grew more warlike. It roamed and claimed. She drooled all over the space between Andromache's legs, her saliva dripping clear from the top to the bottom of her slit, mingling with her juices, and spreading over Andromache's inner thighs and Briseis' chin. Andromache might have come, but Briseis wasn't looking for that at the moment. She wanted her lover to *open*. She leaned back and examined Andromache's opening.

Briseis tested Andromache first with two fingers slipped inside her, then spread apart. She kissed the top of her slit and resumed her tongue's attention, probing to feel whether this pleasure encouraged Andromache's body to let her in.

"Briseis, what are you —"

"Sh. Take me into you." Briseis shaped her hand into a spear again. She positioned at the heated, soaking entrance to Andromache's body. Her fingertips went in easily, but then Briseis encountered resistance. She persuaded with her tongue while persisting with inexorable pressure. Her hand slid in deeper. Andromache's body gripped her now, sucking her in past the resistance with almost terrifying force.

Andromache sobbed a little as she began to open to Briseis' fist. Then something cracked in her voice and her body jerked as her legs spread wide and Briseis' hand sank in wrist-deep. Briseis wriggled her fingers, and Andromache growled low in the back of her throat. She shoved her own fist into her mouth and screamed into it as her body clenched and released in a spasm that radiated from Briseis' hand.

The power of it shot up Briseis' arm and into her own body. She wished she could continue reaching up and into Andromache. Her insides quivered with sympathetic tremors. Briseis straddled Andromache's knee, imagining she could take that in along with Andromache's leg. She imagined Andromache filling her more utterly than she had ever been filled before. Briseis bucked against Andromache's knee until she joined the other woman in orgasm.

Briseis pressed her face to the spot where her arm met Andromache's body. She touched her tongue down tenderly, now, as if licking a wound. Softly, slowly, she eased her hand out of Andromache as gently as she could. "What do you think?" she whispered. "Pleasure or pain."

"Both," Andromache gasped.

"That's the point," Briseis said, climbing up Andromache's body to lie beside her. "I think it's always both." She stroked Andromache's hair again, cradling her like the children she'd never had. Men had satisfied themselves with her, but they had never allowed her to care for them. She had never taken their burdens on as her own.

Andromache began to speak a few times, but drifted off in little groans. They began sated, but soon became anguished. Briseis' forehead wrinkled with concern. "What is it?"

"What do I do about having led us all to nonexistent ships, so we can sail to a place I don't know, where we will build a city that can't exist?"

Briseis kissed the top of her head. "We build that city anyway," she said. "Maybe right here. Achilles and Hector were the greatest warriors of our age, but they both let fate lead them around by the nose. You can be a better warrior than both of them if you take the future in your own hands."

Andromache kissed Briseis long and passionately. "You should have been a queen, not a slave."

Briseis shrugged, but she noticed the way her heart warmed in her chest until it burned. "I can be your queen," she said.

"What are you doing?" No Name said. The old man was doubled over in the mid-day sun. He sounded angry.

Briseis let go of the shovel she held, wiping her bleeding palms on her shirt. All around her, women dug the foundations for the wall surrounding the City of Women. The stream and olive tree would be in the center of the courtyard of Andromache's house, and the rest of the city would radiate from there. "We're tired of the Trojan War, Grandfather. We're tired of raids. We're tired of all the stories that men tell. I'm declaring the end of war." She glanced at Andromache, who was coming toward them. "We're telling our own stories from here on out," Briseis said. "We're making our own world."

Then Andromache was in her arms, and for a moment there was nothing else in the world for Briseis but the other woman's soft mouth and warm skin.

If you enjoyed this story, you can sign up for a free membership at ForbiddenFiction and discuss it with other readers and the author at the *Andromache's Prize* story page at http://forbiddenfiction.com/library/story/AL1-1.000123.

Icarus Bleeds

Icarus, a man on the run, dreams of wings, and of taking flight like the surgically modified rich and famous of Central City. The hacker who harbors him will do anything to keep him, including paying for the dangerous operation in a back alley chop shop. Neither can imagine how much the wings will truly cost. (M/M)

Chapter 1

A Dream of Wings

I will call him Icarus, because he worked so hard to erase his birth name that I will not commit the sin of returning it to him now. The things I said and did when I knew him will only make sense if you understand how beautiful he was, so I will try to force the words of mortals to describe a man who never seemed to belong to earth at all.

Icarus first came to me in the dark, in the rain, passing out of the shadows falling over the street, slipping smoothly into the shadows I made for myself. His eyes glowed from the corner where he took a seat, huddled under shelves loaded with discarded computer equipment. Even then I wondered how a shadow could be so luminous within a shadow, how black could shimmer from within black.

I wasn't in the habit of looking at my clients. They came because they wanted to be forgotten, and they generally did not want to be seen either. I could not help myself with Icarus. He reminded me of flesh I liked to pretend I didn't have. Eyes, lips, fingertips, inner thighs, the sides of my stomach, the soles of my feet. And, yes. Tongue. Cock. Thoughts both crude and poetic competed to distract me from the mechanical process of obscuring someone from all the files and IP addresses that affirmed that person's existence.

I avoided looking at his skin, a lighter shade of what is called black than my own purple-tinged pigment. Icarus's brand of black flowed with honey, shone with sunlight, glittered with the gold that may once have belonged to Pharaoh. Long, thin fingers, delicate as a girl's. Red-gold palms, and the beginnings of a scar, a telltale revelation of a story that started in the hands and parted the flesh of the forearm nearly to the elbow.

He saw me looking, and pulled the sleeves of his sweater down low, clutching bunches of the material in clenched fists. "Can you really make me disappear?"

I snorted. "Of course not. Not these days, not with the backups they keep and the triple cross checks they have to avoid failure conditions. Best I can do is make them forget to look for you."

He nodded, the gesture emphasizing the length of his neck, the quality of his silence. "How much?"

"How much you got?"

He shrank back from me, receding into the forest of parts and cords. "I'm not looking for favors."

"I don't do favors. I do a sliding scale. You pay what you can afford to pay. What you think is fair. I trust you."

"Why?"

I sighed. No one ever understood this when I bothered to explain. "Because I'm not one of them. I don't want to act like one."

He swallowed, his Adam's apple moving gracefully up and down in that impossibly lean neck. "I was going to see what you would take." He bit his lip and didn't explicate, but I got an idea of what he'd had in mind by the way his hands crept toward his fly, the gesture so subtle that I wasn't sure it had been a conscious invitation.

On any other night, with any other man, I wouldn't have. I would have kissed that smooth, wide forehead, done my work for free, and sent him back into the street uttering the vague promise that someday, when he could, he would take care of me. With Icarus, I could not resist the offer. I had to keep him a little longer. Though I hated myself for it, the sentence passed my lips as if it made up part of my daily stock in trade. "After I finish, you'll come upstairs with me."

His bowed head telegraphed his acquiescence well before his soft words. "Thank you."

When I got him to my bed, I knew I should be the one thanking him. He stripped with a benevolent dignity that shamed me. I felt as if I'd brought the Virgin Mary to my room to make a whore of her. Again, I considered releasing him, leaving my work to be my offering to his present and future beauty.

Then his undershirt peeled away from smooth, hard abs, and his boxers fell away from his hips and the thick, dark cock that hung soft between his legs. The shy and lovely youth before me, with his incandescent eyes and visible ribs, brought my own cock surging to life. I could not let him go. My desire made me cruel.

"Get on your knees and crawl to me," I whispered, loosening my own clothing, casting it aside. Hurt flashed through his eyes, and I loved it for the confirmation that it offered. He was open to me. I could touch him. I could make him remember me forever.

His lean, taut muscles rippled. Icarus could not move without grace. He glorified my floor by lowering himself to it. His knees and palms left a trail through the dust of my unswept room as he crossed to me.

I lifted my right foot. He did not need to be told. Icarus lowered himself onto his elbows and pressed a kiss to the arch of my foot. I shivered. The surface of his lips scratched coarsely against my foot, but the soft, hot padding beneath soothed me utterly. His kisses continued up my sole, methodically, their heat lingering everywhere they touched.

"Suck," I said, hissing with pleasure when he took my largest toe in his mouth, then stuffed in smaller toes beside it. I gritted my teeth to avoid kicking him, the warm, wet pleasure of his inner cheek unbearable when combined with the light scrape of his teeth and the rough caress of his tongue. He shifted position and lifted one hand to support my foot. I could not remember a man's hands ever being so smooth, so entirely free of calluses, and yet so strong. He pumped my foot in and out of his mouth, as much of it as he could fit inside, his lips stretching obscenely to accommodate me.

Icarus kissed and licked my calluses, nibbled on them lightly, and opened his mouth and ran his lower set of teeth with exquisite care over my instep and up toward my ankle. His cock had hardened, and my own cock threatened to burst at the sight of his total concentration, and the earnestness with which he sucked on what he'd been given to suck.

"The other one." He moaned and switched. I set my damp right foot on the floor, where it cooled from the fire of his mouth. Bracing one hand against the wall behind me, I fed him the left foot, faster this time, wriggling my toes inside his mouth, wanting him to struggle to take me in.

Icarus gave himself to me, holding the foot with both hands, writhing on the floor below me, eyes closed, mouth and throat open to an alarming degree.

I should have played with him longer, but again I could not. I pulled my foot out of his grasp, leaned over, and gripped him under the armpits, hauling him up and into my kiss. I felt so clumsy compared to him, my hands desperate and fumbling to feel his ass, the subtle muscles of his back, the outsides of his legs. His cock settled against mine, velvet heat to velvet heat. He sighed as he gave his mouth to me, and all I wanted was to push in deeper.

"Get on the bed." My words barely more than a breath. I had no right to this, and yet I would go on taking it until forced to stop. I tore through drawers until I found a mostly full bottle of lube, untouched aside from my infrequent bouts of self-abuse. Unbelievably, I still had rubbers, not even expired.

I flung myself onto Icarus's body, kissing the back of his neck, stroking his sides, smelling the oil in his hair, biting his shoulders a few times. My fingers found his cock and closed around it, but I sought my pleasure, not his, so I did not stroke him. I just held it, enjoying the warmth that radiated from the hard length and into my palm. I reached around him with the other hand and cupped his balls, squeezing them gently so I could relish their vulnerability.

Breath and blood moved through his body as it rested within my embrace. Releasing his cock, I pressed my hand lightly to his throat. He trembled. My balls ached. I kissed the spot beside my hand, then slid down in one firm stroke, gripping the curve of his ass. Firm, ripe muscle filled my hand. Seeking deeper, my fingers parted the cheeks, caressed the valley between them, found his hole.

He jerked when I touched it. He was no hardened whore. "Have you done this before?" I whispered.

"No," he said. It might have been a lie, but it was what I wanted to hear. I petted his head, murmured in his ear, and teased and caressed that hole, its ring of muscle jumping in response to my every movement.

I collected lube on my fingers and rubbed it into him, swirling around his hole, beginning to push the barest bit inside. His body was so hot, its grip so tight, that I wanted to come just imagining what his ass would feel like around my cock.

"Are you scared?"

"No."

"Open up for me."

I pressed one finger in, and his body went stiff in my grip. He drew a shaking breath and writhed to get away, suddenly fighting me where before there had been only acquiescence. My hand froze, then eased out of him. He lay gasping in my arms.

"OK, maybe I am scared."

I managed some compassion for the first time in a while. "Do you want to stop?"

He stayed silent for so long that I was tempted to take the lack of words as tacit permission and start playing with his ass again. I forced myself to wait, clenching my fingers to keep them still.

"No," he said finally, though I had to strain to hear him. "I want you."

"You do?" I could not keep the shock out of my voice. In response, he only nodded, keeping his face turned away. "Why?"

He shrugged, pulled my hand back toward his ass. I wanted to roll him onto his belly and just fuck him. Hard, triumphant victory filled my chest. But his expression of desire had destroyed my appetite for cruelty. I rubbed his back as my finger resumed teasing his hole, as gently and sweetly as I could. "Tell me about a beautiful thing," I said. "Something that you think about that might help you relax."

"Wings." I felt his smile where his face pressed against my chest, but also in the sigh that passed over his body along with the word, leaving Icarus transformed in its wake.

"The wings of birds? Airplanes?" His ass had changed so much that it was almost sucking my finger in. I wanted to keep him talking.

"The wings of men," Icarus sighed. "In the Central City, within the walls, you see them flying all hours of day and night. You know they're not angels, but they look like they are. That's not even the point, though. They go so high. It looks like almost to the sun. And it's got to all look so different up there. You've got to feel free."

I'd gotten two fingers into his ass by then, and had my other hand stroking his cock and balls. He shuddered with pleasure now as I worked my fingers in and out of him and dropped kisses along his neck and shoulder blade. I got a little distracted trying to place his accent. He had the flat, universal sound most of us have picked up from the Internet, but something changed when he mentioned Central City. I didn't think there were any black people in the upper echelon. As a courtesy, I never looked into my clients' histories while I obscured them, but now I wondered who he was.

A little whimper brought me back to more pressing concerns, and the need to help him stay inside his fantasy. "You ever seen one of those angel-men on the ground?"

A nod. "I used to climb up to the top of the Skywalk. They like to land up there. The view is nice, and there's a good restaurant. That restaurant has towels for them, to wipe off the condensation they pick up from flying through the clouds."

I grunted. "To wipe off sweat, more likely."

"No!" The innocent wonder in his voice made me feel old. "Their faces have little frost crystals on them. Their wings are pale because the blood shrinks back in the skin under the feathers when it gets cold. When they warm up again, the wings get a rosy glow from the blood returning."

"You know a lot about this." I slid a third finger into him. At this rate, he'd be ready for my cock sooner than I could have hoped.

"The operation is too expensive."

"It doesn't have to be." I shouldn't have said that, but my pulsing cock had destroyed my thinking by then. I needed inside him, and those words seemed like my golden key. I twisted my fingers, stroking the inner walls of his ass, while I pumped his cock with my other hand. Icarus moaned and pressed back toward me.

"What do you mean?"

"Nothing is impossible, kid. Outside of Central City, we learn to take what we want."

"You really think so?"

"Hell, yes, I think so."

He closed his eyes, obviously caught in his dream of flight. His whole body softened, except for his cock, which had gotten so hard it was quivering. I put on the rubber, lubed up my cock, and took a chance, lining up the head and holding my breath as I eased my way in.

Icarus made a little sound in the back of his throat. "You think I could —"

"Get wings yourself. Yeah." I spoke between gritted teeth, probing ever deeper with my cock. "I can just see how pretty those wings would look on you, spread out to either side of your hot little body, feathers brushing this round ass of yours, your muscles rippling while you pump those wings up and down."

I was fully fucking him by then, gaining confidence in the power of these magical words I had discovered. His ass welcomed my every stroke. Beneath me, he whimpered and arched his back, taking me in to the hilt. "Yes," he whispered. I wasn't sure if he approved of my cock or my words, but I didn't really care.

I grabbed his shoulders. "You could fly up past the buildings. Up even higher than the clouds." I fucked him so hard my words came out as gasps. "Big, wide wings. Tall wings. Whatever color feathers you want."

His ass, for all of its compliance, massaged my cock with such a tight and persistent grip that every inch I sank into Icarus sent nerves tingling down to my feet and up to my head. I was seconds from orgasm, babbling incoherently by then, spewing out whatever wing-related words I could think of. A man will say some stupid things when his cock is happy, especially when it hasn't been for a long time.

"You find somewhere to get wings," I panted. "I'll take you there and help you check them out. Hell, I could even pay for it."

"You would do that?" His cock jumped in my hand. I pumped it faster.

"Yes," I said. His ass clenched around me. My cock had never felt that good before. I pushed in as deep as I could and ground my hips in a circle. Icarus came, pumping his seed out onto my fingers. I felt his balls, drawn up tight and wrinkled near where I gripped the base of his cock.

Icarus reached behind himself for me, face a portrait of ecstasy, and pulled me even deeper into his spasming ass. I growled and fucked myself the rest of the way toward heaven. Who needed wings to fly when I had him?

Only later, holding him in the darkness, did I think about what I'd promised him. I could tell the wings were serious for him. If he trusted me, if he thought I might really give them to him, maybe he would stay. I closed my eyes, clasping the slick, soft heat of Icarus's sweat-soaked back tightly against my chest. I wanted him to stay.

Chapter 2
Wings of Blood and Wax

We talked all the time about how hot it would be for Icarus to have wings, and how beautiful they would look. Wings were foreplay, but they were also hope, joy, and the proof that I wasn't just a horny old bastard taking advantage of a man half my age. I had something good to offer, and Icarus could have it as soon as he found a shop that could do it.

He lived at my place, soft and warm beside me every morning, the light layer of fuzz on his skin already seeming feathery when I rolled toward him for the day's first kiss. I tried not to question it. I didn't want to encourage any line of discussion that might make him realize how much better he could do for himself.

We didn't talk about how expensive wings were, and what I would have to do to actually set him up with them. I stayed up once calculating it. My usual finance policies didn't lead to huge savings. I'd always liked it that way, partly because I could think of myself as a good guy, and partly because it helped me fly under the radar. I would have to behave differently if I wanted to pay for wings for Icarus. I would have to take riskier jobs, for people I liked less.

I saved the calculations in an encrypted file and crept upstairs to bed. Icarus sighed at my touch, snuggling into me, and I couldn't help suckling his cock until he woke up and let me fuck him. I could pretend I had a choice about this, but the truth spooned with me every night in my bedroom. When the time came to come up with the money, I knew I had to deliver. I could never bear to see my image darken in Icarus's luminous black eyes. I could not disappoint him.

"I scheduled the operation for Wednesday," Icarus whispered. I held him a minute before I spoke.

I'd been to check out the shop after he found it, and I hadn't liked the guy in charge. His hands seemed too rough, too clumsy, too uncaring. I didn't like his big-breasted tattoo. I didn't like the idea of him touching Icarus at all, ever. "Can't you look for somewhere else?"

He went stiff and ashen, and pulled back from me. "There's nowhere else, OK? Not outside Central City! Believe me, I've looked everywhere. This guy says he's got state of the art equipment."

"That's what he *says*."

"You don't understand. You don't need this. You don't need anything. You're happy with what you've got right now. You want me to wait so I still need you."

My face must have betrayed me, because Icarus smiled horribly. He turned his back and stripped, then leaned over and spread his ass cheeks — not with his usual innocent sensuality, but lewdly. "Put your clothes back on," I told him.

"What's the matter? I thought this was what you wanted. Don't you get enough of it? Don't you get to fuck me whenever you want?" His voice rose hysterically.

It might have been better to keep my hands off him, but again I could not. I scooped him into my arms, tugged his boxers back up his hips myself, pulled him over to the bed. I clasped him against my chest, rubbing his back, ashamed of my growing erection. "That's not what this is," I said, desperate to soothe him. But my own fears emerged against my will, turning my voice petulant. "I didn't want to force you. You said you wanted me."

"I said what you wanted to hear."

Pain hissed through my chest. I thrust him away from me and jumped up from the bed. I knew better than to think someone like Icarus would really choose me, for my own merits, but I must have let myself slip into the fantasy his ongoing presence inspired.

Regret flashed through his eyes. "Hey. I'm sorry. I didn't mean it."

"Of course you didn't." I kept my back to him. Tears welled up in my eyes, threatening to fall. I couldn't let him see them.

"I'm sorry."

"I know." I sighed. "I'm worried about you, but it's your decision. If you want this guy to do your operation, I'll take you there on Wednesday."

His arms wrapping around my hips could already have been the wings of grace. I even smiled as he pulled me back to bed. He had never been so enthusiastic with me before — his mouth engulfing my cock, hands cupping my balls, legs intertwined with mine — but I could not let myself sink into the sensation of him. He tried to talk me off by going on about the wings, but that wasn't working for me just then. Icarus could tell, and I had to wipe that disappointed look off his face before it broke my heart.

I flipped him onto his stomach and felt up his shoulder blades. I couldn't stop picturing that chop man slicing them up, and my cock wilted completely. I moaned anyway, trying to pretend the whole thing turned me on. I didn't want to think about him scarred. I didn't want to think about him changed.

He was perfect the way he was, but what he'd said about me had been the truth, too. I couldn't understand. As long as I had him, I didn't need anything. He had all of me, everything I could give, but that didn't do fuck-all toward giving him anything he actually needed or even wanted.

Icarus glanced behind him. I'd forgotten to keep up my moaning. I smiled and stroked a finger down his cheek. My perfect boy. Tonight, he was mine, bare and glowing and completely natural. I reached between his legs and stroked behind his balls, and the sweetness of his responding cry got my cock interested again. I spread his cheeks and buried my face in his ass, kissing him, tasting him. I'd never wanted to do things like that before, but there wasn't anything about Icarus that I didn't want to touch or smell or put in my mouth or rub with my fingers or the bottoms of my feet or any part of me that he would allow.

I lubed his ass and tried to fuck him, but he started muttering about wings again. I cursed myself for encouraging that habit.

Eventually, I gave up on coming. I faked my groans of pleasure, wiggled my cock like it was spurting, and jerked him off hard. Then

I lay awake and clutched him so tightly he complained he couldn't sleep.

I liked to fly under the radar. I helped people nobody cared about, people the authorities behind the Central City databases wouldn't mind forgetting. I made sure those people knew how to find me, and nobody else.

See, the systems are more powerful than anybody needs. The computer will flag anybody who breaks any rule, and it's not designed to determine how significant that rule or that person is. Once you get tagged that way, you're make-work for the enforcers. You're effectively a walking pile of paperwork they have to do, an inflated selection of an overwhelming to-do list. For them, it makes more sense to shoot you than to take you in—that's one page of paperwork, versus reams of it.

My usual procedure turned out to help everyone. I made the enforcers happy because I could take you out of the system. A pile of paperwork becomes no paperwork at all—not even the one page that a bullet requires. You were happy because I could sanitize the ID chips behind your retinas, which meant you could go pay cash in the corner store without getting shot by a lazy enforcer. I was happy because I could get by on your gratitude and any scraps you saw fit to throw me.

That was how it used to work. For Icarus, I needed more.

The morning after he told me about his appointment, I worked up a new ID for myself. I posted it on the sites I used to avoid, where people who've actually done something look for someone desperate and good enough to make them disappear.

I knew how to sweep up the refuse that piled up in the corners of the system, but this new work required prying Central City's grip loose from people it still wanted to control. I called myself Daedalus, and my guts twisted as the offers poured in.

"Stay in the room and watch? Are you crazy? I'd have to tie you down and gag you to make sure you didn't do anything to distract me."

"If that's what you have to do," I said. Icarus rolled his eyes as if I were an overprotective parent, but I told myself he would be relieved, too, once it was happening.

The chop shop seemed all too worthy of its name. Through a large window, I saw a room with surgical tools and an operating table—though not the kind you'd find in a hospital. Handcuffs fitted at both ends suggested it doubled as dungeon equipment, or possibly something less pleasurable for the party attached to the table. The room we occupied could have been a machine shop. Rusty gears and rustier circular saws competed for space with outdated cash registers, overturned work tables, radar detectors, and who knew what else. A layer of sawdust coated the floor, and I couldn't vouch for how clean the medical room would be.

I hadn't been able to keep my breakfast down. I wasn't losing this battle. I didn't care what I had to do.

The owner of the chop shop sank deeper into his sales pitch. "I'll give him your money's worth, old man. You don't have to worry about getting cheated. Real titanium-structured wings, feathers harvested from swans and eagles, everything totally legit. Nanocyte healing gels, the works."

"I watch, or it doesn't happen."

The man scowled. "Grab a lollipop and a seat, sweetheart," he said to Icarus. He took me by the arm and pulled me into a side room, this one crammed full of packing material. I wrinkled my nose at the sour smell of his skin. I wondered about his general hygiene, and made a mental note to insist he wear latex gloves, too.

The chop man hawked a little into the back of his throat and squinted at me. "I get it, man. If I was Daddy to that sweet little piece of meat out there, I'd never want to take my eyes off him either. But I'm not going to grab his cock while I'm working on him. He's all yours. He'll be great advertising for me, looking the way he does and wearing my wings. I'm going to do this right."

"I gave you my conditions."

Now, the conspiratorial smile. The pat on the outside of my arm to show that we were both friends, that we were more alike than different. I folded my arms against my chest and cocked my head to hear the next phase of his pitch.

"Why do you want to see this, Daddy? He's going to bleed. He's going to get hurt. You don't want to watch me drilling holes in his scapulas. Do you?"

Of course I didn't. Just the thought of that made me dizzy. But it wasn't as bad as the idea of catching a glimpse through the curtain he would draw over that big window, or of pacing outside over that sawdust-covered floor, wondering about every buzzing sound I heard. I shook my head slightly.

"Have it your way," the chop man growled. "But I wasn't kidding about restraining you. You know that, right?"

"Oh, you're damn right. If you don't tie me down, I'll fucking kill you the moment you touch his skin with your knife."

"Wonderful. We'll call it a deal."

Icarus bled. I bled from my eyes in sympathy, thick drops falling down my cheeks to match the drops that fell from his would-be wings to stain the thick layer of sawdust in the makeshift operating room. When they trickled into the corners of my mouth, they tasted only of salt, only of my sweat and effort, but even if they didn't contain the iron produced in my heart, I know I must have bled.

The chop man drugged him heavily, coaxing needle after needle into the pristine veins of his left arm, then more into the areas around his shoulder blades, but he didn't put Icarus all the way under. I had to listen to his gasps of surprise, odd little moans, and occasional slurring giggles.

It was hell. So much adrenaline pumped through my veins that I worried the man hadn't tied me tight enough. I thought the slightest motion would burst the bonds that held me.

Icarus came apart before my eyes. The chop man opened him, made his shoulders weep fluid down the curve of his back, past his ass. The pinkish mess drooled down his upper thighs and into the backs of his knees. Flesh tore. Bone protested. The chop man drilled and hacked, pinned and sutured. Feathers soaked in pools of wax, waiting to be sealed and inserted.

Bound to the table, Icarus made swooshing noises like a little boy playing with an action hero. He flinched when the chop man fitted titanium rods into his perforated shoulder blades, but then his sighed like an even younger child. "Wings."

"Yeah, buddy. Wings." The chop man shot me a look for the outburst and snapped another rod into place.

The structure dwarfed Icarus, the wings looming over him like a twisted metal angel. "How's he going to move all that?" I asked.

"Questions weren't part of the deal," the chop man said. "I know what I'm doing. He's going to look real pretty."

"Is he going to be able to fly?"

The chop man paused too long. "Sure. Of course. Once he heals."

"He says the wings in Central City let people fly."

"This isn't Central City."

I glared at the chop man's back, focusing on the spot where sweat soaked his grimy T-shirt. "Don't I know it."

That was the moment I knew I was right to despair. The chop man worked for five more hours on wings for Icarus, but I couldn't lift my eyes to look at them anymore. I watched the blood and wax that dripped off the operating table and into the sawdust. The byproducts. The refuse that would never quite be swept away. The things that would stain.

Chapter 3

The Agony of Flight

Icarus required a complex geometric process to get through any door at my place. That didn't matter too much, because he mostly had to stay in bed, gasping and sweating and oozing blood from the holes in his shoulder blades. Most of the feathers on his wings had turned pink from all the mess.

Bed presented its own problems. Icarus could not lie on his swollen back, of course. I could not lie beside him. Even if I'd been able to stand the smell of his infected flesh, I couldn't have gotten close enough to hold him.

Lying on his stomach wasn't comfortable either. To do that without suffocating, Icarus had to twist his head to one side, which engaged the muscles in his neck, which were attached to the screwed-up muscles in his shoulder blades.

Turns out you use the muscles in your shoulder blades a lot. Anytime you want to turn your torso or lift your head or move your arms at all. I tried to find a way to make him comfortable, but his wings prohibited him from sitting in any chair, and when he tried to stand he could not walk more than a few feet without jostling the painful mass of titanium and feathers.

I slept downstairs in my work room. I'd been busy anyway, dealing with the clients I'd had to take on to make the necessary payments to the chop man. Sometimes, through the ceiling, I could hear him crying. Worse, I sometimes heard his moans of agony as he tried to flap his new set of wings.

"You need to eat," I told him one morning. "You can't heal if all you do is drink water."

The eyes that returned my concerned gaze chilled me. Black, dead, and hopeless, they remained empty of both reproach and sign of life. I had to look away from the body I once worshiped.

Oatmeal, sweetened with a little honey. A bowl I hadn't used in a long time, dug out so I could hold it without memories of another, happier Icarus. A spoon, gleaming and fitted to its proper use. I held this up to swollen lips, which responded only slightly. "Please," I said. "Eat for me, if not for you."

His sudden laugh knocked the oatmeal off the spoon and the spoon out of my hand and onto the floor. I bent to retrieve it, trying to clean it with the corner of my shirt, one eye peering up to read his face.

"I still need you," Icarus whispered, his voice cracking from illness and disuse. "I thought these wings would make me free, but now I can never, never leave. You must think it's funny."

Again, the stab of pain. I'd been selfish in my desire for his body, but I'd never wanted to force him, to make him feel trapped. "If there's anywhere else you want to go," I offered, swallowing my fear and loss. "I'll do whatever it takes to get you where you need to be."

For answer, Icarus nudged the bowl out of my hand, hissing with pain at the slight movement of his arm. We both ignored the oatmeal spilling onto the floor. "I'm where I need to be," he said. "I'm where I want to be."

He pulled me close against him, creating an embrace inch by agonizing inch. His arms shook from the strain of reaching around me. His breath caught in his throat. His heart pounded so hard I felt it in my own breastbone. His stomach quivered. I knew better than to fight him or offer to help, and finally, I stood as gently as I could, a little of his blood soaking into the clothes I wore.

My cock proved blind to the tragedy of the moment, hardening in its usual response to Icarus. I winced an apology, but my would-be angel only smiled. "You love me, don't you?" he said. "For real. Like it hurts."

I should have said it back, out loud, but I only ducked my head and nodded, feeling like a pathetic old man. I moved to kiss his chin, and he caught my mouth with his lips. I moaned, startled and excited. I forgot the smell of sickness and remembered all the nights we had been together in that room. I should have given him more pleasure on the first night. I resolved to make it up to him.

Tip of the tongue down his throat, fingers flicking lightly over his chest, watching the muscles twitch in response to my touch. Icarus was always thin, but that time I could taste his ribs through his skin. Fear of disturbing his costly embrace kept me in place for a long time, loving him as best I could with only the edges of myself, and trying not to move him at all.

His cock moved, lengthening and requiring me to carefully adjust to make room for it to rise. I held my breath as I used my lower body to maneuver it into place between our stomachs. My own cock had long ago lost interest, fallen victim to the crimes of concentration and concern.

The heat of Icarus's cock penetrated my clothes. I shifted cautiously so I could slide one hand down to wrap around it. I stroked him awkwardly from the bad angle, until Icarus sobbed from the back of his throat and said, "Please. I need to feel your mouth."

He loosened his arms from around me and let them fall bonelessly to his sides, grunting. I sank to my knees before him. Tilting my head back, I met his eyes. He watched so remotely that I saw him as a broken, bloodied angel in truth. I parted my lips and took his cock like penance.

Little mewls of pleasure from above were interrupted by the occasional click of the tongue or hiss when I jarred his body too strongly. I forced myself to keep my pace slow and gentle, pulling his cock all of the way out of my mouth each time and then letting my lips push his foreskin back as I eased it back inside.

He filled my mouth as much as ever, but the pleasure I gave him seemed far too weak. I flicked my tongue over the head of his cock as it passed on its journey to the depths of my throat. I tried sucking until my cheeks hollowed. I aborted my attempt at deep-throating when it became clear that he couldn't stay standing under the pressure of me pushing his cock through the resistance at the back of my mouth. It made me feel so useless.

I would have caressed him, but I feared hurting that way, too. My hands remained at my sides. My knees began to ache from holding my weight on the wooden floor. Still, I licked him, and fucked him slowly with my mouth.

Icarus made the effort of lifting a hand again so it could rest on the top of my head. His groans as his hand moved back and forth with my bobbing head eventually became too much for me. Releasing his cock, I touched a fingertip to his wrist as lightly as I could. "Doesn't it hurt you?"

Icarus twitched his cock in answer. Remarkably, it hadn't gone soft. "I'm thinking about how you gave me my wings."

The only thing that prevented me from falling back in horror was worry about what that would do to the hand on my head. "That's still a good thing?"

"When I get better," Icarus said, "I'm going to fly." With that, he grabbed the back of my head and pushed his cock deep into me, screaming as he did. I didn't know if it was pain or pleasure, but I wasn't about to refuse him. I sucked him hard and fast, taking his actions as permission to ignore the possibility of causing him pain.

An eternity passed. My jaw ached. The back of my throat burned. I'd sucked saliva up my nose trying to breathe around his cock. I couldn't have gotten off my knees if I wanted to.

Slowly, Icarus's ass began to move, to pump his cock into me. I groaned. I'd gotten hard again. I let one hand make its way down to my own cock as I increased my pace on his. I took myself in my fist and thought of his sweet ass, of the things I hoped to do to him again one day.

I'd learned by then to ignore the harsh breathing above me and the occasional sobs. I just followed the command of Icarus's hand, which still jerked occasionally in my hair. For a moment, I forgot the operation. I smelled Icarus's skin, and anticipated the moment he would come in my mouth.

His cock began to spurt, and my hand moved more vigorously. Victory surged down my spine and into my cock as Icarus came for me.

But my hard-on wilted suddenly as he uttered a little bleat and fell backwards, his terrible, delicate wings crashing into the wall behind him. The cry that followed tore at me.

I tried to scramble to my feet, but my legs had fallen utterly asleep during my long bout of cocksucking. I flailed helplessly on the floor, struggling to master my leaden limbs, while Icarus stood in silent agony, biting a trembling lip and gripping his naked thighs with hands like claws.

"Are you OK?"

He did not respond. Agonizingly long moments later, I finally managed to stand, to go to him.

"The wings?"

I examined his back. Fresh blood flowed from his wounds, but the titanium rods held true. Much as I wanted to murder the chop man, I could not question the strength of the attachments he had fitted onto Icarus. "They're in place," I told him.

To my amazement, a beatific smile eclipsed the pain on Icarus's face. "Thank you," he said.

"For what?"

"For making me come."

"You fell."

"I needed it."

I didn't want to contradict him. I kissed his cheek. Part of me savored the salty-sour semen taste that lingered along the sides of my tongue and toward the back of my throat, but to another part of me, it tasted like guilt.

"I want to do you," Icarus whispered.

"How?" I couldn't have asked it of him even if I thought it was possible.

"Get on a chair. Stand on it. I can't kneel, but if you can get yourself high enough, I can probably dip."

"I can't let you—"

"Please." The naked need in his voice far surpassed the way he'd sounded asking me to suck him. I could not refuse. I went downstairs for my desk chair, hauling it up the awkward, curving stairs and into the cramped bedroom without a thought about how I would get it down again.

I stripped and climbed onto the chair. Icarus's face twisted as he struggled to get into a position where he could reach my cock. He tried bracing his hands against my legs, but his arms began to shake and he eventually pulled back with a gasp. He cycled through a number of difficult-looking positions until he ended up sharing the seat of the chair with me, one knee on either side of my feet. The height of the chair allowed him to kneel without having to press the bottoms of his wings into the floor.

From there, Icarus strained and grunted until he managed to get his face into my crotch. By then, all arousal had left me long before. I felt like a heartless bastard.

"Sorry," I muttered. "Give me a minute."

I closed my eyes and remembered the nights I'd held him spooned against my chest, no wings in the way, and no pain. My hard cock would wake me up at night more often than not, and I would try to pull slightly back from Icarus and jerk myself off without waking him. The times I wasn't quiet or subtle enough, he'd wake, sigh slightly, and slip under the covers to offer me his mouth. The familiar sense of selfishness would burn in the pit of my stomach, but I wouldn't protest. I would stroke his hair, tug lightly on his ears, trace the shape of his lips stretched around my cock.

That soft, hot mouth closed around my cock now. I grunted with lust, even as he whimpered with pain. The erection I had managed slipped. I opened my eyes and looked down. Blood oozed down his wings. His body trembled from holding himself in position. The lines around his eyes spoke of effort and discomfort.

For a moment, I wished for my old selfishness. I would have gladly slid back into the dream of his impossible mouth. But I could not give myself to it. My cock shrank, becoming a soft coil pursued by Icarus's tongue. I touched his head. "Hey. Thank you."

"I can keep trying."

I disengaged myself, removing my cock from him. Careful not to upset the balance on the chair, I lowered my body until I could look him in the eye. I kissed his forehead. "I know you would. But I can't."

A tear slipped down the side of Icarus's face. "I'm sorry," he whispered. "I'm so sorry."

"Hey," I said. "Hey. You try to get comfortable. I'll go downstairs and get you some more oatmeal."

When I returned with a new bowl, he remained in exactly the

same position, and I realized there was no such thing as comfort in his world any longer.

I returned to the bedroom later with a big saw and a bunch of tools. Icarus flinched at the sight of the equipment. "Relax," I told him. "This isn't for you."

I worked fast and hard, relieved at finally having a way to express my anger. Bookshelves seemed weightless as I shoved them out of the way, rearranging furniture to expose the Eastern wall. One deep breath, and I plunged into it.

In a real house, inside Central City, I could never have cut through a wall with nothing but a handsaw, but this wasn't a real house, and we sure as hell weren't among the privileged. The flimsy wall succumbed to me so easily I wondered how it had stayed standing so long.

"What are you doing?" Icarus gasped as he watched me fling rotten wood and nails into the little piece of yard below our bedroom.

When I was younger, I'd cared about things like that, paying extra to have grass below my window instead of another alley full of discarded things and people. I had changed, and there remained no sign of the flowers I used to grow. The lack of pavement hadn't stopped anyone from using the space as a garbage dump, and I'd have to go down, clean it all out, and cut back the overgrown grass. Any number of disgusting things could be lurking under those long fronds.

The big hole I was making highlighted another benefit of my place. It stood a little taller than the neighbors' places, which I'd wanted so I could divide home and shop. I hadn't even looked through the window in years, but now that I was knocking down the wall, I felt free, and just slightly above it all. It wasn't Central City, but in my youth I'd been able to pretend it was.

"You need more space," I told Icarus. He came to stand beside me, gaping, but I didn't say anything else. I didn't tell him the fantasy I had, that someday those goddamn wings would work and he could fly in and out of our house, swooping off to wherever he wanted through what used to be a wall.

I thought I was old and jaded, but when I remember moments like that with Icarus, it seems like back then I didn't even know what jaded was.

Our new deal required me to ignore Icarus's pain whenever and wherever I could. If I could not actually ignore it, I had to pretend I could.

So, he practiced flying, leaping out that big hole I'd made and screaming when he hit the ground. Sometimes, I thought I could hear his bones thudding into the earth, scraping against each other, even breaking. I got up sometimes, went out the front, and walked around to look into that strip of yard, always expecting to see a busted and twisted Icarus, half-alive and crawling or maybe just staring blankly up at that sky he wanted so badly.

Despite the horrible noises, Icarus didn't manage to kill himself.

I hated it worse when he got up the courage to move his wings. Agonized cries rose with every flap of those feathered titanium monstrosities. Once. Twice. The sounds beginning to fade as Icarus ascended. No matter how I tried not to, I always began to hope right about then. I was never prepared for the little squeal he would give when he could no longer stand the pain.

I learned to turn the music up loud so as not to hear Icarus crashing, Icarus slamming into the side of the house and gasping, Icarus beating his fists into the ground and howling because that hurt, too.

I put on a set of earbuds and gritted my teeth. I did not let myself remember the past, either with a healthy Icarus or before him. I refused to question the work I did now to keep up my payments to the chop man. I just kept the roof over our heads and tried to stay out of his way.

Chapter 4

Fallen Angel Finds His Wings

I didn't like the man sitting across from my computer. In the old days, I wouldn't have answered his query in the first place. There'd been something arrogant about the way he used punctuation, and I hadn't liked the fake, archaic way he'd closed his messages. No one these days wrote, "Yours."

I knew those were arbitrary judgments, but the freedom I used to enjoy allowed me to trust my intuition on subtle signals like that. My new debt reality afforded me the opportunity to confirm that sort of gut feeling in much greater detail than I'd ever wished to — to spend enough time with people to find out why I actually didn't like them.

With this guy, my dislike started with the fastidious care that had gone into his clothing, continued with the way he avoided touching me when I offered my hand, and solidified around the sickly triumph in his eyes as he leaned forward in his chair to say, "You're him, aren't you?"

Whatever it was supposed to mean, I had no patience for that kind of drama. "Him, who?"

"Daedalus. Didn't think you'd be so dense. Where'd you learn how to use this equipment?"

That was bad. He was supposed to be an easy job. He shouldn't know anything about Daedalus. And I liked him even less the more he opened his mouth.

I tried not to let it show on my face. I took a slow, deep breath and raised an eyebrow, aiming my expression toward the threatening side of amused. "You've noticed, I'm sure, that for all of our communications so far we've been utilizing secure, single-use identities. I see no reason to change that custom."

I was talking common courtesy and mutual respect for the reasons neither of us would want to share our identities. Anyone who didn't care about that would be a lot of trouble to me.

If anything, the man's smile broadened. "So, you are Daedalus. I've found you."

"A man who's sitting in my office hoping to get lost shouldn't be worried about what he has or hasn't found."

His expression didn't fade, and the air I breathed suddenly got very sweet and sharp in my nose. Adrenaline pounded through me with every thud of my heart. I'd been waiting for and dreading this moment for a good three decades.

"Don't get up, Daedalus. That wouldn't be wise." He shook his arm as if adjusting his sleeve, and a little pocket pistol popped out and into his hand.

"Would sitting here be any wiser?"

"Central City's on its way already," he said with a shrug. "If you make me shoot you, that just means you won't get far when you try to run. And there are reasons a man might want his legs while they're interrogating him. And especially later, when they drop you in the hold."

A paralyzing agent in the pistol, then. Properly aimed, it could disable the large muscles in the legs, and it sounded like the kind formulated by people who didn't care if the effect turned out permanent or not. Based on the rumors I'd heard, he was telling the truth. A man wanted every means of defense available when they locked him in with thousands of other desperate people in the warrens below Central City. I definitely didn't want to find myself there without the use of my legs.

But what the man had wrong was that, more than anything else, I didn't want to find myself in there at all.

Every heartbeat could have been a mallet pounding in my ears, I was that worked up. I ducked my head like he'd cowed me, and as soon as I saw his shoulders relax, I shoved my desk at him as hard as I could and raced up the stairs. My equipment crashed and shattered in his direction. He cursed and jumped up, aiming that little pistol of his.

I'd hoped to make it up to the bedroom without getting shot. From there, I could jump out the big hole I'd made, and have a chance of getting away. No telling what they'd do to Icarus, but I didn't see how I could help him. The thought made my eyes sting, and for a second I slowed my escape. Shouldn't I let them take me? Icarus would know to stay quiet until he got a chance to jump out that window himself and run for it. If I led them up there now, though, I'd be taking that possibility away from him.

A dart bit into the back of my leg, delivering the wake-up call that freed me from my uncharacteristically selfless daydream. Forget nobility and sacrifice. No way could I stand there and wait for Central City.

I burst into the bedroom. Icarus stood at the space in the wall, his wings spread wide, blocking my way. His hands curled around two cylindrical objects that made him look like an angel clutching a pair of scrolls. "We need to get out of here," I said, slamming the door behind me and locking it. That might hold them for a minute, but I thought I already heard boots stomping through the downstairs. "Central City's here for me, and they're not the kind to let you off the hook for being an innocent bystander."

"Central City? For you?"

"I can't explain. Get out of the way, then get yourself out of here, too." Icarus just stared, like he couldn't make sense of anything I'd said. Before the wings, I would have wished for an evening for a proper goodbye, but considering what we'd been going through, most of what I felt right then was relief. However it went down, I wouldn't have to tiptoe around Icarus anymore. I wouldn't have to wonder if I would get him back, and I wouldn't have to keep selling out for his sake.

I started for Icarus, preparing myself to touch him gently despite my panic. Before I could reach him, the poison dart did its work. My legs collapsed under me, so completely numb that I might as well have fallen on a pile of scrap wood.

I knew I was dead.

Fists pounded on the bedroom door. It shook, the hinges complaining. I glanced from the door to Icarus. I'd been careful before him. Whatever he'd intended, he'd ruined me. He must have seen it in my eyes, because he gave a little cry and ran to me.

"Don't try to *help* me, God damn it!" I snarled at him. "Get out! No sense in them killing both of us."

He seemed so wide-eyed and helpless that my anger melted a little. I touched his arm and pitched my voice softer. "They'll be distracted with me. Jump out the window now, and try not to groan the way you usually do. Don't worry if you're not too mobile. Just find somewhere out of sight and wait until you can't hear anything else. It's probably a good idea to find somewhere else to stay. They might come back here."

He nodded, but didn't otherwise respond to my words. He lifted his hands, and I realized he'd been holding a pair of fat syringes tipped with long, wicked needles. He squeezed his eyes shut and stabbed the first into his thigh, sucking air in through his teeth as he pumped fluid into the thick veins there.

"What the hell are you doing? Cut it out and get out of here!"

Icarus ignored me and stabbed the other needle into his heart. I stared bug-eyed. He grimaced and took that fluid in, too. Then, instead of running to the hole like I wanted him to, he hooked me under the armpits and started hauling me in that direction. I struggled with him, even knowing how I might hurt him. "Forget about me, damn it!"

I screamed the rest of the way to the hole, not caring whether the Central City officials could hear me. Icarus dragged me without noting any of my objections.

Someone kicked the door hard enough that it splintered and buckled. If Icarus was going to escape, he needed to leave now. I reached up and grabbed the back of his head, tugging him down far enough that I could lift my eyes and see his face. "Please," I told him.

The dark eyes that had so captivated me blinked once, slowly. They held a feverishness I didn't like, but also the luster I'd seen the first night. Icarus leaned forward a little more and kissed my forehead. "No," he whispered, stroking his fingers down the side of my face.

I stopped fighting him, even when he pulled me to my feet, settling my back against his chest and wrapping his arms across my torso. I had never really let myself believe that he might feel something for me. I had never been worthy of that from him—even moments ago, I'd been ready to abandon him to Central City.

The door split in two, and a pistol came in, followed by a large man. Icarus's arms tightened around me. He coiled low, taking my body with him, then leapt into the air accompanied by a cry. But I was the one who screamed, the beat of his wings ripping through me as if they were my own.

More shots rang out. They must have hit my legs. I didn't feel anything, but I saw something drip from my shoe.

Above and behind me, Icarus flapped his wings slowly, power-fully, and steadily, lifting our double weight with alarming speed. We rose above the Central City police vans parked in front of my home. Men, growing smaller, talked on radios and pointed upward.

Ice ran through my veins, but I could not remain concerned when we rose above the dilapidated roofs of my building and the neighbors'. Finally, we were high enough to see the pattern of the streets, far enough away from the specifics that the brutal design of it all made a cold kind of sense. Central City's spires rose in the middle and everything fell from there, shadow cities produced as part of the great city's half-life, going on into the infinite distance, but possessing less and less of its radiant glory.

"How are you doing this?" I shouted. I wasn't sure if Icarus could hear me over the whoosh of his enormous wings. "I thought you couldn't actually fly."

He gave me a squeeze. "Adrenaline and painkillers," he shouted back into my ear. "Lots of them." He smiled beatifically, as if he'd just declared his love.

I had never thought of Icarus as having much strength, but now his hold on me was the only thing preventing me from falling to my death. I closed my eyes against what waited for us below and allowed his arms around me to be my only reality.

He grunted with effort. His laboring wings lifted us in a slow and straining spiral, higher and higher. The air thinned. His sweat soaked through my clothes, and the elevation's cold air plastered the clammy garments against my body and made me shiver.

Solid ground was the farthest thing from my mind. My eyes snapped open in shock when the backs of my hands bumped against a surface, and Icarus sighed, maneuvered, and set us down.

He did not collapse as I expected. Instead, I was the one who fell. My legs still didn't work. Bullets had grazed my skin in several places. My jeans clung stickily to the holes. I winced and loosened them, wondering if I wanted to find out how much they hurt.

Icarus stood above me. Pain burned in his eyes, but his face glowed.

The world around me glittered, blinding. I blinked and tried to catch my bearings. "Where are we?"

"The Spire. It's a thousand feet higher than the Skywalk." He dropped to his knees beside me, winding one arm around the back of my neck. "You can see that restaurant I told you about from here." He directed my head, but everything looked the same to me—glass and reflected sun.

"We're in Central City?" My head snapped frantically from left to right. "Won't they send someone after us?" Surely, we couldn't be safe up there.

Icarus smiled, his face shining more than the city below. "City regulations prohibit motor vehicles in the sky. The angel-men don't want to deal with police. They want to be free, and they've got the resources to reserve a space all to themselves." His fingers trailed over my skin. "I'm one of them now. I've got the wings to prove it."

I knew better. No one in Central City had ever suffered for wings the way that Icarus had. But I didn't want to spoil his happiness. I kept my mouth shut and kissed him.

He responded with a fire I'd never felt from him before, hands delving under my clothes, tongue driving into my mouth. "You gave this to me," he said against my lips. I accepted his adoration, putting his recent misery out of my mind. He felt good. I closed my eyes, reached around him, and, for the first time, stroked the feathers of his wings. Soft and cold, they sliced my fingertips like the edge of a sheet of paper. My breath caught in my lungs. He seemed so fragile to me. Something that hurt me had to hurt him, too.

But Icarus moaned. "You reach right inside me when you do that."

Watching his face, I flattened one hand against his wing, its titanium ridges pressing firmly into my palm. Icarus sighed, wrapped me in his body, and kicked off from the roof, taking us into a backward dive.

I screamed, struggling mindlessly in his grasp even though I knew that victory would mean my death. Icarus held on, crooning to me within the cocoon of his wings. Fear erased my mind, and all I could do was breathe and wait, clutched against the winged man's chest, wondering what we were to each other.

Then Icarus unfurled his wings with a bracing snap, and we stopped diving, rising sharply on a gust of wind that took us higher than the most exclusive penthouses reserved for the most exclusive denizens of Central City. He started touching me again, one arm securing me while the other fiddled with my pants.

"What are you –"

Icarus just smiled. He couldn't hear me, and what I would have said didn't matter anyway. He loosened my pants from my waist, then used his toes to push and pull them down my legs. Freed from me, they floated and snapped in the various air currents around us, moving slower than I would have expected, but always downward.

My boxers got the same treatment, and Icarus took my hard cock in his hand. I reached around to grip his ass, to start opening him up, but he wriggled it out of my grasp and slid his hands around to my ass instead. I jumped, surprised. Icarus had never touched me there before.

His wings beat in a steady pulse as his hands maneuvered me into position. He hung in the air, facing the city below, and hooked my legs up over his shoulders. I didn't have the leverage or the sensation to move them away from where he placed them. I clung to his neck with my arms, aware that my entire weight now dangled from his upper body.

Icarus slid his fingers into his mouth, then moved the moisture to my ass. Though they'd just come from a warm place, they'd chilled by the time they touched the ring of muscle there. I shivered when he slipped one inside. Icarus leaned forward and kissed me as he probed me. My leg muscles would probably have complained if I could have felt them – I was never very flexible.

217

For all my fantasies about Icarus, and all my lust, I'd never thought about taking him in. But at that moment, rushing through a sky that seemed to belong to him, it seemed only natural that I should belong to him, too.

I wasn't quite ready for him when he fitted his cock to my ass, but I didn't want to make him wait. He held me by the shoulders and hunched his abs up to press into my ass. The display of strength would have amazed me if I hadn't been so distracted by the effort of receiving him. I didn't think I could take it, and I would have jumped away if I hadn't been forced to hold on. Every new bit of territory he claimed overwhelmed me. Every time his cock thrust deeper, I didn't think I could accept it. I didn't know how to open up for him.

But Icarus didn't pull back, and I didn't make him. With every beat of his wings and every tightening of the large muscles along his waist, his cock lodged a little deeper. I didn't realize it at first, but by the time his balls made contact with my ass, fitting his cock into me to the root, I realized I'd never been so hard. My own cock ached and wept, and my balls had drawn up tight against my skin like I was about to come.

Icarus grabbed my ass and pulled me even closer, shoving the final bit of his cock inside me, as far as it would go. And suddenly, the whole thing changed, and I wanted more of him and harder and faster. I couldn't make my knees bend, couldn't drive myself up and down on his cock. I tried to use my arms to swing myself, but Icarus shook his head and fucked me himself. The muscles in his arms corded as he slid me back and forth in time with the flapping of his wings.

I squeezed his neck tightly at first, but the pleasure made me want to arch my back. Eventually, I let go, my torso swinging freely in the air below him, trusting myself entirely to Icarus's hands and cock to hold me up as he flew us higher, and ever higher.

Blood rushed to my head. With me dangling that way, he'd had to stop thrusting, but just the sensation of him filling me began to feel unbearably intense. I'd closed my eyes at some point, and when I opened them, I went immediately dizzy. We'd flown higher than I could comprehend. I gasped. The air couldn't sustain me. I couldn't understand how Icarus's wings could even find purchase in such a thin world.

No matter what difficulties I perceived, nothing slowed his flying or eased the grip of his hands. He groaned above me, and suddenly our angle changed wildly. My head spun as I flipped and twisted on his cock. Then I screamed as my cock began to shoot, my seed freezing almost instantly in the chill upper atmosphere, and the pleasure splitting my head apart as I gasped for air and could not get enough.

Icarus gripped my ass hard enough to hurt. He emptied himself inside me, his cock's pulsing making it feel even larger inside my stretched asshole.

I felt absolutely free. I crunched up toward Icarus for one delirious, delicious kiss. We laughed into each other's mouths.

Then I ran my hand over my thigh and noticed it was wet. I pulled away from Icarus's kiss and found a stream of blood running down my numb leg, dripping off his wing and onto me. Far too much blood.

The mood hadn't yet left him. No strain showed in his face. Though I knew at that instant that he was dead, Icarus did not realize it until after we reached the ground.

We touched down on the outskirts of nowhere, far from where I'd lived most of my life, and far from anything either of us had ever known. I spent the next two days holding him. The wounds from the chop man never again stopped bleeding, no matter how I tried to stop them up.

He'd gotten the drugs from the chop man, after an agonizing limped journey one day while I was working. The chop man told him he would probably only ever manage to fly once, but that didn't stop Icarus. I couldn't bear to ask how he paid the man.

Not long after he told me that, after we left the paradise we'd found in the upper sky, Icarus went away and never returned. His eyes never focused on me, and he never again reached out to touch me.

I tried to keep my legs from getting infected. A jagged, piercing feeling slowly returned to them. Sensation would shoot down one leg or the other at odd moments, interspersed with deadness. I could move them, and I could walk, but it was impossible to accomplish either feat precisely. I did not let this trouble me while I breathed, sweated, and sighed with Icarus.

I was hungry, thirsty, and lost when I closed his eyes for the last time. Sliding out from under him with a lot of help from my hands, I rose shakily to my feet. Had I loved him? I thought love was supposed to be a nobler emotion, so much less selfish. I thought love was about giving not taking, about asking what I could do rather than what would be done for me.

I wanted to kick those wings, which dwarfed his body so utterly. I wanted to tear them off and feed those titanium rods to the chop man slice by bloody slice. It didn't matter that they had made Icarus happy. They still looked alive, while the rest of him had shriveled.

I buried him. I found a piece of scrap that served as a shovel, and I found an alley no one had bothered to pave. I couldn't dig deep enough to get the wings all the way underground, so feathers became his gravestone, poking up from the disturbed earth on either side of him.

If you enjoyed this story, you can sign up for a free membership at ForbiddenFiction and discuss it with other readers and the author at the *Icarus Bleeds* story page at http://forbiddenfiction.com/library/story/AL1-1.000140.

Annabeth Leong

In the
Death
of Winter

In the Death of Winter

As a young woman hangs bound in desperate, hopeful sacrifice, an agéd priestess of the dead god of winter recalls the night he made her his, with his power and his cold passion. (M/F, F/F)

In the Death of Winter

"What if the god does not come?" Sarant asked.

Bolormaa ignored the postulant's words. She pulled the young woman's fur-lined robes over her head and discarded them, revealing a lush body, rosy nipples, and red-brown hair between her legs to match the tresses on her head. Sarant smelled sour under the heavy garment, which did not suit the muggy night. Bolormaa scowled and slapped away a mosquito.

Mud, heat, and rain had no place on this night, and yet they tormented her. The pleasures of the underworld should keep the sun long below the ground. Tonight, frost should crunch under her feet. The winter touch of Erlik should lie heavy on the land.

"Will you send me away if he does not come?" Sarant pressed.

Bolormaa sighed. "Child, he will not come. He is dead."

She uncoiled a rough length of hemp and bound Sarant's wrists with it. The god would have liked this one. The cuts that had covered Sarant's body when Bolormaa found her had nearly healed. Most village men would reject the girl as hopelessly disfigured, but Erlik favored signs of inner strength.

Bolormaa's bones creaked when she hoisted Sarant's hands above her head and fastened them to the branch of a great larch tree. The young woman's nipples had already grown hard. Sarant panted with excitement, and the smell of her arousal stung the old woman's nostrils.

"Why are we doing this if we know he will not come?"

Bolormaa tugged and tightened the ropes, grunting. "Because I am an old fool, and I cannot give up hope that he might."

Bolormaa had seen only twenty winters when her husband stripped her bare and threw her to the mercy of the Longest Night.

"Let Erlik have you!" The slamming door denied her the light of their hearth fire, leaving her under the darkness of a moonless, starless sky.

She shivered against the outside of the heavy door. Bolormaa's feet blushed red, slipping on the thin, knobby layer of ice that had built up across their entryway in the early hours of the night. Chill air whipped past her, chapping her exposed flesh everywhere. She tried to cover herself, wrapping her arms over her breasts. Another blast of wind confused her senses. Her thighs burned with cold, and her back pricked with icy fire. She rubbed her palms against her legs to warm herself, but the next gust hardened her bare nipples to the point of pain.

"Please!" She pounded on the door. "I'll die out here!"

The door quaked dully from the other side. Her husband had dropped the heavy wooden bar in place across it.

Bolormaa slumped in the meager shelter of the doorframe. She hated the man. His reedy looks masked a cruel disposition, and he subjected her to beatings by day and painful rutting by night.

She hated herself more for waiting at the doorstep like a good doggy, praying to be let back in. On impulse, she plunged her hand into a pile of snow beside the narrow walkway to the house, savoring the punishing, clarifying pain.

"Great Lord Erlik," she whispered. "Will you have me?"

Gritting her teeth, Bolormaa lifted her naked body upright and spread her arms. She took one step, then another. The soles of her feet stuck slightly to the icy walkway stones.

Bolormaa could not hope for relief from the cold, so she forced herself to run. Tears formed in the corners of her eyes in response to the dry air, then froze to the sides of her face. The effort did slowly heat her body. Her skin blushed angry red all over. Her lungs opened to bigger breaths, each stabbing into her chest like sharp steel.

She ran from her home, out of the village, and into the woods. Her jaw chattered so violently that she bit her tongue. She sucked on the wound, tasting the metal in her blood, and ran on. The snow beneath her feet rubbed them raw and burned hot as desert sand.

Her body could not take such punishment long. Bolormaa's face had gone numb and stiff despite the furnace in her lungs. She could not tell how each step landed — she could not feel her feet at all. Each heartbeat struck her chest with the force of her husband's fists.

Bolormaa had to rest. She dragged to a stop in the snow, coughing and gripping her thighs. Her confused, struggling body convulsed. Falling to her knees, she could not muster the will to rise again.

The snow here caressed her bare skin. It warmed and comforted her. She sank more of her body into it.

A clump of icicles cracked off the branch of a nearby tree, stabbing the piled drifts. Bolormaa forced her head up. Dull illumination gleamed from the ice in the skeletal branches and ghosted off the snow.

A hand thudded onto her shoulder.

Bolormaa lacked the breath to scream. She craned her neck back and up. The hand connected to a winter-pale arm, which led to the chest of a tall man standing behind her. Ropes of muscle and tendon rippled below his wrinkled skin. He stood naked, hairless except for the thick, jet-black eyebrows that belied his apparent advanced age. Horns grew from the top of his head, tangled like tree roots. His fingers dug into Bolormaa's chest just above her ribs, hooking painfully under her collarbone.

Bolormaa resisted the urge to twist away from his grip. The combination of awe and fear he inspired left no doubt of his identity. "My Lord Erlik?"

The god smiled, pressing a finger the color of packed powder to her mouth. She kissed it reverently, and did not resist when he pried her jaw open into a painfully wide "O." Erlik studied her expression, gave a satisfied nod, and tapped her lips with a chipped fingernail. They rang like glass.

Bolormaa managed to produce a small, terrified sound in the back of her throat. His touch had frozen her mouth immobile. Her saliva transformed to a block of ice that trapped her tongue and radiated aching cold into her cheeks. Erlik kissed her on the forehead and stroked her hair.

Though cold, this contact did not freeze her flesh solid. He ran one finger down her throat, her breasts, brushing lightly over each of her hard nipples. A blush rose to Bolormaa's face and neck when her cunt clenched in response.

He released her shoulder and stepped around to her front. Her eyes widened at the enormous, ivory cock that bounced erect before him.

Shame and fear battled the desire within her and won. Bolormaa scrambled up, her mouth still beyond her control. The god's hands darted out to snatch her wrists before she could get away. She whimpered at his painful hold, but cold had weakened her body too much for her to fight.

Erlik jerked her tight to his chest, his cock a thick column of ice against her belly. "You asked me to take you, did you not?" he rasped into her ear. "To save you?"

Bolormaa managed a tiny nod. Her face contorted around her immobilized mouth. Her eyes poured forth tears that froze as soon as they were shed, coating her cheeks with frost.

"I think you know what to do," the god said. Bolormaa squeezed her eyes shut and sank to her knees before him.

He trailed his fingers over her cheeks. The gentle touch lulled her, leaving her unprepared for when he snatched a fistful of her hair and fed the entire length of his cock into her helpless mouth.

Bolormaa's throat spasmed around his cockhead. She pounded her fists against his thighs and scraped her knees against the snow in her efforts to pull her face off the implacable thing. The god held her effortlessly in place, his freezing cock embedded to the hilt in the deepest heat of her throat.

Slowly, he pumped in and out of her face. His cock skated across her lips and tongue with the unearthly smoothness of ice against ice. Finally, Bolormaa stilled her fruitless struggles and looked up at him. He seemed to have been waiting for her to meet his gaze. His ink-black eyes bored into her as surely as his cock.

"You have a choice to make," he said. He drove into her throat until she gagged. He held the back of her head with both hands and listened to her gurgle around his cock. Bolormaa could not breathe. She choked, alarm heating her numbed body. She clawed at him desperately until he thrust her away, just before she lost consciousness.

Bolormaa lay on her back in the snow, panting through her frozen-open mouth. The god knelt straddling her, his still-hard cock resting on her cheek. "I have three gifts for you tonight, if you accept them," Erlik told her. "You've earned the first. I will bring you safely through this night. The second gift will hurt more, and the third will nearly kill you."

He caressed her jaw. "How much do you want of me?" His touch thawed her mouth. Bolormaa stretched her lips, weak with gratitude. He offered his finger, and she willingly sucked. Warmth spread through her mouth and traveled down into her chest.

Erlik withdrew the finger and raised a thick eyebrow.

Bolormaa considered him. She turned her head slightly to peer at the great cock, its velvety skin smooth on her face. Erlik towered above her. Here was real power, not her husband's cruel shadow of it. Bolormaa kissed the tip of the god's cock. "Please give me all," she whispered.

Bolormaa surveyed Sarant's restrained body. She had lifted the young woman's wrists high enough to force her onto her toes. Sarant's muscles strained to hold her balanced, creating lovely lines around her tensed muscles. The position lifted her breasts and emphasized her height. Blindfolded now, Sarant's head twisted sometimes toward a cracking twig or gust of wind.

Bolormaa stroked the postulant's side, then stretched upward and kissed her temple.

Sarant groaned and turned away. Bolormaa gripped her chin. "Pray to him."

"Lord Erlik," Sarant began obediently. "Winter-touched, dark Lord of the night and the hidden sun, pierce me with your icy spear of truth. Lead me across barren fields and strip me bare of clothes and flesh. Reveal the skeleton of my strength with the harsh caress of your winds. And when my heart has frozen solid from the pain, crush it in your hard hands, Lord, and take me, remake me — to die and be born again forever in the ecstasy of your stern embrace."

That solstice night with Erlik, Bolormaa's stomach burned with the pain of the god's seed. The cold mess of it froze and shattered while traveling down her throat. She feared shards of it would pierce her on the inside.

After emptying himself down her throat, the god removed his cock from her mouth and wiped it against her hair. Bolormaa watched her black hair blanch white at his touch. "You are marked as mine forever," Erlik whispered. "You will gain all the power, respect, and trouble that come of this."

Bolormaa clutched her guts and whimpered. The god's hand on her shoulder stilled her. His fingers found her nipples, circling them with his chilly touch. He squeezed them into thin, aching points, so stiff with cold that they would not return to their customary shape. Erlik gripped both nipples firmly and pulled up.

She gasped and squirmed to get her feet in place under her. "Do you still wish to receive my third gift?" Erlik asked. He kissed her, her still-thawing cheeks so cold that even his icy tongue felt hot and harsh.

"Yes," Bolormaa declared. The god guided her onto all fours in the snow.

Erlik placed the head of his cock against Bolormaa's cunt but did not push inside. He leaned forward and gripped her nipples again, pinching until she screamed and fought him. Slowly, the god increased the pressure, pulling until she had no choice but to impale herself.

The stabbing cold of his rigid member reached steadily farther inside her. "Please," Bolormaa gasped. More and more of it entered her, until it seemed far longer than what had been in her mouth. The god's cock bottomed out inside her, but still he pulled her nipples.

Bolormaa stopped moving, unable to take any more. Erlik did not relent. She feared he would tear her nipples off. Bolormaa could not bear the pain in her breasts, nor the pain of his cock. The torment intensified until it transformed to helpless insanity. She flung herself into both anguished sensations, swinging forward and stretching her nipples to the breaking point, and then slamming back until she

227

thought his cock would rip her in half.

The god toyed with her, sprouting cold claws from his fingers and piercing her body with them. For the first time, Erlik grunted his excitement. The chill he radiated intensified. Bolormaa's skin went numb all over. Aside from a dull pounding at the deepest depth of her womb, she could no longer feel his cock inside her. She could not tell what his hands did to her breasts.

The god moaned and cold surged through her. Bolormaa's body froze solid. She could not speak, struggle, or feel. She heard the god's body slamming against hers. She could not see him or mark the passage of time.

Erlik screamed and rammed against her. The seed he pumped into her womb surged within her. Bolormaa felt as if she could not contain it. Erlik touched between her legs, finding her bud. A sharp poke chipped through the ice that covered it, exposing the tender flesh to the wind and the god's harsh fingers. Bolormaa could feel nothing but the god pinching and tugging on her most sensitive place.

She came, the spasms of it bursting through the icy layer that immobilized her. Bolormaa howled at the pain of her splintering skin.

Erlik withdrew his cock from her. He touched her behind the ear. "Now I will be forever inside you."

Bolormaa collapsed forward into the snow. Through her shock and pain, she smiled.

"Mother Bolormaa, are you still here?" Sarant sounded frightened.

The dark flicker that now passed for night had begun. Erlik would not come, but the solstice must still be celebrated in full. Bolormaa kicked some leaves.

"Why didn't you go to the temple of the Summer God after Tengri murdered Erlik?"

The old woman grunted and spat. "I'm a priestess, not a whore. I will not be passed along with the cheap spoils of war."

Bolormaa squinted at Sarant. The girl should suffer more. Bolormaa had lost two fingers and three toes after her night with Erlik, and the blizzard of his seed had stolen her tongue's sense of taste.

She squatted on the ground beside Sarant and pinched her inner thigh. The girl cried out. Bolormaa did it again, harder, leaving the impression of her fingernails in the young woman's skin. The third time, she drew blood.

Sarant screamed and kicked. Bolormaa dodged the blow easily, cackling. She took out another length of rope. "Do you want me to tie your ankles so your feet can't support you?"

The postulant whimpered. Bolormaa smiled and pinched her side, just under her ribcage. The girl flinched, but bit her lip and took the pain.

Bolormaa wound the rope around the girl's chest methodically, length over length until the rope lifted and squeezed the girl's breasts. Her rosy nipples reddened and grew. Bolormaa shaped Sarant's breasts into cones and bound them tightly with the rope while the girl whined and gasped. Finally, she stood back to admire the purpling flesh.

"Please," Sarant begged.

"Please, what?" Bolormaa tweaked a swollen nipple.

"Please. It hurts."

"It's supposed to hurt. If Erlik had come for you, you would be wishing for mercy right now. But in the end, you would give yourself to him more completely than you thought possible."

"Why are you hurting me so much if he's not coming?" Sarant wailed.

Cold rage rose in Bolormaa's belly. Why, indeed? She had always felt the god's presence in the pit of her stomach. That had ended when Erlik died, obliterated as thoroughly as her beloved snow. She squeezed a tortured breast in the palm of one hand.

"Why did you come to me?" she hissed.

Sarant swallowed, her throat working desperately. "Anything seemed better than my home."

Bolormaa's anger softened. "The pain is what sets you free of that," she murmured. "Remember that."

Her fingers traced the young woman's scarred flesh. She traced the curve of her hips, tickled Sarant's inner thighs, and soon delved into the warm, wet place between her legs. "He would have been pleased with the taking of this virginity tonight," Bolormaa murmured.

Her fingers tingled strangely. She wanted to hurt and help, to strip bare and transform, to destroy and make new. She pushed one finger all the way inside of Sarant. The young woman let out a frightened yelp. "Mother, your hands are so cold!"

Bolormaa slapped the bound girl's face with her free hand. "Do you want the gifts of Erlik or not?"

Sarant's protests fell silent. Bolormaa added a second finger. Sarant's moistening slit provided a pleasant warmth that traveled up her arm. She pounded her fingers in and out of the girl, her aching old woman's joints forgotten.

The postulant struggled against the ropes, her breath hitching. Bolormaa sat on the ground, forcing the girl's legs apart. She easily overpowered Sarant's straining thighs. Reaching up, Bolormaa made her hand into a spear point. She aligned it with Sarant's slit and shoved viciously upward, tearing through her barrier. Sarant shrieked, but Bolormaa did not let up, using her other hand to rub vigorously at the bud between the young woman's legs. She continued to force her hand deeper inside.

"Cold, cold, cold!" Sarant cried. She tried to dance away, but only succeeded at spreading her legs wider. Bolormaa's hand disappeared inside her passage, and the old woman stared in wonder as frost spidered over the girl's legs and lower stomach. She kissed and licked Sarant's bud. The postulant gave in with her entire body, her muscles gripping powerfully at Bolormaa's wrist.

The old woman looked down. Ice covered the larch tree's roots. Bolormaa's arm had lightened by several shades. The hair between Sarant's legs glowed white.

Bolormaa eased her hand out of the girl and stumbled to her feet. Sarant panted and shivered. Bolormaa yanked the blindfold off Sarant's head.

"My Lord Erlik?" Sarant gasped.

Putting her hand to her head, Bolormaa discovered a tangle of rough horns. Exploring further, Bolormaa found a freezing, implacable cock between her legs. Slowly, a smile spread across her face. "You have a choice to make," she said.

If you enjoyed this story, you can sign up for a free membership at
ForbiddenFiction and discuss it with other readers
and the author at the *In the Death of Winter* story page
at http://forbiddenfiction.com/library/story/AL1-1.000042.

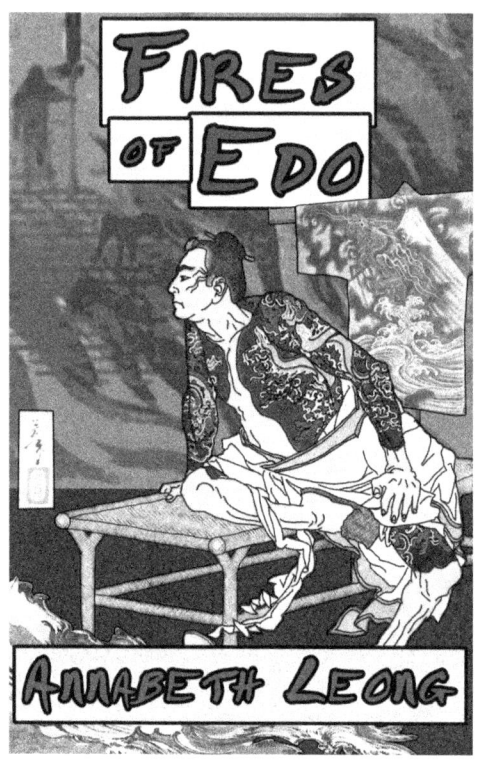

Fires of Edo

Edo, Japan: Isamu, hailed as the veteran of five hundred fires, has spent seventeen years as a machibikeshi, protecting the delicate paper-walled homes of Edo during windy monsoon season. Ryo, the water dragon etched on his skin, has been a source of comfort throughout this time — and an object of longing. The chief of the brigade wants the aging Isamu to retire, but Isamu fears that if he does, the great dragon will no longer be interested in protecting him. (M/M)

Fires of Edo

"Fires and quarrels are the flowers of Edo."
— Traditional Japanese Saying

I. The Hanten

The year died. The monsoon from the north blew strong and cold through the city, never stopped by the paper walls of the crowded *nagaya* where Isamu lived alongside five families. As winter settled over Edo, dread mingled with the smell of oil from his neighbors' cooking fires.

Isamu began to place a small packet of clothing, his good straw sandals, and a paper lantern beside his pillow each night before going to sleep. He packed his few valuables into a wicker basket that he could grab in a moment at any time of day or night. Fire season had begun. He had fought enough fires in his life to know that anyone could lose anything at any time. Isamu suspected the spirits would particularly enjoy the irony of striking down the home of a 17-year *machibikeshi* such as himself, who spent every monsoon season fighting Edo's numerous blazes when he wasn't repairing homes destroyed by them.

This year, Isamu felt too tired to climb up onto the roof of the *nagaya* and check for breaks in the earth layered over the thatched straw. He did it anyway, knowing all too well how a single spark from anywhere at all, borne by the monsoon, could travel from one protruding straw to the next and light half the city.

He eased himself down afterwards, slowly, so that he could keep his face composed. There were too many people around for him to allow himself to groan at the strain he felt in his lower back, or at the

233

ache in joints that had been too well-used in the course of his life. He felt older than he looked, and looked older than his age.

"Isamu-san, won't your water dragon protect all of us who share a home with you?"

Isamu grunted. Daisuke, head of one of the families in the *nagaya*, always had a voice too loud and grating for Isamu's taste, and a manner too intrusive. "There are no guarantees. Not even for me."

He tugged his sleeves down lower. Everyone in the *nagaya* had seen his tattoo of the great blue dragon—it was impossible not to see, for it covered every inch of Isamu's skin aside from his head, hands, and feet. At the age of fifteen, he had nearly sold himself into indentured servitude for it. It had taken years of good carpentry work to dig himself out of the disastrous debt, and yet he did not regret the cost. He called it Ryo, for even a single glance at its smooth blue scales entwined around his flesh made Isamu feel refreshed.

"When does the brigade meet next?" Daisuke asked.

"We will see each other this evening," Isamu replied, running his fingers over his tattooed arm through the sleeve of his workshirt. "The wind will bring the fires soon. It always does."

Isamu washed away the day's dirt and sweat before going to meet the rest of the brigade. He hadn't told Daisuke, but tonight's meeting was being held in Isamu's honor. He might have been able to get over his embarrassment about this fact if he didn't suspect that the celebration was an excuse to force him out and make room for a man with a younger back.

He dressed as carefully as he could, though his commoner clothes would never be elegant enough to compete with the elaborate *hanten* of the *buke hikeshi*, the firefighters drawn from samurai families. Some of those garments were hand-quilted and hand-painted with art so fine that Isamu wanted to grind his teeth when their wearers ventured near a fire.

Nonetheless, you had to have an eye to recognize a firefighter's finery. All the men's garments showed plain on the outside, with simple white chalk stencils to signify brigade. It was within that the wonder of the *hanten* rested — next to the man's skin, where the spirits contained in the art could protect him. The men only revealed the patterns they wore to outsiders after successfully fending off a blaze. Then, to honor the spirits that had kept them safe, the firefighters would turn their garments inside out and parade through the streets, and the people would be reassured that the spirits could indeed hold back the fires of Edo and preserve life in the city.

The parades were the only time that Isamu didn't mind showing Ryo. Since the inside of his own *hanten* was plain, quilted cloth, when the celebrations began, he would pull off the jacket and his shirt beneath and strut beside the others with the great water dragon rippling along with his muscles. It seemed alive in those moments. He always imagined he could feel it moving over him, swimming through his flesh. Sometimes the thought made him shudder with a force that shot to the root of his manhood.

When that happened, Isamu would slip away after the parade had ended to find a willing woman. He would order her to caress the dragon's contours, not his own, and he would concentrate until he could see the creature preening under her touch. He wanted her to feel scales rough against her tongue, and strange, supernatural limbs holding her instead of his mundane human arms.

The trick worked best if they could bathe together. In the water, Isamu would coil his body around the woman's as a dragon would, teasing with his tongue at her spine one moment and at her navel the next. He would intertwine his legs with hers until she gasped and begged for him, but he would not give in and enter her until he could feel Ryo rising up all over his skin. Only then would he close his eyes, imagining that the dragon's cock could burst from amid his tattooed skin to replace his own, and split her thighs, and take her.

"To Isamu-san, the hero of five hundred fires!"

Isamu accepted the toast, forcing his grimace to become a grin. He swallowed hot sake and slammed his cup down on the table. He felt the liquor more than he wanted to, burning his insides like licking flames. He thought of Ryo wrapped around his body, and wished for a rush of cool scales.

Unsteadily, he made his way to his feet. "It's time to toast another man, no? To our brave leader, Masaru-san, who will lead this brigade to victory and reward again this monsoon season!"

The men drank and shouted, but their voices took on a surly tone. Firefighting had always been lucrative work, but the shogunate had been complaining lately about the number and frequency of the fires, and the expense of paying and keeping the men. They'd accused some of the *hikeshi* of arson and extortion, dragging them through the streets in their *hanten* before executing them.

Isamu sighed. Maybe later, when Masaru suggested that he retire, he would accept this time. The other man was talking again. Isamu focused his eyes and tried to pay attention.

"Every year, we firefighters get to see the colors of the autumn leaves come out year-round, and we don't have to leave the city to do it!" Isamu laughed politely at Masaru's tired joke. "Perhaps we would have had more glory battling one of the Great Fires, but even in these lesser times, we've seen our share."

"Especially now!" someone shouted, and Isamu drank to it. There had been so much arson lately. So many times, a fire wasn't an accident anymore. He remembered stopping a woman running from a conflagration with a bundle of spent firecrackers in her hands. "I wanted to see what would happen," she had said. Isamu had simply let go of her, too disgusted to know what else to do.

"How many fires has it been, Isamu-san?"

He realized that Masaru was repeating the question. Isamu teetered, the drink making his balance elusive. "It has truly been five hundred," he said. "Since I've been alive, there are more each year."

"That water dragon of yours has served you well." Envious eyes turned towards Isamu. Other firefighters had full body tattoos, but none could match the artistry and color with which Ryo had been rendered.

"I am not worthy of Ryo's service," Isamu broke in. "It is I who serve him, in whatever way he might wish. Any way. He is as real as the artist could make him, and yet not real enough. I long for just one touch." The room got quieter. The stares changed. He was too drunk.

Masaru cleared his throat, regaining control of the situation.

"Whatever the case may be," he said, "you have served us and the city of Edo long and well. It is time you received appropriate recognition for all you have done."

With a flourish, Masaru held up the finest *hanten* that Isamu had ever seen, dyed with indigo to the exact color of Ryo's scales. Smiling broadly, he opened the garment. Within, Isamu saw Ryo, winding over every available surface. Isamu's face reddened. He felt exposed, as if Masaru had the inside of Isamu's skin on display. "How?" he breathed.

"We've paid a little attention over the years, you know," Masaru said proudly.

II. The Tattoo

The new *hanten* weighed on his body as if it had already been wetted down for a fire. Isamu did not wish to own a garment worth so much more than the clothing of his neighbors. Even if no one would begrudge it to him, Isamu did not feel capable of caring for such a treasure.

It was hard enough trying to keep his skin in a condition worthy of Ryo. He ate carefully, maintained his strength and flexibility, and still he felt ashamed to wear Ryo on a body that had begun to deteriorate.

Keeping his head down, Isamu ducked through the narrow alleyways separating each *nagaya* from the next. It was late enough that everyone else in the long house had gone to sleep. Relieved, Isamu moved silently to his own modest area, delineated by a set of six tatami mats. He moved screens into place to give himself a little privacy. When he was as much alone as possible, he slipped the *hanten* off his thick shoulders.

He turned it inside out. The artist who had painted Ryo onto the garment had done an exquisite job. The dragon's skin shimmered over the quilted fabric. His body lithely wrapped and circled itself so that it was impossible to tell where the creature began and ended. Trembling, Isamu lifted a finger and tried to trace its shape. The fabric of the *hanten* felt silkier than he expected, so that for just a moment he could have believed he touched the smoothest, hardest scale. But as beautiful as it was, he knew it wasn't alive.

Isamu shook himself free of the spell and folded the *hanten* with perfect creases. He set it beside his pillow along with the rest of his treasured and necessary objects. He felt uncharacteristically excited as he undressed, anxious tonight to see the dragon etched into his flesh, to touch his body and feel a warmth that could belong to either himself or Ryo.

He had to focus to maintain even breathing. He forced himself to keep his eyes on the tasks at hand as he prepared for bed. All the while, he felt Ryo waiting, part of him and yet entirely too divine to belong to Isamu's flesh.

Finally, Isamu lay down naked on his sleeping pallet. Light flickered from somewhere nearby. He thrust his stomach upwards, so that Ryo's painted silver eyes caught the gleam. Isamu stared at the dragon and felt it staring back.

Slowly, trying to match the grace that Ryo would certainly have, Isamu moved his body in a ripple, watching the play of light against perfect blue scales. He undulated his arms and legs as if moving through water. He arched his back and neck, stretching up toward the ceiling and then curling back down. Never before had he felt so much nobility in his body.

His cock stirred. Isamu imagined the dragon's scales, wet and smooth against his lips. He envisioned his fingers finding the sharp edges of the polished, blue, bony plates, his legs wrapping around the coiled power of Ryo's body. He imagined feeling the dragon's muscles surging against his inner thighs, settling firmly against his balls.

Isamu suppressed a moan. He let his fingers play over the head of his cock. He watched himself. His hand, bare of markings, was that of a man, but the tattoo of Ryo extended even over his cock. Isamu made love to the dragon, but he also became the dragon. He felt the softness of human skin against his reptile body.

He was rock hard by now. His hand fisted and began to pump. Isamu continued to ripple his body, thinking of how Ryo's long, serpentine form would surge up and down in the waters of the Sumida River, teasing in and out of sight.

In his mind, he joined in the swimming, clinging to Ryo because he could not otherwise match his speed. Isamu thought of how water would rush over his body, the droplets chill, sharp, and precise. The only heat would come from Ryo. Seeking warmth, Isamu would squirm against the dragon, rubbing his entire front against water-slicked muscle.

Then, Isamu imagined, there would be an even greater heat, powerful enough to boil the water around them. Without having to look, he would recognize the source of the heat as Ryo's cock. Isamu tried to picture what the dragon's cock would be like, but here his mind always failed him. He knew it would be majestic, impossibly velvet, and strong, but he could not reconcile the contradictions it would embody. It would need to be hard, and yet how could a hard cock match the lithe movement of the dragon as a whole?

Isamu knew that, given the opportunity, he would have no care for his safety. Even if the water steamed and bubbled from the heat of Ryo's cock, he would reach in to touch, to feel, to stroke.

He gasped and came into a cupped palm. Isamu lay resting a moment, feeling his body cool as whispers of the monsoon caressed his lightly sweating skin. Then he rubbed his palm against his stomach, picturing the dragon's tongue licking up his most heartfelt sacrifice.

III. The Matoi

"You're sure I can't convince you to help with the paperwork?" Masaru asked.

Isamu pulled a face, not deigning to respond. He poured Masaru a fresh cup of tea and got one for himself as well. Already, he felt old and irrelevant. He should be out on the streets looking for signs of blazes, not sitting indoors in Masaru's home making conversation.

"We've been drawing up some detailed maps of the patterns the fires travel every season," the other man wheedled. "It's not just work for the idle. It requires knowledge of history, and the final products will be beautiful."

"You didn't ask the other night at the party," Isamu said finally. "I might have said yes then."

"Are you a woman now? Must I court you and follow your whims as I might watch the direction of the monsoon winds?"

Isamu grunted.

"That dragon of yours won't protect you forever, you know. Not even with the beautiful new *hanten*."

He couldn't think of a way to explain. The other night after the party, after touching himself, Isamu had felt serene certainty come over him as he fell asleep. Ryo would never leave him as long as he lived with purpose. It was only in the morning that the opposite thought had come to him. If he gave up his duties, perhaps the dragon would no longer be interested in protecting him.

Isamu opened his mouth for a sentence that hadn't yet formed. He was saved by a rush of activity at the door.

"Masaru-san!" the newcomer panted. Isamu recognized Kaito, a new man on the brigade.

He jumped to his feet and, before Masaru could respond, barked a reply. "Pull yourself together and tell us what's going on."

The newcomer swallowed and took a deep breath. "We saw fire in the southwest district. We planted our *matoi* in the roof of a nearby house like we're supposed to. We wanted to do it before anything else so that everyone passing by could look at it whipping in the breeze and know without a doubt that it's our brigade that deserves the reward for dealing with the blaze."

Isamu had no patience for the young man's obsession with credit and rewards. "Tell us why you ran to Masaru-san's house."

"We had begun to do our work when we looked up and saw the *matoi* had been taken down. We couldn't believe it at first, but then we saw Manabu the steeplejack's crew around the spot where we'd left it. Our men went to talk to them, and it was worse than we thought. They were standing there with fireworks and other explosives — they must have set the fire so they could put it out and claim the reward."

"So turn them in to the authorities," Masaru said.

"Our men started fighting them and it all fell apart from there. They said they would claim we were the ones with the explosives — and our *matoi* is the one people will have seen. We could be executed!"

"What about the fire?" Isamu itched with eagerness. He needed this fire like he needed Ryo's embrace. He needed for Masaru to stop trying to convince him to retire.

Kaito took a long, shaky breath. "While we fought with Manabu's crew, we forgot about the blaze. I looked up at some point and saw it had spread to a whole cluster of *nagaya*. It's headed for a row of shops." The man appeared to be near tears. "Please," he said.

But Isamu had already pulled on his *hanten*, and had begun dragging Kaito out the door.

IV. Ryo

When Isamu and Kaito arrived at the fire, the battling crews had been forced to set aside their differences. People ran to and fro carrying wicker baskets on their backs. A few girls who hadn't been evacuated for fire season stood in the shade of nearby shop doorways and wrung their hands.

Heat from the fire blasted Isamu's face when the wind turned his way. He thought he felt Ryo twitching with anticipation. He surveyed the tactics the men used to battle the fire's spread. Blood drained from Isamu's face. "Get those girls out of here," he said through gritted teeth.

"What?" Kaito shifted his weight from foot to foot.

"They're not controlling the flames at all." Isamu pointed. From where they stood, it was so clear that he couldn't understand why the others didn't see it. Instead of pulling down buildings in a ring to stop the fire from moving out of a defined area, the *hikeshi* worked in a haphazard pattern, leaving plenty of room for the flames to travel whatever disastrous path they wished.

"They must not have a leader," Kaito said. "We could go down and help them reorganize."

Isamu shook his head. "No time. If we don't want the fire to grow beyond this district, we have to pull down that building right there."

"The fire's headed right toward that! No one could—"

Isamu had already left, running toward the big jugs of water stored where his brigade had initially set up its base. He poured one over himself, soaking his *hanten* and buying himself a little time up close to the blaze. He wrapped a wet *tenugui* around his head, grabbed his long, hooked *tobi*, and raced for the fire.

He kept his eyes focused on the *nagaya* he had identified as a target. All he had to do was reach that place, he told himself. But every time he glanced up, the flames had formed a bigger wall, and they seemed to get faster the closer they got to him.

Isamu lurched at the *nagaya* he had chosen, tearing it with his *tobi*. The tool plunged through the paper walls and flimsy straw roof. Isamu wasn't satisfied. He whirled and destroyed like a demon. Still, the fire advanced.

If he had been just a little earlier, he thought, his plan would have worked. As it stood, he should have picked a row of *nagayas* farther out. His *tobi's* handle scalded his palm. The air burned his lungs and the skin inside his nose. Isamu whispered Ryo's name like an incantation, ceaselessly.

He scanned his surroundings, blinking away smoke. If he took down a few more buildings, there might still be hope. Isamu leapt into action. He nearly hurled his *tobi* at the next set of walls. He realized too late that he needed to have a care about how its tiled roof fell. A piece of ceramic hit the top of his head with a sharp thud.

Isamu would have continued to sleep, but he couldn't breathe at all. Everything hurt. His skin felt crisp and brittle. It wanted to curl away from his bones.

He licked his lips with a tongue as dry and unfamiliar as the clay of a foreign city's streets. "Ryo," he said. He touched his stomach, as if he would be able to feel the delicate cheekbones that adorned the dragon's face.

But there they were, beneath his fingers in accordance with his delusional expectation, angled and interesting and, above all, cool. Isamu moaned with relief. Gently and with wonder, he explored the dragon's face and jaw. His pain dulled as he pressed against the creature. Its scales were like balm.

Something whispered and rustled around him, then that cool, refreshing body wrapped and embraced him, coil after coil, shielding him completely from the blaze. "I am still protecting you," Ryo said, in a deep voice that Isamu knew from dreams and fervent wishes. His ribs resonated in sympathy with it.

Isamu couldn't bear the thought of anything separating him from the dragon. He shrugged off his *hanten* and pressed his bare body against its coils. "Ryo," he whispered.

"Old friend." The dragon squeezed him. Isamu wanted to sink into its flesh. He wanted Ryo to wear him the way he had worn Ryo for so long. He wanted to be within the dragon, and to hold the dragon within him.

Ryo slithered tenderly over him, cradling him in its heavenly cool embrace. Isamu could hear the flames still raging beyond the dragon. Its scales slid over the bottoms of his feet, and Isamu screamed from the pleasure of it—an ice-cold silky slicing that cut and healed him in a single motion.

He thought the dragon chuckled. The very tip of its tail snaked up into the cocoon to toy with Isamu's foot some more. It slid between his toes and stroked his ankle. The sensation made him ache all over. He struggled within Ryo's coils, but his motions only drove him to greater ecstasy as he felt that same teasing touch all over his naked body, breaking over his flesh like tiny shards of ice.

Isamu wanted the dragon to feel him, too. He worked his hands up so that he could slide them over Ryo's coils, squeezing and massaging its firm muscles. Ryo's response seemed half-involuntary, the skin clenching near Isamu's probing hand, then easing away and shifting him into a newly formed coil.

Isamu felt as if he were constantly falling and constantly being caught. Ryo's body pulsed around him, sometimes so tight that he could not quite catch his breath, and sometimes loosening until he thought he would tumble free. Ryo seemed very male to him, and yet he felt as if his body had sheathed itself in the dragon like a cock inside a woman.

Isamu licked a nearby scale, cautious of the edge. He expected salt, but instead purest lake water burst over his tongue, chilling his mouth numb. He opened wider and sucked at the scale, and icy liquid ran through him, soothing the tenderness of his skin and freezing him hard.

Gently, he parted two scales and worked his tongue between them. The dragon's flesh twitched beneath the probing, impossibly soft and slick and tasting of rivers and wind. Isamu licked until he could not feel most of his face. He shivered from cold and longing.

The shiver passed to Ryo, and its body rubbed against more of Isamu's exposed flesh. He could not bear the touch, and also could not do without it. He felt his skin parting for Ryo, opening to him, then knitting together again the moment the dragon passed beyond it. Isamu felt as if his body were the water the dragon swam through.

He wanted to worship the dragon, but lacked the words. The coils shifted, and Isamu found himself pressed against the coolest, slickest surface yet. The dragon's cock was not hot, as it had been in his fantasies, but was as cold as a mountain spring. It stole his heat and yet made Isamu long to pour himself into it.

Isamu fumbled for his own cock. He had almost forgotten what warmth was until he touched himself, and the burning evidence of his need made him cry out in shock. He guided his cock to press against the dragon's. The sensation was too intense for Isamu to bear more than a few thrusts. His seed burst from deep in his balls. Isamu felt every inch of his skin pulsing with the force of his spend. He turned his cheek to rest against the dragon's sleek body and sighed as he lost consciousness again.

V. The Anagura

"Isamu-san! Isamu-san!"

Isamu blinked. He couldn't see anything. Kaito's voice came from above. He felt around him, disoriented and bereft now that he was no longer in Ryo's powerful embrace. His fingers landed on a latch and a trap door. He poked his head up into a much cooler world than the one he had left. The fire was out.

"What are you doing in the *anagura*?" Kaito cocked his head.

Isamu hauled himself the rest of the way out of the underground storage unit. He had no idea how he'd wound up there, locked inside. It would have been the only safe spot in the burning *nagaya*, but there was no way he could have dragged himself there after being hit in the head by a ceramic tile.

He was naked and covered in soot. Isamu smeared his hand over the black dust in disgust. "What happened?"

"You charged into the blaze. What you were doing was helping, but not fast enough. I thought you were going to die."

"And?"

"Then there was this—explosion. But not of fire. Of water. I saw blue scales, indigo like your *hanten*. Then all the fire went out. The blaze didn't even reach the line of shops in the first alley. I've never seen anything like it."

"Ryo," Isamu said.

"If your dragon's that powerful, it's no wonder you're the veteran of five hundred fires." Kaito's expression turned strange, and Isamu frowned.

"What is it?" Isamu asked.

"Your Ryo. Where is he?"

"What?" Isamu looked down at himself, at the place on his arm where he'd smeared the soot. A thrill of panic ran through him and he smeared at his stomach and his legs. The blue scales were gone, from every place he checked. His skin was as clean and blank as the day he'd been born.

Isamu let himself collapse into a sitting position amid the rubble. The dragon had been real. The incredible memories of its touch were also real. Isamu didn't know whether to laugh or cry. He rubbed his new skin slowly, dreaming of rivers and wet places. It was time to retire.

About the Author

Annabeth Leong has written erotica of many flavors. She loves shoes, stockings, cooking, and excellent bass lines. Forbidden Fiction publishes many of her dark erotica titles. She can be found online at annabetherotica.com or on Twitter @AnnabethLeong.

Other works by Annabeth Leong

Right Message, Wrong Man

About the Publisher

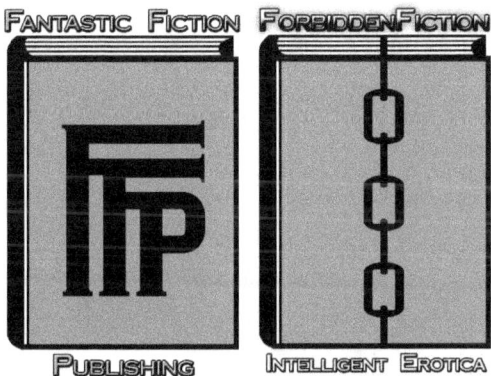

ForbiddenFiction.com is a publisher devoted to writing that breaks the boundaries of original erotic fiction. Our stories combine intense sexuality with quality writing. Stories at ForbiddenFiction.com not only arouse readers through sensations, but also engage them emotionally and mentally through storytelling as well-crafted as the sex is hot.

ForbiddenFiction.com is also designed to be a social reading environment. You'll have fun even if just reading the latest post each day, yet you will have the chance for so much more. Readers and authors can be part of ongoing discussions of specific works and individual authors as well as more general topics.

Sign up for a FREE Membership today at ForbiddenFiction.com